A MERMAID IN T
Love, mermaids and alter
a philosophical novel with some jokes

Reviews from Wattpad.com readers around the world

All of the following comments were unsolicited and no-one was either paid or prodded with a stick by the author.

Laughing hard—mission accomplished xD.—Ana Ribeiro, Portugal

I think it is all allegory for deeper journeys within the psyche and the self, the search for identity, love and spiritual awakening.—Takatsu, Toronto, Canada, author of Espresso Love, Of Forests and Clocks and Dreams, and Secondhand Memories.

This is one of my favourite stories on Wattpad! It's original, witty, and it really has a sense of its own style. I love how vividly it portrays Cornwall as well as all its colourful characters! Myfanwy is an absolute dear and adding her notes at the end of each chapter was a stoke of genius.—Rose Wick, Scotland

Response to chapter 2: Love this and especially the line, "But you don't smoke" and all that follows. And the whole Quantum and Schrödinger's cat paradox... —Mary L. Tabor, author of The Woman who Never Cooked and (Re)making Love.

What do you call a potpourri of humour, good prose, excellent story arc and relatable characters? A Mermaid in the Bath. This book manages to impart some morals which we could benefit from and all this without being preachy. I liked the crisp tone the story is written in. The chorus, the comic relief, the layered characters—well done.—Shrijana Subba, India, author of Bottle Green Daffodil.

...like Roald Dahl for grownups—Jennifer Cooreman, Colorado, USA, winner of the @MargaretAtwood #Freeze-DriedFiction contest for Sister of the Bride.

Enchanted already—John M. Gilheany, UK, author of Not a Stone Left Unturned, Library Dandaical and other works.

Undignified squeal—I love this book! I can't wait to get my hands on a copy.—Austin Malcome, USA

A Mermaid in the Bath

Love, mermaids and altered consciousness:
a philosophical novel with some jokes

(an everyday story of a man
who finds a mermaid in his bath)

Milton Marmalade

with footnotes by Professor Neville
Twistytrouser, Professor of Logical Pescatology
and Warden of St Doris College, Oxford

Narrow Gate Press, London
MMXVI

Published by Narrow Gate Press,
BM Box 6798
London
WC1N 3XX

www.ngp.co

www.MiltonMarmalade.uk

All rights reserved. No part of this publication may be reproduced or transmitted (other than for purposes of review) in any form or by any means, electronic or mechanical, including photocopy, recording, or any information storage and retrieval system without prior permission in writing from the publisher or the copyright holder where applicable.

The author asserts his moral right to be identified as the author of this work.

Cover design and illustrations: Martin Dace

Copyright © Milton Marmalade & Martin Dace

Set in Linotype Joanna Nova, Joanna Nova Sans and IM Fell (The Fell Types are digitally reproduced by Igino Marini. www.iginomarini.com)

Thema classification: FU (Humorous fiction)
BIC classification: FA (Contemporary fiction)

ISBN: 978-0-9565497-6-1

www.miltonmarmalade.uk

To Ann
and to all my teachers
without whom I could have done nothing

Contents

A note from the author	8
A note from Milton Marmalade's exotic Welsh secretary	9
Boring copyright notice from Milton Marmalade	9
Acknowledgements	11
1. A mermaid in the bath	13
2. The curious suggestiveness of numbers	20
3. A policeman calls	24
4. The disquieting nature of love	28
5. A mysterious stranger	31
6. The mermaid is arrested	36
7. Puce-on-cream toile de jouy wallpaper	39
8. Tea and St Doris	42
9. First news of St Doris Island	45
10. Love at first sight and a dark warning	50
11. A hidden passage and an old book	55
12. Love and fear in Castle Drog	59
13. A pasty can be the difference between life and death	63
14. Let your body do the driving	66
15. An Englishman's right to keep whatever one wants in one's bath	69
16. Sir Henry Herring's account of St Doris Island	73
17. Lola	80
18. A brush with officialdom	86
19. The beauty of melancholy	93
20. Psychiatric indeterminacy	95
21. When your fate calls, do not fail	97
22. Union Jack underpants	102
23. El Sueño de la Razón	110
Illustration: A mermaid in the sea	113
24. The immutable law of the universe	114
25. A woman loves a man in uniform	120
26. How to diagnose imaginary illnesses	130
27. A further history of the Selkies	137
28. The abduction of Lola, and a note on solipsism	148

29. Hallucinogenic tea	151
30. Useless are the thoughts of mortal men	159
31. Follow your soul	166
32. Snooping around at night	177
33. "Nothing can stop me"	185
34. High noon at the pink clinic	188
35. A car chase and a meeting of souls	195
36. Dr Squidtentacles escapes	200
37. A lesson in seduction	209
38. Being out of time	215
39. How not to do seduction	217
40. The fight on the beach	224
41. The first thing to do is to pray	230
42. What to do when you have nothing left	236
43. The vision of St Doris	242
Illustration: The mermaid asleep	246
44. The mermaid's sleep	247
45. Inside the Kraken	248
46. The missing mermaid	253
47. The song	256
48. The quiet exercise of free will	261
49. The power of nothing	265
50. The last temptation	269
Epilogue	276

A note from the author

Dear Chums,

Milton Marmalade is my pen name. I'm not certain what my real name is but I suspect that both parts of it begin with M. I leave all that sort of thing to my secretary, since what's in a name, after all?

Myfanwy is my secretary. She keeps interrupting the inspired flow of my writing with cups of tea and descriptions of Welsh cooking, and generally hovering over me. But at least she is very good at thinking up names for me that begin with M. Also she types up my manuscripts to send out to you, dear reader.

When I started the story about the mermaid in Lionel's bath I had no idea how it would end. Luckily though I have divine inspiration from Aerfen, the Celtic goddess of Fate, who sends me plot details in dreams and also when I am in the shower. I try to make myself a clear channel for the goddess, since the merely human imagination is only capable of recycling old stuff.

Now all the loose ends have been woven by Aerfen into a single pattern, made by your humble author into the flawed masterpiece you now hold in your hands.

Myfanwy asked if she could leave in all the notes that were sent out to my readers during the process of composition. I told her not to, of course. It would interrupt the flow of the story and it's not a normal thing in a book to do that.

love to you all,
Milton Marmalade
"An idiot at the height of his powers."

A MERMAID IN THE BATH

A note from Milton Marmalade's exotic Welsh secretary

Hello Sapient Selkies,
I call you that because if you understand everything Milton Marmalade has written then you will rightly be called wise, that is, sapient, and you may, like the Selkies, shed your old skins to become something that can move between two worlds.

Nice bit of writing that, Myfanwy, though I say so myself. I feel a bit inspired just being around Milton and his creative outpourings. Women can write, of course, but I'm more of the muse type. Still, you never know.

Mind you, Milton Marmalade can be rather stuffy and wrapped up in himself. It is a mystery to me that the goddess chose to guide his pen rather than choosing someone a bit more charismatic. There's no accounting for what goddesses do a lot of the time.

love and kisses,
Myfanwy Merioneth

Boring copyright notice from Milton Marmalade

You want to know how an ordinary and rather dull man is transformed into someone passionate and with a certain quiet power after he finds a mermaid in his bath. Of course you do, because when the unexpected happens to you, you will want to know how to deal with it.

It is a tale of love and struggle, no more surprising and absurd in its way than real life.

So you will want skip this bit since it's just the legal stuff that you're supposed to put in. You can skip this section as long as you are not a bad person or a lawyer.

This is just where I point out that this whole story is copyright and all rights are reserved. In addition all characters are fictitious and any resemblance to real persons living or dead is coincidental (except the bit about Stalin). All right, there are bits of satire where I have a dig at such things as payday loan companies and coffee houses that don't know how to make really good coffee, but if you think it's you then either it isn't or you have a guilty conscience.

One more thing. This story is in fact mostly safe for children, but since there are a couple of mentions of droplets of water on the ends of nipples I had to classify it Parental Guidance. If your little ones are suddenly going to ask you, 'what's a nipple, mummy?' you need to have a prepared answer, so that you don't blush and tell them to ask the other parent. Also the word 'orgasm' has crept in a couple of times, but only in a totally innocent context. On second thoughts, best not read it to the kids.

You may now read on, even if you are a bad person or a lawyer acting for a payday loan company.

May you also be transformed as Lionel will be, by meeting the unexpected with an open heart.

Acknowledgements

For help with occasional phrases in Spanish I am indebted to my good friend Jorge Terren, the wonderful Colombian poet, singer and guitarist, and to my Wattpad acquaintance and author @AndRigelVega.

I am also grateful to my many readers on Wattpad who have given me encouragement by reading all the way to the end, and to anyone who has pointed out errors whether textual slips or inconsistencies in the plot.

I am particularly grateful to Jenny Lineham who supplied many jokes under the pseudonym of Jel E. Fish and also encouraged my secretary Myfanwy when she was at a low ebb, and to Robin Dace otherwise known as HRH Reuben Dogsandwich III who also gave invaluable advice on the layout and typography. I also take my hat off to my late grandfather Charles Braybrooke, book designer to Jonathan Cape. I hope the present humble effort will not disgrace his memory.

Needless to say any remaining errors are entirely the responsibility of the author.

1. A Mermaid in the Bath

Lionel Fortescue was taken aback one day when he found a mermaid in his bath.

"How the devil did that get there?" he thundered. "And she's borrowed my rubber ducky! The impertinence!"

The mermaid was pleasantly well-formed to the point of being Rubenesque and she had a sweet smile. She looked at him with round eyes. The water glistened on the orbs of her breasts, and her tail swished gently at the tap end near the plug-hole. However she said nothing.*

"Give me back my ducky at once!" Lionel said commandingly, but the mermaid merely looked at him demurely. He made a grab for the ducky, but she would not let it go, and he found her grip to be unbreakable. In pulling harder on the ducky he was necessarily drawn towards the bath and found his face closer to the breasts than decorum would allow.

Lionel's face was full of steam, whether from the moisture rising from the bath or from an exhalation from his own pores he could not tell.

"If you do not give me back my ducky I shall have to call the police!" Lionel tried to control the passion in his voice.

The mermaid said nothing, the soap suds caressing her breasts as they rose and fell slightly with each breath.

Lionel went into his study and lifted the handset on his telephone.

---

* Footnote from Prof. Neville Twistytrouser: Close reading of later chapters suggests the possibility, indeed likelihood that, although the mermaid is of Cornish ancestry, she may have some African blood. I feel I should mention this now in case someone makes a film out of it and overlooks this at the casting stage, an oversight that would sooner or later be spotted by attentive readers.

"Police please. Yes it is rather. My rubber ducky's been taken. Yes well it has sentimental value. Yes I did see the thief, she's still here, in my bath. Well of course the rubber ducky is still in the house, the thief is in my bath as I just told you. Long hair, well-built, totally naked and with a fishy tail. Why not? Signs of breaking and entering? Well no, not as such. Why isn't it your department? Well whose is it then I'd like to know?"

Lionel stormed back towards the bathroom, then hesitated at the door, and knocked. There was no reply, only the gentle splashing of water in the bath. He paused, uncertain of what to do, then took a deep breath and strode in.

The mermaid was now sitting forward washing her hair. Lionel noticed one or two tiny crabs being washed out, wriggling in the stream of dilute shampoo flowing through her long wavy locks, together with a few strands of seaweed. There was a small sea anemone stuck to the side of the bath near the tap end. His bath was beginning to resemble a rock pool.

Little cascades dropped from the ends of her tresses and wound down her back in ever-changing sinusoidal courses.

Pulling himself together, Lionel exclaimed, "This won't do at all! This is my bath you know." The mermaid ignored this remark as if it were irrelevant to the task at hand, which was the restoration of her hair to its proper glory.

Lionel noticed that with her hands occupied with her hair, her raised arm revealed an incurved armpit like a gentle harbour in some sleepy Cornish village. He thought of fishing boats and ice-cream.

At this point the rubber ducky was floating on the far side of the bath next to her silvery thigh. He noticed that her thighs were covered with thousands of tiny scales like mother of pearl. He paused, vaguely enchanted by the way each scale glistened with a point of light. Then, breaking though his sense of wonder, he made a lunge for the duck.

The mermaid was too quick for him. Lionel missed the duck, his hand plunged into the bath meeting no resistance and he fell. He found his face under water. His nose was pressed against the shallow groove where the mermaid's big fishy tail was not quite separated into two thighs at the top. The mermaid did nothing.

Retrieving himself with as much dignity as he could manage he flicked the wet hair out of his eyes and ran out of the room.

"Coastguard? You see, there is a mermaid in my bath and she's taken my rubber ducky. Yes, my bath is in my house, where else would it be? Well of course the house is on dry land. *Yes but there is water in the bath*. So would you be able to help me if I lived in a houseboat? Well really. My taxes pay your wages, you know! I demand to speak to your superior. [pause] There's a mermaid in my bath and your junior says... Well no the ducky isn't contraband as far as I know. I bought it in British Home Stores although it does say made in China on its bottom. I see. Try Customs and Excise. Well thanks for nothing. Goodbye."

Lionel paused. This was not going well at all. The mermaid was firmly ensconced in his bath with his rubber ducky. How would he shower in the morning before going to work? Lionel was a chartered accountant, and under no circumstances did he want to turn up to work looking less than pristine.

Perhaps, he decided, she would eventually finish her ablutions and be content to return to the sea by whatever route she had arrived in his bathroom. This was indeed a mystery, since he could not imagine so buxom a creature coming up through the plughole as spiders are sometimes alleged to do. Likewise the idea that she had been dropped through the skylight by a passing seagull seemed moderately improbable.

Musing on these and other possibilities Lionel decided to try a different tack. He boiled a kettle and found a fish stock cube in the kitchen cupboard. This he put in the teapot with the union flag printed on it. He wondered vaguely if by this ruse he might detect from the mermaid's reaction whether or not she was loyal to the Crown. This might come in useful as evidence if and when he took up the Coastguard's suggestion of ringing H. M. Customs and Excise, since they might take interest in the problem if he could convince them that the mermaid was not from British Territorial Waters. This line of thought did seem a little tenuous even to Lionel, since there was no evidence that she carried any baggage that might be liable to duty, other than the comb and mirror he had seen resting on the soap rack.

Putting the teapot and a cup and saucer on a tray together with a small salt cellar and a little silver teaspoon he re-entered the bathroom, not knocking this time but pushing the door open with his foot.

The mermaid appeared to have finished washing her hair and was now combing it with the little tortoiseshell comb in one hand and holding the mirror in the other. The water ran down her forearms and trickled off the ends of her elbows. Her tail flicked back and forth gently, sending speckles of reflected light onto the walls and ceiling. Her body seemed abnormally real, living, more alive and immediate than anything Lionel remembered seeing before. He found himself trying to tally the number of drops of water on her shoulders. Wisps of steam were rising from her back and from her breasts. He wondered if mermaids were in any way tax-deductible. Perhaps if they were an endangered species he might at least claim for the shampoo.

As if in a dream he set down the tray on the bathroom stool. "Fish tea," he said. "Tell me if it's too strong."

The mermaid said nothing but turned to look at him with those big round eyes. She smiled briefly and then turned to look at the tea tray, her body curved and counterpoised into as near a mannerist contrapposto as it is possible for a mermaid in a bath to have. Lionel was not familiar with mannerist contrapposto and so this was a new experience for him. He found himself saying a little huskily, "Shall I pour?"

Since the mermaid said nothing he poured the fish tea into the cup. As he handed it to her the cup rattled slightly as it had not been placed squarely on the saucer. "Salt?" he offered, and she held the cup and saucer steady as he stirred. The teaspoon tinkled against the sides of the cup. Even the fish tea winked in the sunlight.

She drank the tea with an audible slurp and with evident satisfaction. Some of it dribbled down the sides of her mouth. Having drained the cup she floated it in the bath next to the rubber ducky. She then resumed her ablutions in a kind of lazy way as if time were endless, squeezing the soap between her hands until it popped up towards the ceiling and landed in the far end of the bath with a plop. With her lathered hands she then caressed her whole body slowly, starting from the back of her neck and working down and around, cupping her breasts meditatively for a while then moving on down towards her navel and beyond.

Lionel stood there not knowing what to do, his mind a blank. Part of him felt he should not be there at all and another part of him did not want to move or even think.

Without knowing how, he found himself again in his study. He had already dismissed from his mind the possibility of ringing Customs and Excise, sensing in advance another pointless defeat. It crossed his mind to try the Ministry of Agriculture and Fisheries, but he couldn't think of a way of presenting the facts that would goad them into action. There was no evidence at all that she had imported any Colorado beetles nor was she infested with oak processionary moths. Besides, he had now given her tea, and it was not the British way to report guests whom you have invited to tea to the Ministry of Agriculture and Fisheries.

Well, he hadn't actually invited her, but tea had been served so the point was now moot. A fine legal mind might be able to untangle it, but alas, Lionel was only an accountant.

Lionel sank down into his study chair and leaned back, resting his hands on the leather-topped desk. He stared out of the window to the shimmering sea beyond. Clouds passed, each momentarily obscuring the sun.

"What am I going to do?" he thought.

A note from the author

Dear Fishy Afficionados,
One of my early readers, Ann Chovy, has said: "Silly man! He could just get into the bath with her."

Another correspondent, one Jel E. Fish, says: "Is it possible that the previous week a charity worker came round collecting for the Marine Environmental Rescue Mission or MERM Aid? He may have ticked the box pledging support."

As to the latter, this may well have been the case. We shall see. It is possible that the mystery of exactly how the mermaid came to be in Lionel's bath will never be completely clarified. Not everything is revealed, not even to me, the writer.

As to why he didn't just jump in the bath, there are any number of reasons why this did not happen, an aversion to sea anemones perhaps being the least of them. In general accountants do not normally leap into baths with mermaids, as the topic is not covered in their accounting manuals.

Respectfully yours,
Más de Merengue

A MERMAID IN THE BATH

A note from Myfanwy

Hello Seaweedy Sweethearts,
That's the trouble with men isn't it? If you don't want them then they're all over you, but on the other hand if you take the trouble to turn up in a fellow's bath naked he still doesn't always take the hint.

Men can be quite bad at interpreting a woman's signals, even when we're not that subtle.

I think this tale is a bit odd, although in regard to the mermaid in the bath it's very true-to-life, isn't it?

A kiss,
Myfanwy

2. The Curious Suggestiveness of Numbers

Lionel found it difficult to settle at work.

Something had prevented him from going into the bathroom the previous night and he had gone to bed unwashed. Mercifully he had a separate toilet where he had sat for longer than necessary staring at the back of the door and thinking about nothing in particular.

If the thought came to ring the authorities he dismissed it as pointless. There seemed to be no official mechanism for dealing with mermaids. He supposed that at the time when mermaids were a common problem on the high seas there would have been little incentive to draft legislation about them, as most of those who tangled with them were probably buccaneers whose own position in the eyes of the law was at best ambiguous.

When he had awoken he had crept to the bathroom door and listened intently. There was no longer any splashing, and at first he thought the mermaid was asleep, or even that she had slipped away by whatever means it was that she had first arrived. This latter thought gave him a strange feeling in the pit of his stomach that he could not quite identify. Then he had heard singing, almost inaudible but very beautiful, with no words, or none that he could pick out.

He had tried to look through a thin crack in the door. It was an old cottage and the doors were original, with the consequence that there was a very narrow gap between the boards in one place. By moving his head from side to side slightly a reasonable image could be formed of what was on the other side. The mermaid was now sitting on the ledge of the square window with only the end of her tail still dipped in the bathwater. The bath itself now seemed to have acquired a lot more fauna and flora than he remembered from the previous night.

He had dressed and gone to work unshowered.

The curious suggestiveness of numbers

At his desk he found the long columns of figures on the screen staring at him meaninglessly. The 9s reminded him of seahorses and the 6s of hermit crabs sticking one claw out of their shells. The zeros reminded him of the mermaid's eyes and the 3s he tried not to think about at all. By a supreme effort of will he made himself concentrate on the task in hand, which was to offset the cost of barnacle removal from a fishing boat hull against profits but taking into account the European subsidy for not fishing on prescribed days. This was for Captain Kipper of the *Saucy Jellyfish*.

Owing to an oversight in Brussels in failing to remind the French government to repeal the legislation of 1793 and also owing to the mandate of pan-European harmonisation this had to be calculated according to the *calendrier révolutionnaire français*.

This of course meant creating a new cell in the spreadsheet and applying the formula creator, which regrettably did not have a built-in function for translating dates in the French revolutionary calendar into a form compatible with a UK 5th of April year end. After three failed attempts Lionel felt he needed to clear his head.

He wandered over to the water cooler but a glass of cold water did nothing to settle his thoughts, which were of tiny crabs being washed out of long hair in rivulets, and thighs covered with iridescent scales. Most of all, that moment repeated itself when he had handed the mermaid fish tea and she had looked at him with those big round eyes, and the cup had rattled because it had not been set squarely on the saucer.

"Mavis, I'm going outside for a smoke," he announced to his secretary.

"But you don't smoke!" she replied, wide-eyed.

"No, but I'm entitled to a smoking break just the same as the smokers. If it isn't in the European Working Time Directive then it should be!" he said defiantly. This was a side of Lionel that

Mavis had not seen before. She had never known he could be so masterful.

He walked distractedly down to the promenade and then down to the beach, and since it was low tide he walked for some distance away from the town, inhaling the clean sea air with its tang of salt and hint of decaying seaweed. A flock of small cumulus clouds drifted slowly across the sea horizon like sheep in no particular hurry.

Lionel felt that he had a problem but he could not say what the problem was in precise terms, or perhaps he was avoiding saying what it was since to do so would have required him to do something, and he was far from convinced that he would want to do whatever it was that saying what it was would imply he should do. Once you formulate a problem in precise terms the answer nearly always pops up with surprising inevitability, like a bar of wet soap when squeezed, Lionel thought, so if you don't want to do anything it's best not to think too carefully.

As he was thinking these things, or to be more precise, avoiding thinking these things, the solution to his accounting problem came to him with the suddenness of a seagull's message landing on the head of an unsuspecting tourist drinking a pint of cider in the forecourt of a harbourside pub. It was both simple and exhilaratingly bold. He would claim on behalf of his client on the basis that in order to have a subsidy for not doing something you had to have the means of doing it *all the time* otherwise no-one would pay you for not doing what you weren't going to do anyway. Therefore barnacles were claimable not just in proportion to days spent at sea but in *toto*. Captain Kipper of the *Saucy Jellyfish* would be pleased.

With that revelation he turned and walked back along the beach, a new firmness in his step. Something, at least, had been resolved.

The Curious Suggestiveness of Numbers

A note from the author

Dear Mermaid-loving Chums,
Another correspondent writes:
   "Has it crossed your mind that the sudden and unexpected appearance of this mermaid might have been due to quantum intertwingling? Thus, there will be no need to squeeze her voluptuousness through the plug-hole."
   As to that, you should understand that mermaids are not to be tampered with lightly, irrespective of any quantum indeterminacy. We all know that we don't know what happened to Schrödinger's cat, and I think we should leave it there.
   Yours,
   Morgan Mountebank

A note from Myfanwy

Dear Ubiquitous Urchins,
"She had never known he could be so masterful."
   I like a man who is masterful, don't you?
   A kiss,
   Myfanwy

3. A POLICEMAN CALLS

SOLVING THE BARNACLE PROBLEM had put Lionel in an altogether lighter mood. Somehow the problem of the mermaid seemed less urgent. He even whistled a little on his way home.

"She might be hungry," he thought. There was nothing to eat in the bathroom, and he doubted the mermaid would be able to get into the kitchen as there was no way of swimming there. Mind you, you never know.

Indeed you never know anything, or hardly anything. You have an intractably difficult accounting problem, and then the answer just pops into your head when you're least expecting it. And again, you can be an ordinary fellow and even perhaps rather dull (Lionel, whatever his other shortcomings, was at any rate not conceited) and then for no reason at all you find a mermaid in your bath.

Why, Lionel wondered, do strange things happen to some people, yet other people can pass their whole lives and nothing out of the ordinary ever happens to them? It seemed on the face of it a little unfair.

Anyway, his way passed the fish and chip shop and Lionel went in and ordered two large portions of cod and chips. "Wrapped, please," he specified. He left one of them without vinegar in case the mermaid didn't like it.

On entering the house there was indeed no sign of the mermaid in the kitchen and no evidence of rummaging in the fridge. He tapped on the bathroom door and gently opened it. The mermaid was now back in the bath watching the sea out of the window. She turned as Lionel came in, a question in her eyes on seeing the newspaper parcels, from which a very promising smell of cooked cod was emerging.

Lionel sat on the little bath stool and opened up one of the packages (the one without the vinegar) and handed it to her. She was clearly puzzled but the smell convinced her to bite into the fish, which she then finished as fast as its temperature would allow. The chips she handed back with the sweetest smile Lionel had ever seen. Her chest heaved as she took in a deep breath and let it out again with a sigh, gazing at him. Droplets wobbled on the ends of her nipples, which Lionel could not help seeing but pretended not to.

He met her eyes for but a moment and almost immediately dropped his gaze to the floor, not knowing what to do next and feeling acutely uncomfortable. He sat there in silence studying the grain pattern in the polished wooden floor for what seemed like an hour but was probably about a minute. Suddenly there was a loud knock at the door.

Relieved, Lionel rushed out of the room and downstairs and opened the front door. Standing there was a small policeman.

"Constable Figgis of Pengoggly Police. I have come to investigate a complaint." The policeman wasted no time in coming to the point.

"Yes?"

"A person or persons has or have complained that you are running a disorderly establishment."

Lionel looked blank.

"To whit, a lady of negotiable affections disporting her mammaries to the general public from your upstairs window while dressed as a mermaid. Might I come in?"

Lionel stood there for a moment taking this in. The presence of the police the previous day would have been welcome, at a time when Lionel merely wished his ordinary existence not to be interrupted by mythical creatures. However the police had proved most unhelpful and now the damage was done and Lionel had been irrevocably changed into someone to whom unusual things happen. The moment had passed.

Lionel did not move. "Do you have a warrant?" he asked.

"Not as such," replied the officer, "but I was hoping that as a respectable citizen you would comply with my request, coming as it does from one whose remit is to protect decent people from unwarranted intrusions into their quotidian existence."

"Well yesterday when I rang, you said that it wasn't your department," said Lionel huffily.

"Well it is now."

"What's more, she isn't a lady of negotiable affections and I resent that remark," said Lionel stoutly. "I merely gave her fish and chips out of the goodness of my heart and I can assure you that at no time did she solicit these from me nor did I extract any recompense in kind or otherwise, so there, with all due respect, officer."

"Fish and chips, is that what you call it!" said the officer with a sneer.

"A piece of cod, if you must know."

"I wouldn't mention your codpiece too much if I were you. Don't think you have heard the last of this," said the officer, "and I'd advise you if she does want to sit in public view pretending to be a mermaid you should at least make her wear a cockle shell bra, like on Disney." With that the officer turned to go.

"Cockle shell bra!" Lionel felt an unfamiliar warmth of passion arising within his chest as he shouted after the retreating policeman. "If you were a mermaid glorying in your carefree nakedness would you wear a cockle shell bra? I doubt you've even tried to wear cockle shell underpants!" Lionel heard himself say these things with some surprise as he had never heard himself say anything like it before. The officer looked back over his shoulder and hesitated before getting into the police car, a grim expression on his face.

A note from Myfanwy

Hello Corruscating Cockles,
Cockle shell bra? You won't find that in Marks and Spencer. You've only got to think about it for two seconds to realise it's a non-starter.

"I think there's a real gap in the market for cockle shell bras, Lord Sugar."

"You're fired."

A kiss,

Myfanwy

4. The Disquieting Nature of Love

LIONEL CLOSED THE FRONT DOOR firmly behind him and walked up the stairs.

"It's all right, he's gone," he shouted through the bathroom door, but he didn't go in. Instead he went to his study and sat once more at his desk. The problem of the mermaid was getting more complicated, and the time for thinking clearly had come.

Why, in just over twenty four hours had the mermaid gone from being an unwanted nuisance to being something or someone he had, at least temporarily, saved from the police? What would the police do to her if they discovered she was a real mermaid? Nothing at all good could come from that, Lionel thought, imagining scientific investigations or the circus as possible outcomes. He also realised with a start that he had quite forgotten about the rubber ducky and didn't care much if he never saw it again.

Which brought him to the most difficult question of all. His feelings for her. The fact was that visions of her repeatedly intruded into his thoughts: little crabs in her long wavy hair, rivulets down her back, her beautiful scaly thighs, droplets—he had to admit to himself that this made him feel weak at the knees —droplets on her nipples, her smile which could melt an ice cream cornet at a hundred paces and most of all her deep sea eyes. The columns of figures all added up. It was very disturbing, but there was no doubt about it.

On the negative side of the balance sheet were the following. Item: she hasn't spoken one word to me. How do I know what she thinks of me? Does she even understand English? Item: she has a fishy tail. How can there be any future in a relationship between a man and a maid with a fishy tail? And most serious of all, item: why would any woman have feelings for me, a dull and in no wise handsome chartered accountant, who is neither tall nor rich and drives a very ancient brown Morris Minor with rust in the front wings just behind the headlights?

One thing Lionel was now sure of. Whether the mermaid liked him or not, whether there was any future in their relationship beyond this brief encounter, these moments stolen from time over fish tea and cod in newspaper, he was determined to let no harm come to her.

To love—Lionel dared think the word—to love is a risk. Most of all it is a risk of being rejected, of being hurt to one's core. To love is also to risk loss. He was used to his life being grey—comfortable in a dull kind of way, like those days when you don't go out because it's the weekend and it's raining and no-one's called, so you stay in and play patience.

With those thoughts turning in his head Lionel felt there was nothing more he could do, now that he had confronted some of the truths of the situation. He felt overwhelmingly tired. On his way to the bedroom he knocked gently on the bathroom door and heard in response a little splash.

Taking this as a signal to open the door he peered cautiously in. As his head rounded the door his gaze met the mermaid's. She fixed him with those deep sea eyes and this time he did not look away. It was not that he felt brave or that he was steeling himself. It was simply that he had no energy left for being embarrassed, that he was tired of being Lionel, that he had no energy any more for being the dull and in no wise handsome chartered accountant who is neither tall nor rich and drives a very ancient brown Morris Minor with rust in the front wings just behind the headlights. What happens will happen.

He stood in the doorway a long time, and all the time she looked into his eyes. Her face was open, guileless, almost expressionless, almost serene yet betraying a sense of longing. It would be a cheap metaphor to say that he was drowning in her eyes, but he wanted to.

"Goodnight," he whispered softly. He felt her eyes still on him as he gently closed the door.

A note from Myfanwy

Hello Littoral Luminaries,
Well I like it so far. It's kind of a love story isn't it? Boy gets girl then loses her almost immediately because she's a mermaid. Sort of like when you fancy someone in spite of the fact that there's an insurmountable problem, like the boy being English and stuffy and the girl being Welsh and passionate.

Anyway, Marin Marinade has asked me to send you the next chapter, in which Lionel takes the accounts to Captain Kipper. Don't worry, it's not about accounts, it's about *feelings*.

love,
Myfanwy

5. A MYSTERIOUS STRANGER

THE NEXT MORNING Lionel got up early and ran down to the supermarket to buy some fresh oysters for the mermaid's breakfast, some haddock for her lunch and some sole for their supper. The Chinese takeaway was open early today for the fisher folk, so he bought a box of crispy seaweed as well.

The sun shone brightly through a sea mist and Lionel felt unaccountably happy. Only the sight of the police patrol car parked near the harbour cast a cloud over his mood. P.C. Figgis was in it, and wound down the window.

"I'm on to you," said P.C. Figgis menacingly. Lionel ignored him and walked on. "You watch your step," the constable called out to Lionel's retreating back.

Once Lionel was out of sight, Figgis drove off. A stranger dressed in what looked like a tattered naval uniform tried to flag him down.

"What do you want?" Figgis called out.

"A lift to Kasteldrog, if you're going that way," the stranger requested.

"No, you may not have a lift. I am in a hurry."

"I should be indebted to you for a lift part-way, as I am weary and a stranger in these parts," the stranger persisted. "Will you not help an old naval officer fallen on hard times?"

"Do you imagine I am a taxi service? You can walk there for all I care!" Figgis exclaimed, and with that he sped off.

When Lionel got back the mermaid did not answer his knock. Quietly opening the bathroom door he saw that she was asleep, her head resting on the bath sponge and her breasts rising and falling gently with her slow breathing, her tail twitching occasionally. Her face was impossibly beautiful. He set down the oysters, the haddock and the crispy seaweed on the bath stool and went back out again.

It was time for work. It was not a busy time of year so he decided he would take the completed accounts and draft tax return to Captain Kipper of the *Saucy Jellyfish*. Lionel was very proud of these accounts because he had solved the barnacle problem, and a chat with Captain Kipper was always a pleasure.

The *Saucy Jellyfish* was moored near *The Frothy Coffee With a Bit of Coffee and Quite a Lot of Milk Café*. Lionel sat down at his usual table outside, ordered two coffees, *macchiato* so that they wouldn't be too milky, and waited. He noticed a man in an oversized raincoat sitting at the next table reading a newspaper, but thought nothing of it.

Captain Kipper was every bit the archetypal fisherman, with his ruddy face, large trousers and navy blue polo-neck sweater. "Ahoy there, Leo!" he addressed Lionel loudly before plonking himself down on one of the thin metal chairs, which creaked slightly. The man with in the oversized raincoat looked over the top of his newspaper and then continued reading. The front page headline read, "Marina development approved."

They went over the accounts together, but this did not take long because Captain Kipper frankly did not understand accounts and he trusted Lionel to do a proper job. The barnacle issue he understood was a *good thing*, but he would not have been able to explain it to anyone five minutes later. The man in the oversized raincoat ordered another coffee.

"Well now, me lad, how are things with 'ee these days?" Captain Kipper enquired.

"Well," began Lionel, lowering his voice, "there's a small problem I'd like your advice on, strictly between you and me."

Captain Kipper smiled knowingly. "Ah harr!" he said, "you have finally fallen in love."

Lionel was startled. "What makes you say that?"

"You have a twinkle in your eye that I h'ain't seen before, and you have a problem, which is a rare thing with 'ee. So tell me all about it!"

"Well," began Lionel, not quite knowing how to begin, "thinking back it might have been when I ticked the box on the form."

"Form?"

"Yes, that must have been it. Someone came to the door with a form asking for a donation to the Marine Environmental Rescue Mission or MERM Aid. She was a sweet looking young woman and you know how sometimes you do things just to get a smile, so I gave a donation and ticked the box agreeing to receiving further information."

"Donations to mermaids, is it? So you're in love with this young woman and don't know what to do about it, is that it, me salty lad?"

"Not that young woman, although come to think of it there was a remarkable resemblance. No," and here Lionel dropped his voice further because the man with the oversized raincoat was still there, "there is a mermaid in my bath."

"Mermaid?" said Captain Kipper, rather too loudly. "Have you been drinking too much o' that Caribbean rum?"

"Maybe I ticked the wrong box and they have sent me a mermaid," whispered Lionel. Captain Kipper looked thoughtful.

Lionel put down enough money on the table to cover both their coffees and tugged Captain Kipper by the sleeve. "Let's go," he said.

As they got up to go Lionel noticed out of the corner of his eye that the man in the oversized raincoat had also got up. "Who is that man?" he asked.

"Arr," said the Captain, "that be Sidney Sinister, private eye. On a case, no doubt."

A MERMAID IN THE BATH

A note to the author from Jel E. Fish

Dear Marzine,
Good chapter—especially the rather brilliant bit about the form!
 Teehee,
 Jel E. Fish

From the author

Dear Frolicking Fish Fanciers,
I need to add the following sentence, highlighted below, to the end of the relevant paragraph of chapter 5.

The man in the oversized raincoat looked over the top of his newspaper and then continued reading. The front page headline read, "Marina development approved."

That's because I haven't fully figured out the plot yet and the present tends to influence the past, contrary to what most people think.

On another topic, one of my correspondents, Ann Chovy, suggested that P.C. Figgis can't have been loved properly as a baby which is why he is so bad-tempered, and so he needs to be taken in hand by a voluptuous woman.

I must say I had originally assumed that all the bad guys would be properly routed, but then there are some comedies in which a happy ending for all concerned is possible—or maybe that only happens in Gilbert and Sullivan. Well it's better than all those mad Italian operas where everyone dies miserably owing to multiple misunderstandings. Since this is a British story I think it is only right that the worst effects of multiple misunderstandings should be that various characters' trousers fall down revealing spotty boxer shorts. We are, after all, a cultured nation.

Anyway, I am currently working on the Figgis problem.

A MYSTERIOUS STRANGER

Any further comments are welcome, although I do not guarantee to include them if they are contrary to British decency or infringe any provisions of the Underwater Pastimes Act (Tiddlywinks Amendment) of 1863.

In the next chapter the mermaid gets arrested. I just hope I don't paint myself into a corner with this. It's going to be awfully tricky to get all this sorted out, and it's getting more complicated by the minute.

Sincerely,
Mordred Mevagissey

From Myfanwy

Hello Denizens of the Deep,

Morton Murgatroyd has no idea what he's doing, does he? He's making it up as he goes along. I hope he really does have guidance from a goddess because otherwise this is going to end up a right muddle.

Between you and me, I expect a happy ending, but I can quite see how it could all go wrong.

You know what I think? I think some sad endings are where the storyteller has got lost and just decides to end it any-old-where because they are too lazy to do it properly. That's what.[*]

Defiantly,
Myfanwy
xoxoxo

---

[*] Footnote by Professor Neville Twistytrouser, Warden of St Doris College, Oxford: Tragedy does have a place in culture. It's just that it doesn't make you smily. More a sort of catharsis (from the Greek *katharisteria*, meaning the dry cleaners).

6. The Mermaid is Arrested

WHEN THEY GOT TO THE HOUSE there was a crowd outside and a police van, but the window was empty of any suggestion of the mermaid. The front door was open and P.C. Figgis was standing outside.

Lionel rushed up as if to go inside but Figgis stopped him with an outstretched hand.

"Where do you think you're going?" said the officer.

"If I might enter my own house?"

"You may, but she's gone."

Lionel rushed upstairs and burst into the bathroom. There was a young woman with a press camera photographing the bath, but no mermaid. Of the oysters only the shells were left, but the haddock and crispy seaweed remained uneaten. Grabbing the haddock he rushed downstairs again only to see the police van disappear up Harbour Lane.

Without a word Lionel flung the haddock onto the back seat of the Morris Minor (with the rust in the front wings just behind the headlights) and he and the Captain took off after the van.

When they reached the police station Lionel was just in time to catch a glimpse of the mermaid being hauled out of the back of the van trapped in a large fishing net, although Captain Kipper could not see clearly as his view was blocked by the van. The mermaid caught sight of Lionel and the pleading expression on her face was unmistakeable. There was bleeding from some of her scales. Then she was lost to view.

"What be going on?" Captain Kipper frowned.

Lionel had no hesitation. He bounded up to the police station door and on entering, stood at the glass window and rang the bell. A police officer strolled slowly over.

"And what can we do for you?" It was P.C. Figgis looking slightly out of breath and with damp patches on his uniform.

"What have you done with my mermaid?" Lionel demanded loudly.

"Your mermaid is it? And you would be?"

"Lionel Fortescue of 7 Marine Parade, Pengoggly, as you well know."

"Ah. Do you have a mermaid licence?"

"No, do I need one?"

"Do you *need* one? I think it is your business to know the law before embarking on keeping mermaids, sir." Sergeant Spriggan had entered the room behind P.C. Figgis and they exchanged knowing smirks.

"Now then," continued Figgis, "this has been very entertaining so I shan't charge you on this occasion, but it doesn't do to waste police time with made-up stories about imaginary creatures, or as you might say, fishy tales." His shoulders shook with mirth at his own joke. "I suggest you run along now and sleep it off. Mermaids! Very droll I'm sure."

By now Captain Kipper had caught up with Lionel and was standing behind him holding the haddock.

"I don't know what be going on here," he said, "but whoever it is you got in custody there, we should like to see her."

"You too?" said P.C. Figgis. "I seem to recall your boat licence is up for renewal. It wouldn't do for a person prone to hallucinations taking a boat on the high seas and being a potential danger to shipping, now would it? Run along, both of you, and go easy on the cider."

"But we both saw you at my house!" protested Lionel. "What was that all about, then?"

"A routine matter I assure you. We had complaints about a young lady disporting herself in an unseemly manner, which I warned you about as you recall. I am happy to inform you that the young lady in question has removed herself to a more appropriate premises. Of course we have on record your recent request for assistance and I am happy to have been of service on this occasion. Your problem is thus resolved in a satisfactory manner. Good day to you both."

Captain Kipper stood his ground. "Well I don't know what be going on but it be you that smells o' bad fish. Give this haddock to your prisoner, whomsoever she be, as it do belong to her as I believe."

He pushed the haddock through the gap under the glass window. Figgis and Spriggan did not move, but stood there, arms folded in silence. After a long pause Lionel, fuming, turned to go, and Captain Kipper followed him out.

As Lionel started up the Morris Minor, Captain Kipper noticed a figure in an oversized raincoat entering where they had just left. Lionel paused, handbrake on, the engine still in neutral, his hands tense on the wheel.

"Leave it for now," Captain Kipper advised, "we'll come back later. There be something amiss here, and be of no doubt I'll stick by ye till we sort it out, me salty lad."

As they left, Lionel thought he heard faintly above the engine noise and the sound of seagulls, the sound of singing, beautiful as a girls' cathedral choir and mournful enough that it squeezed the heart like a sponge.

A note from the author

Dear Salty Sea Anemones,
The goddess Aerfen has indicated to me that this should have a happy ending, but that's about all I know at the moment.

As to Myfanwy's little outburst, I think she should confine herself to typing the manuscripts and making the tea, rather than taking on herself the role of literary critic. I do know what I am doing, at least some of the time.

Huh,
Mellifluous Mollusc

7. Puce-on-cream toile de Jouy wallpaper

AFTER SUNDOWN Lionel picked Captain Kipper up from the harbour and drove slowly towards Harbour Lane and on towards the police station. He had with him in the car a bag containing a flashlight, a metal file, a crowbar and a set of screwdrivers.

Lionel switched off the headlights as they approached and parked the car just before the bend, out of sight if anyone should have been watching. They crept out, taking the bag with them.

The police station was in darkness save for a single light in the office at the front of the building and the blue light over the door. An approach from the front was clearly doomed to failure.

"We must go round the back," Captain Kipper whispered, "but I don't see how."

To the Captain's surprise Lionel walked softly through the front garden of the house next door and tapped on the door.

After a while a little old lady answered the door. "Lionel!" she said at once, "what are you doing out so late?"

"Ssh!" whispered Lionel. He indicated the presence of the Captain and the little old lady ushered them in.

"Come in come in!" she said, excitedly. "Any friend of Lionel's is a friend of mine! Lionel looked after my cat when I was taken sick in the hospital you know. Nothing too much trouble! Why he's still single I don't know—such a lovely man. Would you like a cup of tea?"

Lionel explained the situation. "You see, Nellie, there was a mermaid in my bath..."

"A mermaid?"

Nellie looked shocked. A strange mixture of emotions crossed her face—anxiety mostly, and surprise, and something else. She struggled to recover herself.

The motifs on the chintz on closer inspection proved not to be the usual flowers, but fishes with floral fins in reds and greens.

This marvellous fabric covered the sofa, the armchairs and the curtains, with the same design in yellows and blues for the cushions. All this glory clashed wonderfully with the puce-on-cream toile de jouy wallpaper which, rather than the expected nymphs, shepherds and pagodas, showed instead affecting scenes of handsome sailors caressing winsome mermaids under palm trees, these vignettes interspersed with flying fish.

"... yes, P.C. Figgis has taken her and put her in the cell, so I have to rescue her."

The Captain looked doubtful at the mention of the mermaid.

Nellie looked at the Captain. "I don't know about any mermaid," he said slowly, "but something's amiss, and this Figgis is up to no good ..."

"What was she like?" Nellie cut in. The Captain raised an eyebrow.

"She has sea deep eyes," Lionel explained, his voice suddenly calm and full of presence, "and sometimes she sings so that the sound would either send you immediately to heaven or else break your heart."

Nellie got up. "Something must be done."

She led them to the back door and found a ladder in her garden shed. The two men clambered over the side wall and into the grounds of the police station, pulling the ladder after them. There was a low grumbling as of a sleeping dog somewhere.

They could see in the moonlight where the cell should be, but there was no light on. Lionel called out in a loud whisper.

"Mermaid? Are you there? It's Lionel. From the house. You were in my bath?"

She had never spoken but he knew that she could sing. They listened.

"Mermaid? Mermaid?"

There was no song.

Immediately the dog started growling more loudly and was joined by another—the police alsatians Fenrir and Ragnarok now awake in their pen at the end of the police station garden. The growling turned into loud and persistent barking and the pen rattled.

The Captain and Lionel quickly manoeuvred the ladder under the window of the cell and Lionel climbed up while the Captain steadied the foot.

Since neither Spriggan nor Figgis had spent any time repairing the dog pen it wobbled and creaked under the repeated impacts of the two now frantic beasts.

Lionel reached down and Captain Kipper handed him the flashlight. He peered through the window and shone the torch into the blackness, illuminating in turn each corner of the cell.

It was empty.

As Lionel descended the ladder a light went on at the back of the police station. Kipper grabbed the ladder, set it up against Nellie's garden wall and started to climb, Lionel following. At that moment the dogs broke down the pen and sprang as one in the men's direction. As Lionel neared the top of the ladder Fenrir leaped, grazing Lionel's ankle as he bit. Fenrir was left with a piece of Lionel's trouser leg in his snarling jaws.

A note from Myfanwy

Hello Saline Sirenophiles,
Confine myself to typing and making tea? I'm supposed to type this stuff and not have an opinion? And why can't he make tea sometimes?
    love,
    Myfanwy

8. Tea and St Doris

THERE WAS NOTHING MORE TO BE DONE.

Nellie cleaned Lionel's wound and bandaged it up as best she could, then she insisted on making them both tea before they left. Lionel felt hopeless and tired beyond endurance and would rather have gone straight home to sleep, but consideration for Nellie made him stay.

"Well," she said, pouring, "I was young once and I know what it's like." She turned to Captain Kipper. "You'll have a little whisky in yours too, Captain? Earl Grey and Bruichladdich. Nothing better in an emergency," she went on.

"Aye," said the Captain, smelling the mixture of peat and smoky tea with satisfaction.

Despite the Earl Grey tea with its strong hint of Hebridean mystery, Lionel's face was suffused with despair. "Breath in the vapour!" Nellie commanded, "It will give you strength."

"Strength for what?" Lionel muttered, his shoulders hunched in defeat. He coughed a little as the heady aroma of transformed Islay water went up one nostril and down the other.

"For whatever comes next, of course," said Nellie. "You can't give up now."

"It's all so worrying," Lionel said. But the warming effect of the tea was already extending into his chest on its way to his fingers and toes.

"Worrying?" Nellie said. "No sense in worrying! As Saint Doris says, there are only two kinds of problem: ones you can do something about, and ones you can't. The ones you can't there's no point in worrying about. The ones you can do something about, you go and do it."

"Saint Doris?" the Captain raised a quizzical eyebrow.

"And you a seafaring man!" exclaimed Nellie. "Patron saint of sea slugs..."

"Arr, slimy things!"

"...And anyone in danger in or near or of the sea in and around the Celtic fringes of the British Isles in all cases not already covered by St Brendan. St Brendan can't be doing everything now, can he? And I'll have you know sea slugs are very pretty creatures indeed!"

At this Nellie walked over to what looked like a very shallow wooden wall cupboard with double doors, on the outside of which were painted an anchor and a mermaid in blue and white. Reverentially she opened the doors to reveal a painting in deep medieval colours showing a lady with a mysterious smile riding the waves on a scallop shell, drawn by the most brilliantly patterned sea slugs imaginable. The lady had a halo, and under the picture in gold half-uncials was written, 's. doris pengoggly.'

Lionel was not a believer in the paranormal nor in obscure Celtic saints but curiously this cheered him a little. Nevertheless it was with heavy hearts that he and Captain Kipper finally crept out into the darkness. The barking of the dogs had stopped and all was silence. Around the corner the trusty brown Morris Minor (with a bit of rust in the wings just behind the headlights) waited for them.

By a little pushing with the door open and deft steering Lionel managed to turn the car around in neutral without switching the engine on, and only when they were rolling downhill and well out of sight of the police station did they jump in and turn on the ignition and the headlamps. Almost at once they saw a shadowy figure in what looked in the darkness like a tattered naval uniform walking by the side of the road.

The figure turned and put out a hand to wave Lionel down.

A Mermaid in the Bath

A note from the author

Dear Egregious[1] Echinoderms[2],[*]
I am figuring out who the old sailor is, and then I have to write about Castle Drog, Lola "Hot Stuff" Tabasco, and a sinister pub.

How can I be expected to make tea when all this is going on and the story is all but out of control? Really! And often Myfanwy will keep a running commentary while making the tea, about whether the milk should go in the cup before or after pouring and the finer points of broken orange pekoe, lapsang souchong and assam tips.

A good secretary should just make the tea quietly and put it without comment where I can reach it.

Yours,
Merlin Monkfish

---

[*] A footnote from Professor Neville Twistytrouser:
[1] egregious (adjective)
1 outstandingly bad; shocking : 'egregious abuses of copyright.'
2 archaic remarkably good.
[Oxford English Dictionary]
(take your pick)
[2] Echinodermata (Zoology)
a phylum of marine invertebrates that includes starfishes, sea urchins, brittlestars, crinoids, and sea cucumbers. They have fivefold radial symmetry, a calcareous skeleton, and tube feet operated by fluid pressure.
[Oxford English Dictionary]

9. First news of St Doris Island

LIONEL SLOWED THE CAR and Captain Kipper wound down the window. "What can we do for 'ee?" asked the Captain, somewhat quietly.

"A lift, if you please, as far as you can go without undue inconvenience towards Kasteldrog. I have no money to get there by cab, and it is a long way."

"Get in," said Lionel, feeling that at least he could achieve something useful today. "Captain, shall I drop you off home first?" The stranger had a kindly face, open like a child's, yet his wrinkles suggested the simple wisdom of a life well-lived.

"Not me," said the Captain. "Let's finish the day's work properly and take this fine gentleman all the way, what do 'ee say?"

Lionel nodded and the stranger settled himself in the back seat as the Captain turned around to look at him. Lionel could see in his rear view mirror that the nautical gentleman's cap was emblazoned with the name 'H.M.S. Higgs' in gold braid.

"Arr," the Captain ventured, "the legendary H.M.S. Higgs. Went down with all hands in that there Bermuda Triangle, so they say. I hope 'ee be not some kind o' ghostly apparition."

"Ha ha! I'm as real as you are. The ship went down all right, but we all swam ashore, not a single life lost. There's a little island there, we called it St Doris. Strange it's not on any chart, but there's an extinct volcano on it which is the source of an anomalous magnetic field. Local legend has it that the navy chart makers once visited the island but their measurements were so confused that they couldn't make their charts join together properly in the middle, where the island should be. Since they were coming to the end of their assignment and were looking forward to a holiday in Cuba they decided the easiest thing was to leave out the island altogether. They said to each other, no-one would ever notice so no harm done. Besides, they rather liked the island and couldn't bear the idea of it being overrun with tourists, or at any rate, that's how they reasoned it out afterwards."

"Local legend?" asked Lionel. "So there was someone there already?"

"Well now, perhaps we'll come to that later, as that is delicate information." The stranger lapsed into silence. The little car was now on the main road heading out of Pengoggly on the A-road towards Pentingly, and as they left the edge of the town the street lamps stopped, the only light coming from the headlamps. Even the scattered houses they passed were asleep, and the moon was disappearing behind clouds.

After a while the Captain started up conversation again. "By your uniform you are some kind of officer," he remarked.

The signpost to Kasteldrog came up and Lionel turned into the side road. Almost immediately the road narrowed to a single track with tall hedges on either side, and apart from where the headlamps illuminated the road a little distance ahead, there was utter darkness.

After a pause the stranger replied, "Indeed, I was the bosun."

The Captain started. "Arr, shiver me jellyfish! So it be you they be looking for all this time!"

Lionel, too, was taken aback. "So," he ventured, his voice measured as though speaking quietly in a cathedral, "you are the God particle."

"And so are you and so are all of us," replied the stranger in a quite normal and jolly voice, "but what you mean is, yes, I am the Higgs Bosun. You can call me Alf."

They drove on in silence for some miles, the road twisting and turning. Occasionally there would be a fork in the road and Lionel would have to slow the car to read the signposts. At each fork the road to Kasteldrog seemed to get narrower than before so that at times it scarcely seemed possible for the little Morris to get through at all. At other times the road turned to dried mud and the wheels were forced into ruts that had been formed earlier by tractors.

"So," ventured the Captain again, "'ee be staying at Kasteldrog? It be lonely enough and far from anywhere where 'ee might buy a fish supper! They do say it be infested with pestilential piskies. But tell me to mind me own business if 'ee don't want to say."

"I am on a quest," Alf responded. "There is something important I must find. Something lost from that island many years ago that I must have, if it be granted to me by the powers above to have it, or perish. But enough of me. What are you two about this dark night?"

Lionel spoke. "We also are on a quest, or were, but we have lost." Here he stopped as the risk of tears choked him up and he could not speak. Some part of him watched this with surprise, as though the intensity of the emotion were unexpected and unfamiliar. Yet there it was. Only now did Lionel fully understand the depth of his attachment to the mermaid and the void created by her loss, a void that must have been there all the time but which he never saw, as though one had papered over a huge hole in the floor and by some physical impossibility never fallen through it.

"A quest for what?" Alf enquired. "Ah, but all quests are one quest."

"One quest?" Captain Kipper asked.

"A quest may appear to be for many different things." Alf's voice was calm in the darkness. "A jewel, a mythical beast, a lost island, the eternal city. But it is the quest that is important. For at the end of it a man finds himself."

"But he knows himself all along!" Lionel found his voice again.

"That's where you're wrong. A man's real self is unexpected. Totally unexpected."

This made no sense on the face of it, yet Lionel couldn't help remembering that moment when he had given up being Lionel through the sheer weariness of it, and he and the mermaid had stared silently into each other's eyes.

"A mermaid," Lionel said, almost inaudibly.

"A mermaid," echoed Alf.

There was a long pause. The headlights momentarily lit up a sign reading 'Kasteldrog' and the hedges were now replaced by low dry stone walls, but there was as yet no sign of human habitation.

"Why I'm going along with all this mermaid nonsense I can't figure out rightly," said the Captain suddenly. "I never seen a mermaid in all my years at sea."

"But you're here anyway," said Alf, "and I'm grateful for that."

As the car rounded another bend the dry stone wall gave way to nothingness, then suddenly the headlights illuminated the foot of a white post with a sign above it, displayed under a flickering light.

"Here!" Alf said suddenly. "Stop the car!"

"We'll be blocking the road," protested Lionel.

At the top of the post was a pub sign showing a Cornish pixie sitting on top of a pasty, with the legend, *The Piskie and Pasty* in black gothic letters underneath.

The nothingness was the forecourt of a pub, still apparently open judging by a dim light coming from the downstairs windows. Lionel eased the car off the road.

"I need to find the castle itself," Alf said, "and I can walk from here."

A note from Myfanwy

Hello Finny Friends,

I'll try to be kind, but really Melvyn should make an effort to be a bit more gracious. I've been very attentive. It's not every secretary

who would even bother to make a proper cup of tea, especially when he's so grumpy.
    love,
Myfanwy

10. Love at First Sight and a Dark Warning

"Castle?" Lionel turned off the engine.

"Arr, that be Castle Drog," explained the Captain. "Had a reputation for things that go bump in the night once upon a time. Strange goings on. Poltergeists moving things about some say, or piskies say others. They say the old Lord of the Manor, Arbuthnot Fumble, used to sleep in the east wing, but one morning they found his false teeth in the attic in a glass on the bedside table of the Mexican kitchen maid, one Lola 'Hot Stuff' Tabasco. No-one could ever explain it. Some of the other servants reported a creaking of floorboards, thumping noises and strange cries. Lola herself seemed oddly changed in her mood and would not be drawn on what she had witnessed that night. Right peculiar."

"What did Lady Fumble have to say about it?" enquired Lionel, whose sharp accountant's mind had fastened on a theory.

"Lady Lucretia Fumble had passed on some years before," answered the Captain, "although no-one has ever seen her grave. The whole thing were a bit mysterious, because according to the Pengoggly Post her death certificate said she died o' The Twinge. The coroner did query it, not finding The Twinge in his medical encyclopaedia, but by that time the doctor who signed it, a Dr Squidtentacles, had disappeared without trace, so the coroner passed it and that was that."

The darkness was oppressive, and not much lifted by the dim light coming from the windows of the *Piskie and Pasty*. The loss of the mermaid felt like a weight on Lionel's chest when he didn't think about it, and a sharper pain when he did. He now felt that any adventure not involving his own problems would take him out of himself, which would be some relief. "Whatever your business with Castle Drog, I'd like to help if I can," he addressed Alf.

"Aye, count me in too. But I think we could all do with a drink first," said Captain Kipper.

There were few customers in the *Piskie and Pasty*, and they were all sat in corners, crouched over pints. As the three men walked up to the bar all eyes turned on them suspiciously. The landlord heaved himself up from his stool and leaned on the bar, hands resting on the beer-soaked mats, and stared at them.

"So... what be you doing in these parts?" The landlord spoke slowly, as though he had seen too many Westerns. His accent was local, but there was something about it that did not quite fit.

"My round," Lionel turned to the others. "Alf?"

"Just a single Antiguan rum to warm me up, thank you very much. Must keep my wits about me tonight. Oh, and a pasty if I may beg of your kindness."

"My pleasure. And a pint and a half of *Hideous Pigsty*, please," Lionel added, knowing the Captain's taste in local bitter. The half was for himself, as he was driving.

The landlord did not move. "You bain't from around here," he stated in the same slow drawl, fixing Lionel with an emotionless gaze.

There was an uneasy silence. Then Captain Kipper spoke up. "I be a Cornishman as much as 'ee!"

The landlord appeared to ignore this. The men stood there, saying nothing more. Lionel felt a previously unknown courage surging within him, and held the landlord's stare. An unreasonable amount of time passed.

Finally the landlord appeared to waver. "Woman!" he cried loudly, his head jerked back in the direction of the back room.

Almost immediately emerged a woman who struck something deep within Captain Kipper. She seemed overwhelmingly sad, dressed in a simple off-white smock and a dull brown skirt, her eyes downcast and her face expressing defeat. Yet something about her lit a fire in his simple fisherman's heart. Her wavy raven hair framed a dark complexion and her fine features might have been somewhere between African and Hispanic. Her body, too, was well-formed.

"Serve these gentlemen!" the landlord ordered, "A single rum and a pint and a half of bitter. And a cold pasty." He then slumped back on his stool and seemed to stare into space.

Silently the woman brought the drinks to the bar, making brief eye contact with each of the men as she did so. There was a pleading in her eyes. Captain Kipper touched her hand briefly, almost by accident as she handed him the pint of *Hideous Pigsty*, and he held her gaze longer than the others. There was an unspoken promise in the Captain's expression. Sometimes a lot can happen in the time of taking a breath.

They took the drinks over to an unoccupied table and sat. Alf simply put the cold pasty in his jacket pocket. After the three men had been sipping in silence for a while, one of the denizens of the pub shifted slowly from his place and shambled over.

"You lookin' fer summat?"

Lionel spoke. "Castle Drog. Is it far?" Alf kicked him under the table but it was too late.

There was a stir amongst all the other drinkers.

"Arr!" they all said in near unison, like some rustic Greek chorus,

> "don't 'ee be goin' to that haunted place!
> Cursèd be the day when Arbuthnot
> the Lord and longtime ruler of this land
> did sell his birthright for a pot of gold,
> abandoning his castle, friends and folk,
> into the merciless hands of greedy men!"

"What happened to Lord Fumble, then?" asked Lionel.

The first denizen raised a warning finger. "Sold the castle and all his lands to the Devilipers."

"Developers?" ventured Lionel.

"No, Devilipers."

LOVE AT FIRST SIGHT AND A DARK WARNING

"Don't you read the newspaper?" the Captain chipped in, addressing Lionel, "they're going to build a marina in the harbour, complete with multi-storey hotel, amusement arcade and a giant aquarium. Make Pengoggly into a major tourist resort. Although what they want with the castle I don't know."

A cold stab of fear went through Lionel's heart. First, the loss of the mermaid. Now this, the destruction of the beautiful harbour and the sleepy fishing village that he had grown to love.

"That's it," a second pub denizen picked up the conversation, "sold his birthright and moved to Chelsea. They say when Lady Lucretia died his mind turned dark, and now he be decayed aristocracy, so he be gone to Chelsea to decay some more. The previous landlord of this pub disappeared too, good old Ben. Incarcerated in an old folks home, is what I heard."

At this the landlord looked round darkly, but said nothing.

Lionel said in a faraway voice, "All that gone..."

At this the chorus started up again.

"Arr!

"When those who rule let darkness overcome
"their raddled minds, then rising from the mud
"come fearsome creatures in the shape of men
"who trample beauty in their lust for gain."

"Arr..."
"Arr..."

Alf put a hand onto each of the other men's arms. "It's time to go," he said. Lionel looked around and noticed that the landlord was no longer there, only the woman. She hesitated, looked behind her, then lifted the bar flap and approached the men. She handed a small slip of paper to Captain Kipper. "Your receipt," she said, loud enough for the rest of the drinkers to hear.

"But it were Lionel..." the Captain began, but she was gone.

The men rose slowly and bowed to the denizens. "We thank you for your company, but now we must be on our way," Alf addressed them.

"Whatever 'ee do, don't go to the castle. It be an evil place!" All the denizens rose as one as the men went towards the door.

"Don't go there. No. Arr."

A note from the author

Dear Pulchritudinous Periwinkles,
Another chapter of this thrilling yarn.

I have to inform you that owing to an oversight the purchase of a pasty by Lionel for the Higgs Bosun was omitted from the original text of chapter 10. This is the kind of error that can creep in during long nights in the study.

I am happy to report that Myfanwy at least has stopped giving a running commentary while making the tea, but she still breathes heavily when putting the tea right in front of me instead of slightly to one side, as I asked.

Pip pip!
Melodious Mackerel

11. A HIDDEN PASSAGE AND AN OLD BOOK

ONCE OUTSIDE, ALF GAVE DIRECTIONS in a low voice. Lionel retrieved the flashlight from the car and led the way.

After about a quarter of a mile they came to a high stone wall. Further on still was a set of huge iron gates, through which was blackness, except when briefly the moon shone through the edges of a cloud. Set back a long way they could sometimes make out the silhouette of a large building with turrets and strange spires. Oddly the iron gates were not locked.

Alf gently pushed open one of the gates, which squeaked on its hinges, and went in. The others followed.

The gravel drive crunched underfoot, so they took to the lawn. Every so often their way would be met by a large obelisk of topiary, and they would feel their way round. Coming at last to where the lawn gave way to more gravel in front of the house, they turned left, following the lawn around to the side. Here they met a neglected knot garden. Out of respect for some unknown past gardener they all tried not to trample the low box hedges. Sometimes there was the scent of lavender.

Finally they reached the back of the house where they found a large conservatory. The doors were shut, but Captain Kipper found they gave way with a slight splintering sound on a modest heave of his shoulder.

A dim light was coming from somewhere inside the building. They pushed their way through the shoots of neglected vines hanging with clusters of dried out grapes. Large fan-palm leaves and spiky cycad fronds brushed their faces. When at last they left the tangle behind them they entered a long corridor lit at the far end with a single lightbulb hanging without a shade.

There were signs of former glory in the encaustic tiled floor and the wooden half-panelling of the walls, but the paintwork above the dado rail was cracked and stained, and there were marks on the wall where once pictures had hung. Leading off the corridor were a number of doors, all painted in the same pale green, giving the impression of a stately home turned into a neglected military hospital.

One by one each of them tested one or other of the doors. One was a broom cupboard. Another led into darkness which Lionel's flashlight revealed to be an abandoned library festooned with cobwebs. He called Alf over in a whisper.

"It would help if we knew what we're looking for," Lionel said.

"Don't worry about that," replied Alf, "we'll know it when we find it."

The Captain shrugged and kept opening doors then closing them again.

Lionel paused a little longer in the library. A flash of gold-tooled lettering on the spine of a small book had caught his attention. Closer examination showed it to read 'Seynt Doris Ilande.'

Someone once said that chance favours the prepared mind, and perhaps this was one of those chances.[*]

The leather was hardly worn but it looked dry, ancient and dusty. Lionel picked up the book, and opening it the spine creaked as though it had not been touched in several hundred years. At the title page Lionel read, 'Seynt Doris, an Ilande in ye Westerne Indies, its Historie Geographie & divers Marvells founde therein together with a Description of its Aboriginall Salvages, set down in all Veritie by Henry Herring, Earl of a Bit of Cornwall and not the Other Bit, who went there with Francis Drake, Kt. in the XXI year of the reine of Her Glorious Majestie Queen Elizabeth whom God preserve. Printed and sold at St. Doris-by-the-Fishmonger Churchyard, London MDLXXXXIX.'

---

[*] *Footnote:* 'Dans les champs de l'observation le hasard ne favorise que les esprits preparés.' Louis Pasteur, Lecture, University of Lille, 7 December 1854.

The frontispiece facing the title page showed a woodcut, primitive and wonderful, of a volcanic island fringed with palm trees, in the distance a little ship much like Drake's *Golden Hinde* and dominating the foreground a triumphantly naked mermaid.

Lionel closed the book and put it into his pocket.

It was the matter of a moment. Lionel was an habitually honest man, and had he thought about this at all he would have determined to return the book at the earliest opportunity. It was not greed for a rare manuscript that motivated him, but the promise of information which, while it might not help him, seemed closely related to the story Alf had told them. Also he wondered greatly at the mermaid picture.

He closed the door on the library and continued past Alf and the Captain, who were trying other doors, dependent on the light from that single ceiling bulb. At the far end on the left an opening led to a large hallway dominated by the foot of a grand staircase, but there was no additional lighting, and where it went could not be seen.

On the right the door opened onto a narrow wooden staircase of the sort servants use when they require not to be seen.

Lionel beckoned to the others and led with the flashlight, trying not to make the boards creak. Part way up they met a narrow corridor leading off the staircase to one side. Following this they came to another door set into the wall. Opening this carefully Lionel could see yet another door about two feet in front. He had seen things like this in stately homes before. Often such a door would be decorated on the other side to resemble the rest of the wall so as to be all but invisible, allowing servants to appear and disappear without discommoding the occupants of the room. There was a small crack in the door, evident from a bright light that shone through it from the other side.

Lionel held back and Alf peered through. There was a long moment of silence broken only by Alf's breathing, that sounded almost like a sighing. "You should take a look," he whispered finally to the others.

Captain Kipper looked. "Shiver me jellyfish!" he exclaimed in a hoarse whisper. He turned towards Lionel, his face lit by the sharp sideways light from the crack, his expression like one whose whole understanding of the world has just been entirely demolished. Finally Lionel looked.

A note from Myfanwy

Hello Littoral Literati,
Well, the chapters are coming thick and fast at the moment, although some of them are quite short. When I've typed up the one after next you will learn why sometimes keeping a pasty in your pocket can make the difference between life and death.

It can be very lonely looking after a genius, if that's what he is. Having not even thanked me for the numerous cups of tea, he is now asking me to make him a sandwich. I am somewhat put out and I think I shall wait until he says please.

love,
Myfanwy

12. Love and fear in Castle Drog

WHAT LIONEL SAW WAS THIS. The room, like the corridor downstairs, had the appearance of a space that had seen much better times. Large rectangles edged with dust stains showed where ancestral portraits and paintings of mythological scenes had once hung. Above wooden panelling that could have done with a thorough waxing was what had once been fine silk wall-coverings, now decaying into ribbons. But in the centre of the room was the thing that had caused Alf to pause and the Captain to change his world view. It was a huge fish-tank of thick plate glass, and inside was almost certainly Lionel's mermaid, sitting motionless on what looked like a plastic rock with her back to them. Her tail was partly covered with water clouded with an algal bloom, and her shoulders were hunched.

Lionel pushed open the door. At first the mermaid did not notice. Then as Lionel walked round the tank she caught sight of the movement and started in fear. At last she saw who it was, and her face lit up in a combination of joy and alarm.

Lionel stared, not knowing what to do.

She pressed the palm of her hand to her lips for several seconds, as though her hand were some lover in whose kiss she was passionately engaged. Then she lifted her eyes to Lionel, held his gaze, and very slowly, very deliberately blew him the kiss. This was not the kiss of a coquette, a thing of a moment, disposable. This was palpable. He could sense the velocity of it, its slow trajectory through the air, slowed further as it refracted through the thick glass of the aquarium and on through the air again. He felt the moment it impacted his cheek. At that moment a warmth began to infuse his whole body, radiating from the kiss, like the burning of the first sip of a fine whisky but more penetrating, more complete. Finally it concentrated in the place where his heart lived.

Once again, this was not Lionel as he knew it. Lionel for those endless seconds was not there. As the Higgs Bosun had told him: the real self is unexpected.

Then the thought intruded, "Why me? Who am I to deserve this?"

Alf and the Captain were now beside Lionel, looking at the mermaid. Captain Kipper looked simply astonished. Alf's expression was harder to guess, but there was awe in it and recognition, as if some ancient memory had been reignited.

The mermaid now gesticulated wildly, and pointed towards a door on the far side of the room. Then she pointed back towards the door the men had just emerged from. There were noises, approaching footsteps, voices.

Captain Kipper was the first to snap into action. "Quick, back into the wall!"

The three of them stepped rapidly back behind the false door and closed it. Lionel pressed his eye to the crack.

The mermaid had resumed her former pose, as if nothing had happened. Three men entered the room together with a large dog.

"What makes you think they'll come? They were warned, weren't they?" A large man was speaking and he had his back to them.

"They'll come all right. A few rustics mouthing rubbish won't put them off." The accent was a crisp Home Counties one, but the speaker was unmistakably the landlord of the *Piskie and Pasty*.

"Well, whatever happens they mustn't see the mermaid," said the big man. "This thing needs to be kept quiet until we have the whole development in the bag, everything. We don't want any animal liberation busybodies claiming rights for fish at the last minute. How many people know?"

The dog started sniffing around. It was an alsatian.

"Only Fortescue." It was Figgis. "I can deal with him. No-one's going to believe him. If he causes trouble I'll put it about that he's mental and then get him on a section 136."

The dog started sniffing round the fish-tank and growling, and the mermaid recoiled as far back in the tank as she could, but the dog was not interested in her.

The big man addressed both of them. "What does Kipper know? You said Kipper was with him, and a third man. Who is the third man?" He turned to Figgis.

"I don't think Kipper saw anything," Figgis said.

"Think? That's not good enough. Find out. If he knows, arrest him."

"On what charge?" Figgis asked.

"Do your job, Figgis. Do I have to do everything? You think this is going to fall into your lap without you doing any work?" Here he started to shout. "WHO IS THE THIRD MAN?"

"I don't know anything about any third man," said Figgis.

The landlord spoke. "Old chap in a tatty naval uniform. H.M.S Higgs on his cap."

"THE HIGGS BOSUN!" The big man was incandescent. "Where'd he come from?"

The other two men looked at each other and shrugged anxiously. The big man spat.

"Do whatever you have to. Get rid of him. I want him gone. At all costs. By any means. Do you understand?"

The dog ran from the fish-tank towards the hidden door, barking furiously, and started pounding the wall with his front paws.

"Down boy!" Figgis shouted, "Fenrir, heel!"

The dog would not be pacified. Figgis grabbed Fenrir's collar and pulled him, growling, from the wall.

"Are you stupid?" the big man shouted, "the dog's onto something. Let him go." The big man walked towards the wall and pushed.

From the author

Dear Corruscating Catfishes,
In which our heroes are chased by a dog and there isn't a car chase. Oh no. Too cliché.

If any of you gentle readers have any clue how this should work out please let me know. I've got some vague ideas but a few pointers would help, especially if they are completely improbable.

Just now I'm writing a chapter in which Mavis shows an unexpected interest in Lionel and we hear more about Lola "Hot Stuff" Tabasco.

As you can see, I am working furiously without so far having received the sandwich I asked Myfanwy to prepare for me. That woman is exasperating at times.

Your friend,
Malodorous Mackerel

13. A PASTY CAN BE THE DIFFERENCE BETWEEN LIFE AND DEATH

LIONEL, ALF AND KIPPER had heard it all, and when Fenrir had started pounding the hidden door they had started back down the corridor as quickly as they could with the least sound possible.

Luckily the door was made to open outwards into the room, so the big man's pushing was of no avail, and he didn't know the trick of opening it from the room side.

"They're in the festering wall!" the big man shouted. "Figgis, get 'em! Smithers!" addressing the landlord, "go! You better catch them or it's all up with you two!"

Figgis stood for a moment dumbfounded, staring at the wall with Fenrir pawing the woodwork frantically. Then, before the big man could pile on any more invective Figgis attached Fenrir's lead and dragged him through the doorway into the next room and on towards the big staircase.

Smithers, however, went straight to the small wooden knob by the fireplace and turned it. The hidden door opened and he ran inside, hesitating as not knowing which way they had gone, then taking a guess and running on.

Sensing a fight, Fenrir ran ahead. By the time the dog had reached the top of the staircase dragging Figgis behind him, Lionel, Alf and the Captain had reached the door into the ground floor corridor. Figgis at the top of the stairs was in darkness but he glimpsed the men's feet as they passed under the lightbulb. Fenrir dragged him downstairs so fast he nearly fell over several times, and in his panic it had not yet occurred to him to let Fenrir off the leash. At the bottom of the stairs Smithers ran out of the servants' corridor crashing into Fenrir's lead.

By this time Lionel, Kipper and Alf were already passing through the conservatory, the crowding leaves whipping their faces.

When the men were already half way across the lawn towards the iron gates, Smithers, Fenrir and Figgis emerged from the conservatory. Only now did Figgis pause to release the dog, who took off like a bolt from a crossbow.

"We're done for!" Lionel panted.

This was when Alf reached into his pocket for the pasty and threw it behind him. Despite the quantity of potato in the filling, it had enough meat in it to interest Fenrir. Figgis's neglect of the dog compound at the police station was matched by his lazy attitude to regular dog food, and Fenrir was now caught between his lust for blood and his desire for meat. The dog hesitated.

As the men reached the iron gates Figgis caught up with Fenrir, who was licking the last of the meat out of the pasty. "Go! Kill!" Figgis shouted, and kicked the dog who looked up and snarled. If a dog can snarl derisively it was definitely a derisive snarl.

The three friends kept running. From somewhere behind them they heard Smithers shouting at Figgis, and a little later they heard the big man shouting at both of them. Then silence, and later still the sound of an expensive car starting. By this time they had reached the little Morris and jumped in. It started first time.

From the author

Dear Marine Marvels,
Next chapter: not exactly a car chase.
    That's it.

Sorry I'm a bit busy just now working on the rest of the story. I shall have to delegate writing messages to you, my dear readers, to my secretary Myfanwy. It'll keep her out of my hair anyway.

Yes of course it's lovely having you around, it's just that... I really am grateful... Anyway... Yes I'm sorry I didn't mean it that way, it just came out all wrong. These things happen when you're a struggling genius working on what will later be hailed as a flawed masterpiece. Yes. All right. You're right of course and I apologise unreservedly. A sandwich would be really nice. If you have time. I really appreciate it. Thank you.

Yours in haste,
Melton Mowbray

14. Let Your Body Do the Driving

GENTLE READER, if you are Jeremy Clarkson you may at this point be expecting a thrilling car chase, preferably with explosions and bits falling off. If perchance you are not he then you will understand that not every matter of life and death is solved by driving unreasonably fast.

You will recall that the Morris Minor is a car both ancient and humble, the sort of thing your grandmother would have driven had she afforded a motor vehicle at all. It was produced from 1948 to 1971, has a sweet rounded shape and is powered by a 918cc side-valve straight-4 engine producing 27.5 hp and 39 lbf·ft of torque, achieving a maximum speed of 64 mph and delivering 40 miles per imperial gallon. There. I think Jeremy Clarkson has gone away now, so we may continue.

Lionel reversed the little car onto the road and started off back the way they had come. At the fork in the road where turning right would point them back towards Pengoggly, Alf suddenly ordered Lionel to turn left. Lionel could see the intermittent twinkle of headlights through the hedges some distance off. He turned as instructed, at the same time switching off the lights on the car, realising that if he could see them, they could see him.

"Good move," said Alf.

"But now I can't see," said Lionel. The tyres were hitting the bank. In a panic Lionel overcorrected and the tyres hit the opposite bank. This happened several times.

"Relax," said Alf, "what will happen will happen. Let your body do the driving."

Lionel reduced speed. He didn't understand what Alf meant, but panic was blinding him and he had nothing to lose. With an effort he let his mind relax and stopped trying to drive with his head. He watched as his body took over. There was enough moonlight that sometimes the road ahead could be glimpsed, and his hands on the wheel held the car steady, a little movement now and then keeping the car on track. When a tyre did touch the bank it did so gently and was instantly corrected. Lionel noticed that the engine ran sweeter and quieter too.

"Here!" commanded Alf.

There was a dirt track off to the side, leading perhaps to a field or a distant farmyard. Lionel turned the car onto the track and down it a little way, then stopped and switched off the engine.

"Now we wait," Alf said.

The headlights of the other car were clearer, still flickering through the hedges. The purr of its engine was audible. It slowed.

"It's at the junction now," Alf whispered.

They watched the lights to see which way the car would turn. For Lionel it was now as if in a dream, or rather, it was reality, and worrying about it was the dream. What would happen would happen. He felt neither fear nor anticipation, merely curiosity.

The headlights turned away. Now they could glimpse only the red tail lights, shaking a little as the car negotiated the rough road, shrinking out of sight towards Pengoggly.

"Arr! They've gone!"

"What now?" asked Lionel.

"We wait some more," Alf replied.

From Myfanwy

Dear Fishtastic Finny Fans,
Manfred von Mittelerde is having a lie down, having strained something trying to invent all these alliterations, so he asked me, his exotic Welsh secretary look you, to pen the message for the latest episode of this thrilling adventure. I wanted to include my

recipe for mutton cooked with cheese in the Welsh manner, but he forbade it, I don't know why.

Anyway, here is chapter 15, in which Mavis gets interested in Lionel, Lionel talks to the press and Captain Kipper gets an unexpected message.

Coming soon: Henry Herring's 16th century account of St Doris Island.

Just between us, Manfred is a dear, but I do need to give him a hard time sometimes, otherwise I don't know whether he cares or not.

love and kisses,
Myfanwy,
Mwah mwah

15. AN ENGLISHMAN'S RIGHT TO KEEP WHATEVER ONE WANTS IN ONE'S BATH

LIONEL, CAPTAIN KIPPER AND ALF returned to Pengoggly very late and by a roundabout route. It was obviously unsafe for Alf to stay at Marine Parade, but at the same time they reasoned that Figgis couldn't do much by himself in broad daylight and the other two would probably not want to create a disturbance in Pengoggly itself. It was decided that Alf would stay the night on the *Saucy Jellyfish* and the Captain and Lionel would return each to their own homes. They were not disturbed.

The next morning Lionel went to work as usual. As he walked into the office Mavis stopped what she was doing and her eyes followed him. As he sat at his desk she was still looking at him with big eyes until he caught her glance and she looked down quickly and started shuffling papers on her desk.

Mavis was a large woman and not unattractive. A man who appreciated large-breasted women would have appreciated her. She had a winning smile. She also kept a cat and had a picture of it on her desk. It is a truth universally acknowledged that a single woman in possession of a picture of a cat on her desk must be in want of a man.

At mid-morning Mavis offered to make Lionel a cup of tea, which she had never done before. There were tea bags in the kitchenette and mostly he made his own tea. He wondered what could have changed her attitude towards him so suddenly.

"You seem different," she said as she handed him the tea together with a plate of bourbon biscuits. This in itself was odd, because if anyone ever brought bourbon biscuits into the office they were gone almost immediately, and all he would usually find were those thin plain biscuits that smelled vaguely of camphor.

He wondered who ate them, or whether they were always the same ones.

"Do I?" he asked, "in what way?"

Mavis thought for a moment, then said, "I don't know. Have you had a haircut?" Of course she knew perfectly well that he hadn't had a haircut because it's only men who are vague about things like that, but she had to say something.

"No," Lionel replied, "but thank you for the tea." Then he resumed his work, and conversation ceased.

At lunchtime Lionel felt he needed some air, and strolled down to *The Frothy Coffee With a Bit of Coffee and Quite a Lot of Milk Café*. The coffee was not so good, but it was drinkable, and he ordered a sandwich too.

As he was about to bite into his sandwich a young woman approached him with a little notepad. "You are Lionel Fortescue?" she asked.

"Yes," he replied.

"The police raided your house yesterday and one of our reporters got a photograph of your bath. P.C. Figgis said you were keeping a prohibited creature, a shark or an octopus or something. Do you have a comment for the Pengoggly Post?"

Lionel considered telling the young woman the truth but thought better of it. "No, but don't you think that in England one may keep whatever one wants to in one's bath provided it does not pose a nuisance to others? That is one of the freedoms that this country is known for the world over."

"Do you want to tell the readers what was in your bath?"

"What was in the photograph?"

"Some sea anemones and a bit of seaweed."

"I'm afraid I can't add anything useful to that," said Lionel with a smile. She was a rather junior reporter and had not yet learned to be pushy, so she went away.

Soon the Captain appeared and sat down opposite. Over on a far table was Sidney Sinister, still wearing an oversized raincoat, although it was quite a warm day.

"What now?" Captain Kipper frowned.

"I don't know. What happens, happens, but I have a feeling we have to make it happen."

"Talk to the press?"

"I've done that. If I tell them the truth, they will make it into a joke."

"Go to the police? ... oh."

They lapsed into silence. Lionel stared out to sea, his mind a blank. Something had to be done. He had no idea what. A shadow fell across the table.

Lionel looked round and Alf was standing there with a smile. He sat.

"That piece of paper in your pocket?" Alf was looking at the Captain.

"What piece of paper?"

"In your left jacket pocket I believe."

The Captain felt in his left jacket pocket and retrieved a small crumpled piece of paper. "It's just the receipt from the *Piskie and Pasty*," he said.

"Open it."

Captain Kipper opened the receipt. He read out loud: 'Please help. St Doris Church, Ankarrek, sunrise. Lola.'

Lionel glanced anxiously over to where Sidney Sinister was sitting, but he was reading the paper and seemed oblivious of them. Lionel hoped he was too far away to hear.

"Which sunrise? It's after noon!" The Captain started to stand up, but Alf put a hand on his arm.

"Calm yourself. If she meant today and you weren't there, she'll likely understand the difficulty. She'll try again."

Captain Kipper sat down. "Tomorrow it is then."

From Myfanwy

Hello again Watery Whelks, Myfanwy here,
Some people imagine that the mermaid's name is Lola. This is not correct, as the mermaid's name has not been established at all. No. Lola is the dusky Mexican barmaid. Now pay attention. Mervin Mollusc the redoubtable chronicler of these events has taken pains over this story, so notice the details, isn't it?

Chapter 16 is copied down with great care from a sixteenth century book.

After that is coming some more stuff about Lola, but you'll have to be patient, as Melville Montague the redoubtable chronicler of these events has his work cut out just keeping track of his own name, look you.

from Moldywarp Menzies' exotic Welsh secretary,
Myfanwy
xxxxxxxxxxxxxxxxxxxxx

16. Sir Henry Herring's account of St Doris Island

THAT EVENING Lionel settled down to read *Seynte Doris Iland*, of which I here set down several extracts.

> Thus we landed in severall small boats leaving the Hinde at anchor some distance from the shore, on account of the gentle slope of the bottom. It was a verdant iland all set around with fronded trees and in the midst a great volcano, the which we thought extinct, there being no show of smoke or fire therefrom.
>
> Drake at once leapt from the boat and planted the flagge of England in the sand, claiming the iland for Gloriana our gracious Majestie Queene Elizabeth. We then on our knees offered up a prayer to Almightie God for our safe deliverance to this place, and I also quietly did offer thanks to our own Seynte Doris, thinking that if I were to pray out loud some might think me a Catholick, but knowing in my hart that I am a true Protestant and loyal subject of the Queene of England.
>
> What shall we call this place? inquired Drake. I made bold to say it should be called Seynte Doris as many of the crew were from my Bit of Cornwall and therefore such a name were fitting.
>
> Ha, quoth Drake, thou shalt have thy way Fisheface (for thus he did call me in jeste on account of my name of Herring, that being a fishe), and so did I humbly

accept the jeste with a smile so that the iland could be thus named. For by occasion humilitie can achieve more than the posturing of coxcombs.

Searching about we did find many things that were good to eat, such as the fleshe of huge woody nuts that must needs be cleaved with a sword, sea weed that when cooked put us in mind of the cabbage that was the customary fare of our school dayes, and a great quantity of fishes. Thus hungry and weary from our travells we did make a feast on the beach.

Now I must tell of the most great marvell of that place, hearing the which the honest reader may well doubt of my veracitie. Honest Cornishmen have spoken of suchlike things and been laughed to scorne, thus to this day they do hold their tongues. E'en so I shall now set forth the truth of the matter, let he who will, gainsay it. If thou believe it, so, and if not, then do as thou wilt.

The cooking of the fishes did cause such a wondrous pleasant smell that presently came some of the natives of that land most curious to see what should be occurring on their beach. But came they not from the land but from the sea, and wonder to behold they were of the form of beautiful maidens, clothed scantilie in sea weed and otherwise in little more than the apparell in which they had been borne.

This caused a most mightie stirring among the sailors, but Drake did not wish to mar the reign of her Majestie upon this new Dominion with any kind of impolitick controversie, so he did order the crew to throw buckets of water over each other untill their vegetable passions be safely diminished to proportions proper for social intercourse. This did indeed dampen the sailors ardour, though we nobles were much discomfited by the persistence of water in our codpieces.

Thus calmed into gentilnesse the sailors intreated the maidens with all civilitie to join them in the feast, whereupon some of the maidens lifted themselves onto rocks nearby but came no further in, the reason being much apparent by that their thighs and legges were joined into the form of fishey tails.

At this some did say that this was the worke of the Evil One but others said that nothing so beautiful could be made by the Lord of Darknesse for it is not in his power to do thus and therefore it is godly. At this all the mermaids, for such they were, began to sing a most melodious and plaintive song so that even the rudest member of the crew was much affected by it.

During all our sojourn on that iland peaceful relations persisted between the sailors and the mermaids, the sailors being much changed in their manners and showing much courtesie. By moonlight each would wade to the rock of his favourite maid and feed her with fishe the which he had first cooked with spices on the fire. She in turn would sing for him at which he would gaze upon her most tenderlie.

At length the sailors began to teach the mermaids to speak in their own tongue, some in English and some in the Cornish or Kernewek as it is called. Some of the sailors claimed afterward that their mermaids spoke the Kernewek passing well, which did surprise them greatly. For their part the mermaids did teach the sailors some words of their own language, which however had no ready translations into English or Cornish and which the sailors could but understand when the mermaids spoke it. For my part I could only remember the speech of mermaids at dawn for at other times it left no trace on my memory.

Nor was I unaffected by all this but found myself with a deep affection for one of the mermaids. I never knew her name but she sang to me and then I understood many things that I have since forgot. Whether it be folly or no I must one day return to that iland, for there it is certaine my hart remains. For her part I know that she will not forget me, though I know not how I deserve it.

After many dayes passed in replenishing the stores of the ship and mending our bodies and most of all our soules, for such was the effect of the mermaids on all of us, Drake did address the crew thus:

It is not for idlenesse that Her Majestie hath entrusted me with this journey, but for to enrich oure nation with all manner of foreign things, not least by the plundering of Spanish gold. Therefore must we leave this iland on the morrow.

This speche did the sailors receive with much lamentation, albeit talk of gold did begin to revive their

Sir Henry Herring's account of St Doris Island

avarice. Therefore did Drake order an extra ration of rum and full many of the crew forgot their mermaids that night and did slepe until dawn.

For myself no gold and no rum could quench the longing in my brest and I did steal away to my mermaid, who seemed to understand that we must parte, and sang so sweetlie that I thought I should dye, nor would such a fate at such a time have been unwelcome.

Lionel closed the book, unable to read any more, and a mixture of emotion and weariness overcame him.

He awoke with his alarm clock at a dark hour, wondering at first where he was. Then he remembered Captain Kipper's meeting at St Doris's church.

A note from Jel E. Fish

Dear Myfanwy,
Fear not. I am quite aware that Lola 'Hotstuff' Tabasco is not our enigmatic mermaid.

I find sailor Herring's account very moving—he has touched me to the core.

I have never come across the words 'Welsh' and 'exotic' in the same sentence before. Myfanwy, you are indeed intriguing yourself—could you be yet another distraction for our doughty Moldywarp?

Well I am, as always, all agog for the next thrilling instalment.
Jel E. Fish (née MacKerel)

P.S. I think the MacKerels may have been known to the Herring family in the distant past but I'm not sure.

From Myfanwy

Hello again and iechyd da, chèr(e)s Saltimbanques de Mer, (French is so chick isn't it?)

Myfanwy yer,

Well I'm glad somebody recognises that I am intriguing, but if I am distracting as well I can't help that. Some of us are born to be exotic, and we must make the best of it.

Moving on.

Recipe for cawl. Take a sheep and feed it a remarkable quantity of cheese. Tie a wreath of rosemary round its neck and walk around it three times chanting the name of that famous Welsh railway station backwards (you know, Llanfair-pwllgwyn-gyllgogery-chwyrndrobwl-lllantysilio-gogogoch—only backwards that would be chogogogoilisytnalllwb...), then...

Oh, sorry. Mervyn Mildew says I'm not to put recipes in these letters. Why not I'd like to know? My Welsh exoticness is wasted on him. Wasted.

Anyway, there is a Cornish and Welsh goddess called Aerfen who weaves the fates of each person, and she appeared to Mervyn in a dream and told him that however complicated the weaving becomes in this story it has to be straightened out again at the end, see? Tidy. So he's working on it. It's a great responsibility being a writer isn't it?

Aerfen has painstakingly dictated to him the next charming chapter about Lola, also mentioning Ramón Pimiento el Picante and Edwin Sharck, bad people who will certainly get in each other's way later on if I know anything about it.

After that Lionel and Captain Kipper visit the planning office—a very exciting chapter but with no car chases in it.
Mwah mwah,
Myfanwy
xoxoxo

17. LOLA

ANKARREK WOULD HAVE BEEN ABOUT A MILE walk from Kasteldrog but not quite so difficult as that place to get to by car, there being a decent B-road off the main road. Alf was off on some mission of his own, so it was just Lionel and the Captain in the car as they approached St Doris's. It was cold, and some pale yellow clouds on the eastern horizon showed where the sun would come up.

The church was perched on top of a tall inland crag. Looking from below, its steeple seemed to pierce the clouds, and the tower was joined to a gaunt gothic nave.

Lionel drove the Morris up the steep slope and parked in front of the western face. Over the main doors in a niche was a stone statue of St Doris standing in a seashell drawn by giant sea slugs marvellously carved, just as Lionel and the Captain had seen in the picture in Nellie's front room. The double doors were closed. Quietly the two men approached and the Captain pushed on one of the doors, which opened gently with a creak.

As they entered all they could see at first was the pre-dawn light filtering through the stained glass behind the altar, but then they could make out the silhouette of a figure sitting in one of the front pews apparently praying.

The inside of the church was filled with hints of intense colour, quite unlike most English churches with their whitewashed walls. Such light as there was showed patches of red, green and blue, and everywhere were sharp glistenings of yellow gilding. There were paintings on the walls too, but what the subjects were they could not see. From the ancient hammer-beam roof hung wooden sculptures of coloured fishes of all kinds, which seemed by their grouping and by their very splendour to be eternally at the point of subduing the monstrous grey squid that also hung in mid-air, its tentacles reaching out over the pews. A painted wooden statue of St Doris was there also, facing the squid with the calm all saints have.

At the sound of footsteps the figure looked round. It was the woman from the *Piskie and Pasty* wrapped in a brown cloak.

She turned back towards the altar, crossed herself and stood up. She peered closer and when she saw that it was indeed the Captain her eyes widened and a smile filled her face with beauty.

"I knew you would come!" she said in a whisper, out of respect for the place they were in. Her accent was Mexican and her eyes flashed in the half-light. "Come," she said, I must explain everything to you outside. Are you a religious man?"

Captain Kipper thought for a moment before replying quietly, "I do my best, that's as much as I can say. I try to be a decent fellow and be useful to my friends. I work hard and listen to the wind and the seagulls' cry. I hope that may be enough."

Without another word she grabbed him by the wrist and started up the aisle towards the entrance to the church. He followed in the sort of daze that is not so much a daze as a heightened sense of reality, his heart pounding a little. Before leaving the church she turned again towards the altar, bowed and crossed herself once more. Captain Kipper bowed out of respect rather than belief, although at that moment, though he had no words for it, he too had become a believer. Lionel also bowed.

Once outside the Captain could see that beneath her dull brown cloak Lola wore a brilliant white blouse embroidered with big flowers in blue and red. There was a glimpse too of her skirt in rich cobalt blue, which looked brighter than it should in the early morning light, much as moss among the dark roots of trees sometimes seems to glow. She had put on her best clothes for this meeting. He could tell that under the cloak her figure was full and sensuous. She was younger than the Captain, but her face had some hints of having lived through many escapades – a little sorrow, a lot of endurance, and eyes that were gentle and passionate by turns.

"My name is Lola Tabasco," she began, her words tumbling out. "I love your Cornwall, even though the sun don't shine so much and you no have churches filled with flying cherubs and colourful saints, except Santa Doris of course. You have pretty fishing boats, and everything is green, and the people they are mostly kind."

She was happy but nervous, as though there were not much time. "I need your help but I don't know if you can give it. You may misunderstand me and you may suspect me. ¡Pero mi corazón dice la verdad! My heart is true!"

She looked up to the still half-lit grey-blue sky and with her left hand she cradled her right fist over her heart, as if asking heaven to witness her words.

"When our eyes met in the Piskie and Pasty my heart tell me what I must do. There is nothing I can do to prove I am true but all I can do is tell you everything and then I place my faith in Santa Doris and what will be, must be."

Lionel held back a little, feeling that he should not interfere. The Captain stood as if transported into a magical realm he had not dreamt of before, full of silent wonder. He looked like a man who had seen his soulmate for the first time, never having considered the possibility that she existed.

"I come as chamber maid to Lord Fumble," Lola continued, "to escape from Ramón Pimiento El Picante the international chilli dealer. He run illegal chilli farm. It is in secret valley where many chillies grow, but they are bad chillies that make people go loco and see chillucinations. He think I am his woman, but I find out about his bad chilli dealing and I tell him, you no do this no more. And he say, where you think the money for your diamond necklace come from? And I say, I no more want your diamond necklace. I throw it to him. Pah. Then he beat me black and blue."

She paused for breath.

"I come here very early to pray. Mister Smithers, he make me work all day in the pub, clean the whole place, make the pasties, take deliveries of the beer, then every evening to serve the customers. He treat me like a slave."

"Arr, Smithers," remarked the Captain, "a bad fellow. He be mixed up with some goings on at the castle, too."

"Mister Smithers he was butler to Lord Fumble," Lola continued. "Lord Fumble was never the same after Lady Lucretia Fumble die. Later Fumble sell the castle and the *Piskie and Pasty* to someone else, no-one know who, Fumble go off to Chelsea, the new owner he send Old Ben away and put Smithers in, so to hear all the local gossip is what I think." She took another breath. "And he is in with this man Edwin Sharck who come round the pub to talk big money property schemes with him."

"Is this Edwin Sharck a large man?" Lionel enquired, thinking of the man they had seen ordering Smithers and Figgis about at Castle Drog.

"Si, a big bad man."

Captain Kipper spoke up again. "Why don't 'ee just leave? Ye could get a job in the town!"

"Ah! Smithers have my passport and I no have visa. If I cross him, he turn me in and they send me back to Ramón."

Now she stopped talking and looked at the Captain with pleading eyes.

"How can I help you then?" he asked.

"I don' know. But when I see you I see a kind man. I am thinking, I cannot stand this life any more, I must do something. And when I see you, I see my destiny. I say to myself, Lola, this is a man you can love. Even if he cannot help me, I must see him. I know as soon as look at you—sometime a woman know these things. Then I pray."

There was a pause in which no-one spoke. Lionel still stood apart, listening, trying not to take the space and the moment that belonged to them.

The Captain seemed stunned. He knew he had loved this woman from the moment their eyes had met in the pub, and now she was offering herself to him. Should he doubt her intentions? Was he just her passport out of her present hell, and nothing more? Yet deep inside him he felt there was more to it than that.

Lola spoke again, "If you no want me, I understand. I have to take my chance. You guess of course that I am, some people say it like this, 'damage goods.'"

He coughed nervously. "I be not without a chip or two meself."

Silence again. Neither of them moved. There were but three feet between them and the very air seemed to want to pull them together, she being held back only by her need to know that she was wanted, and he only by his incredulity that she would really want him.

The sun was now half-risen, shining through distant trees. Lola spoke. "I must go back to the *Piskie and Pasty* before Smithers come in and find me not there." She turned slowly to go.

The Captain still stood there, uncertain what to do, or knowing what to do and being afraid to do it, or doubting that he knew anything at all. Lola paused, turned around again. Captain Kipper remained as if his feet had stuck in the soil. She turned away again and started to walk.

"Lola," he said.

She stopped and turned to look at him.

"Lola, I won't forget you," was all he could manage.

She turned, and walking round the hedge at the side of the church, was gone.

Lola

A note from Jell E. Fish

Ooh, I loves a bit o' romantical stuff. Not a dry seat in the house!
 Xxx

From Myfanwy

Hello again Oceanid Observers,
This next is a really exciting chapter but still no car chase. I think Marvin Molecule has done quite well really this time, in spite of his obvious deficiencies.

I notice some of you are asking what if anything I do. Well, apart from being exotic which as you can imagine can be quite tiring, I have to type these emails, and what is more Mervyn Marbles has altogether given up the effort of making up alliterations for the greeting on these messages, so I have to do that as well. Sometimes it takes a week with the dictionary, and what with making tea and repressing the urge to communicate a Welsh delicacy you can see I have my work cut out.

mwah mwah!
Myfanwy
XOXOXO

18. A BRUSH WITH OFFICIALDOM

THE TWO MEN HEADED BACK TO TOWN IN SILENCE. Lionel had a view on what had happened but thought it wise to say nothing until asked. He parked the car on the quay and they found a table at *The Frothy Coffee With a Bit of Coffee and Quite a Lot of Milk Café* for breakfast.

The sun was above the horizon now, and the breeze from the sea was still pleasantly cool. The beauty of the scene was marred by plywood boarding enclosing a large area on the far side of the harbour, and the fenced-off area included a piece of the sea. There was scaffolding and heavy machinery. Lionel didn't remember all this being there yesterday. He walked briskly over for a closer look.

Peering through a gap in the boards he could see that a sea wall had been constructed of concrete and there were extensive foundations below sea level with clusters of brown steel rods jutting vertically out of them. An impressive framed poster on the boarding announced the name of the architects and contractors, together with a computer-generated picture of a shiny high-rise hotel looking out over the ocean.

"In conjunction with Pengoggly Town Council, an exciting development designed to put Pengoggly on the map as a major resort, comprising a new hotel with underground car park, leisure facilities and a holistic health centre. Tourist attractions will include the largest public aquarium in England."

Next to it another building was already complete—single storey, flat-roofed and in the New Brutalist style, but with bright pink walls. Lionel took the long walk round the fence to look closer. Another poster announced, "Pengoggly Holistic Health Centre now open. Dr Fluffycardigan M.D, M.A (Eel Pie Island University), Dip. Woo (California Institute of Woo). Axolotl therapy, nasal hair analysis, psycho-omphaloscopy, quantum intertwingling, toenail reflexology, traditional English medicine,[*] swimming with eels." Then there was a long list of ailments treated, one for each letter of the alphabet including some imaginary ailments for which imaginary letters of the alphabet had been added.

"Why didn't we notice all this before?" Lionel asked the Captain as he returned to their table.

"Why would we?"

"Well, there might have been a planning application notice or something."

"I don't remember seeing one."

Lionel looked tense. "It's obvious they're going to make the mermaid the star attraction. They'll put her in that aquarium with a plastic rock and a cheap mirror and comb." He thumped the metal table and the coffee cups jumped an inch into the air before returning to their saucers with a rattle and a small scattering of milky coffee droplets.

The two men sat in silence for a while, Lionel's face grim. "We'll go to the Council Planning Office and find out if there ever was a planning application."

Blocking the way through to the main door of the Town Hall was a small knot of local men and women, several of whom Lionel recognised from the *Piskie and Pasty*.

"Gentlemen and ladies, we need to pass," said the Captain.

"Arr, so you might. We been waiting here half an hour and they won't let us in. We come about the highway"

"Highway?" asked Lionel. There was a chorus of replies.

"Arr. Dual carriageway right through Kasteldrog village green and the demolition of the *Piskie and Pasty*."

---

[*] Something to do with leeches

Others chipped in, one following the other without a pause. "Road widening it be." "Countryside narrowing it be." "Arr. They say it be for the tourist trade to Pengoggly. They say that there new development will put Pengoggly on the map." "We say Pengoggly be on the map already, at least I seen it on the inch to the mile version that you get in the village post office." "It'll wipe Kasteldrog village and the *Piskie and Pasty* off the map, right enough." "They be turning the castle into a funfair!" "Arr, so it be."

Lionel interrupted: "Did you put in an objection at the planning stage?"

"We never saw the notice. Danzel here found the notice the other day, posted with drawing pins behind the oak tree under a bramble hedge."

"That I did. O' course, the deadline for objections be long gone. And so be our land, 'less something can be done."

At this the assembled villagers started up in unison:

"The land that's given by the gods to man
Is sacred, and our lives are rooted here
In every field and tree and winding track
And every rock that's beaten by the sea.
When mortal men blinded by hope of gain
See naught but profit in the gentle cove
And lure of money in the timeless sea,
Unleash their serpent road through ancient hills,
Corrupt with ven'mous noise the limpid air,
Then all things go awry, and what is lost
Is not recorded in the banker's book."

"Why do you all sometimes talk in a chorus like that?" Lionel asked.

"Arr," responded Danzel, "'Ee knows that in ancient times Phoenician traders come to Cornwall to trade for tin from the mines. Once they brought with 'em some Greeks who'd got on the wrong boat by accident at Syracuse, and to pass the time they put on a play by a tragic playwright that were with them, Nobblinnees* he were called. I don't think they'd invented chick flicks in them days, so it were fairly intense. Anyways, that's how our ancestors learned the rhythms of the chorus art, handed down ever after, to be used in times of woe."

"Arr. Times of woe," the crowd chorused.

Lionel and the Captain eased their way through the little throng and rang the bell.

"I told you, we're closed," came an annoyed voice from inside.

"My name is Lionel Fortescue and I have come about a different matter," said Lionel loudly.

"That's right," added the Captain, taking his cue from Lionel, "completely different. A matter that will be of great interest to your boss, no doubt."

The heavy oak door opened a crack and the pale face of a minor clerk peered out. Immediately Lionel put his foot in the door, and the crowd at once surged forward.

"So you'll let us in?" enquired Lionel, but it was more a statement than a question. The added weight of various members of the crowd on the door made it easy for Lionel to push it open and they all tumbled into the double-height hallway. It was lined with wooden panelling and there was a grand staircase in the middle. The tiled marble floor was illuminated with spots of colour from a large stained glass window in which the heraldic arms of Pengoggly and the Bit of Cornwall and not the Other Bit were prominently displayed.

The clerk looked distinctly uncomfortable.

"So," said Lionel, taking command, "I've come to see the Chief Planning Officer. It's a matter of great importance affecting the seafront development."

---

* Nobblinnees (Νοβλινης): dramatic poet flourished in the 5th Century BC.

"What about us?" cried Danzel. The crowd grew restless with cries of "Arr! What about us? What about Kasteldrog and the *Piskie and Pasty*? What about the village green?"

He turned to the crowd. "We'll all go together. Once the Planning Officer hears that the planning notice was hidden behind a tree and that we haven't seen one in Pengoggly at all he'll have to take action. We live in a democracy after all. It's just a matter of bringing things to the attention of the proper authorities and then they'll have to put a stop to it."

"Arr. That's right."

The clerk ran ahead as there was nowhere else for him to go and the crowd surged up the grand town hall stairs, Lionel in the lead.

"Where now?" asked Lionel. The clerk mutely indicated a door on the left, and they all barged in. A large man in a smart suit sat behind a correspondingly large oak desk. He looked up slowly, as though the crowd were a fly which while unwelcome might be swatted at any time and so did not merit any expression of disquiet.

"We have come about the Pengoggly and Kasteldrog developments," began Lionel. "We'd like to see the planning notices because we don't think they were properly displayed."

The Chief Planning Officer spoke. "Don't you now? I can assure you notices were properly displayed near to the relevant sites. What is more there was an advertisement, admittedly in six-point type, but nonetheless plainly visible, on page 23 of the *Pengoggly Post*, next to the much larger advertisement for the holistic health centre, which I'm sure you'll agree is a good thing and of which this planning department is particularly proud. Now if you'll kindly let me get on with my work?" He started to shuffle papers on his desk and paid Lionel no further attention.

"But the notice were behind a bramble bush!" protested Danzel.

"Look," said the Chief Planning Officer, looking up once more with a bored expression, "if you're too lazy to take an interest in local affairs there's not much I can do about it."

Captain Kipper spoke up. "What about our harbour? It'll spoil the whole place! Why here?"

The Chief Planning Officer turned slowly to look at him. "What about local jobs? Have you thought of that? It will be a boost to the local economy such as Pengoggly has never seen. Don't you care about that?"

Captain Kipper looked grim. "Spoiling the place we live in to make jobs. Jobs that no-one cares about because it's just a way of making money instead of doing something that means something. Then going home to a place you no longer recognise and no longer love?"

The Chief Planning Officer did not move and said nothing. There was a long awkward silence. It appeared he was simply waiting for them to get fed up and leave.

Lionel was perplexed. He hadn't expected such total obduracy. His mind whirled. He had to do something, say something. "Look," he said, "this may seem to you out of line, but there is a mermaid, a real one, and the developers have captured her and mean to use her as a circus attraction. Which is cruel, because she's a real person, like you and me. It's not right! It's false imprisonment! I know this sounds crazy to you, but I can prove it. I don't expect you to believe me now, but if you would give me a chance you can help me prevent a terrible wrong!"

The Chief Planning Officer looked at Lionel impassively, his eyebrows raised just a little. He leaned back in his chair.

"I think I've heard quite enough of this nonsense for one morning," he said. "You either leave now, or I call a psychiatrist to commit you and a policeman to take you away to a secure establishment. Your choice."

For a moment there was silence. Only now did Lionel's head clear enough for him to take in his surroundings more calmly. He looked at the closed face of the Chief Planning Officer, sensed the bewilderment of the crowd behind him. Sensed the Captain standing at his side, similarly quiet but ready to support him in whatever came next.

Then Lionel read the name plate on the desk. It read, "Chief Planning Officer Edwin Sharck."

From Myfanwy

Hello again Fishy Fans,

Well, Marvin Marmalade is labouring away in all available spare moments to continue the story of Lionel and the mermaid. He is diving fearlessly into the subconscious looking for the illuminated deep sea denizens of dreams and coming up again to view the flying fish of fate. Every time he surfaces his swimming trunks get full of bubbles and so the added swimwear buoyancy gives him a wedgie. It's a tricky business I can tell you.

Now then, while he's underwater, here's my recipe for Welsh Rabbit. Take a Welsh rabbit and feed it an unconscionable quantity of cheese. Then tie a sprig of rosemary to its tail and ... .

Oh, he's come back again dripping wet and says it's time for a cup of tea and a digestive biscuit. So much for Welsh cuisine then.

kisses,
Myfanwy
xoxoxo

19. The beauty of melancholy

Meanwhile Alf had been doing some investigations on his own. At dawn he had borrowed the little rowing boat from the *Saucy Jellyfish* and rowed out to sea, following the coast and staring into the green water as if looking for something. Now he had returned. It was low tide and it had started to rain, and the Higgs Bosun stood on the shingle among the hulls of the boats, staring out to sea.

No-one was watching, unless the presence of Sidney Sinister leaning on a railing on the harbour wall high above, with his back to the sea and his oversized raincoat flapping in the wind, was more than coincidental.

It was as though Alf were looking for some clue to something beyond the harbour. He seemed to be studying the sea itself, its ripples and areas of smoothness, as though the surface might reveal a clue to some mystery. Here and there were rocks jutting out of the water, marked by nearby orange and white buoys to warn the boats. The sorts of rock a mermaid might sit on.

Meanwhile up on the quay, quite unnoticed by Alf, was Nellie. The old lady of the vibrant wallpaper for some reason was drawn to the railing and to the view.

Sidney Sinister seemed to take her arrival as his cue to leave, as if this place, otherwise deserted apart from a few gulls pecking at scraps under the awning of the café, were too crowded now. Perhaps whatever it was he had come there for had been accomplished and he wanted his tea.

Nellie absorbed the luminous greyness, enjoying the way the line between sea and sky was blurred by the coming rain. Sea and sky at one. Not all beauty has to be in a major key. Without melancholy, joy might seem saccharine.

Then she took in the huddle of boats, their bright colours more harmonious because of the moist air, and the figure of Alf himself standing among them. She stood awhile transfixed, filled by some intense emotion, old yet familiar.

Alf remained gazing out to sea. His gaze was both relaxed and intense, his senses keen and his mind quiet. He stood there for a long time.

20. Psychiatric indeterminacy

"It's no use." Lionel addressed the little crowd. But they were no longer paying attention to him.

"Mermaid? Mermaid?" A hubbub arose among the Kasteldrog folk.

"Arr. That be the legend of Lyonesse, long ago."

"Arr. Lyonesse. My grandmother said it were all true."

"My grandmother too. She said they'd come back one day, to the place of their ancestors. That were foretold in the lost book."

"Foretold! Arr! Then there will be a time of woe!"

"A time of woe! Saint Doris preserve us!"

They all crossed themselves. Lionel and the Captain stood there, simply looking on. Edwin Sharck looked suddenly uncomfortable as the situation seemed to slip from his control. It would be hard to convince a psychiatrist to take Lionel away if the mermaid business were a genuine local belief, and to get them all taken away was impossible, since there is rumoured only to be one actual psychiatric bed in the whole of England. Beds in psychiatric hospitals suffer from quantum indeterminacy: it is claimed there are many of them but they disappear when you try to locate them accurately, especially in an emergency.

Slowly he lifted the phone. "Spriggan? Yes, Sharck here. Send a patrol car to the Town Hall would you? Yes now. Bring Figgis with you. And the dogs." His voice was measured and with an edge of sharpened steel. He put down the phone and sat still, staring at the assembled villagers.

The little crowd backed towards the door. "Seems like we're not wanted here," said Danzel. "Seems like our democratic rights have been trampled on."

"Arr, but this isn't over," said another.

"We'll pray to St Doris, that's what we'll do," said a third.

Edwin Sharck leaned back in his chair as they left, and smirked.

From Myfanwy

Hello again Twinkling Teleosts!
Mephistopheles Mortlake has released another chapter for your delectation. He's typing away furiously still sitting in his wet bathing trunks.

It's not a sight you'd particularly enjoy. That's why I'm explaining it to you like in a Greek tragedy you see, when all the horrible stuff happens off-stage and then someone comes on and says, 'you'll never guess what I just saw! Oedipus just burned the sausages and the frying pan caught on fire and there was smoke everywhere and then a spark caught his underpants on fire and then he had to jump in the swimming pool and stubbed his toe on the bottom. O woe that I was ever born to see this day!'

Something like that anyway.

I'd better make his tea now. Not that he'll notice. He's in a fury of creativity. When he's in a fury of creativity he doesn't notice anything much at all. I think I might put something interesting in his tea. Like a plastic spider.

Kisses,
Myfanwy
mwah mwah

21. When Your Fate Calls, Do Not Fail

IN EVERY SPARE THOUGHT Captain Kipper's mind had been returning to Lola. Doubts clouded him. He was an escape for Lola, nothing more. She wouldn't want him for himself, why would she? A woman like that. He was an ordinary fellow, sometimes smelling of fish.

Even so, the image of Lola haunted him. Her smile when she had recognised him in the church had melted his heart. He could not imagine her playing false—she felt too real to be other than what she said she was. Her eyes showing her sorrow, too, were beautiful, signs of a sorrow nobly borne.

It had been a long day. After the debacle at the Town Hall it was too late to take the boat out, so he had contented himself with mending his nets on the harbour-side next to the *Saucy Jellyfish*. He was feeling rather than thinking, because his thoughts were contradicting themselves and swimming about like shrimps in an aquarium. His feelings were more like the sea snails that wander lugubriously up the sides of the glass, so he just bore them as best he could while focussing on making knots.

The view from the harbour was marred by shuttering and cranes, but he looked up occasionally to watch the other fishing boats coming in. After some hours the last one had unloaded its catch and the tide had turned. The weather, too, had changed and the air, now halfway between mist and rain, suited his mood. He continued working until the tide was low and dusk was coming.

Almost everyone except the occasional tourist, determined to enjoy Cornwall whatever the weather, had gone home. Even so he noticed two figures on the far side of the harbour, round by the café: a man in a flapping raincoat with his back to the harbour, who eventually left, and the small figure of an old lady leaning on the railing and gazing at something or somebody he could not see. Eventually she also went home.

Then something caught his eye. A dot on the horizon, too small to be a tanker, seemed to be getting larger. He watched for a long time as the boat came closer. It was white and gleaming in the rain-soaked light, not one of the colourful fishing boats but something new and shiny.

At the same time the Captain became aware that someone had come up behind him. The energy was gentle. Without turning Captain Kipper knew that it was a friend. Whoever it was took two steps forward and rested a hand on the Captain's shoulder. It was Alf.

"Where have 'ee been?" asked the Captain.

"Early this morning I borrowed the lifeboat, looking for something. Later I was down there on the far side of the Saucy Jellyfish this last hour or so," Alf replied, "thinking."

"Thinking?"

"Yes, thinking. Pondering."

"About what? 'Ee told us you had a quest. 'Ee never said for what."

"For something close to my heart. Something without which my heart will one day break."

"Something? There can't be any such thing," Captain Kipper asserted. "It must be some*one*." He sighed, thinking again of Lola.

Alf was silent for a while. Now he knew the Captain understood him. The Captain had guessed the secret of his soul from the secret of his own.

Captain Kipper said nothing further, but listened to the sound of the wind rattling the rigging on the sailboats and the seagulls crying, and watched Alf's face, an almost expressionless gaze that said so much.

"She was the most beautiful creature I ever saw," Alf began slowly. "It was on St Doris Island. You've seen what you've seen, you know they exist." He paused and took a deep breath.

"Mermaids?" queried the Captain.

"She looked into my eyes and I saw her soul and mine, all in one moment," Alf continued. "I loved her at once. She spoke to me in a strange mixture of some Celtic tongue and English which I barely understood, but I understood her look, the gentle way she stroked my hair. And she had a brilliant smile and she would without warning jump into the sea, the water sparkling on her body, and pull me in too, and we would romp and play, and I marvelled. I did not know before that time how much love I had in me. But I could never understand how it could work, she with a fishy tail and I with two legs."

"Did she love 'ee?" the Captain asked.

"I think so. I hope so. But what could we do? The crew made a raft of wood and coconut shells and wove a sail from banana tree fibres and we sailed away. We headed for whatever inhabited island we should first chance upon. On our way we were picked up by a navy vessel and from Nassau we flew back to England. At the time I thought it was for the best, but ever since I have been thinking it was the worst mistake I ever made."

"'Ee met her on St Doris Island? So why look for her here?"

"I did go back to St Doris. I tried to forget her at first, because it was all so impossible. But I couldn't. I thought about her every day and dreamed about her at night. In the end I got a job on a cruise ship and jumped ship at Nassau. I hired a little sail boat with a motor and went back to St Doris Island to look for her."

The shiny boat was now no longer just on the horizon and its shape was a little clearer. At that distance its size was difficult to guess—a large pleasure boat perhaps. It seemed to be heading for the harbour. The distant sound of powerful engines began to reach their ears.

"And?"

"Some of the mermaids I'd known before were still there. But not her."

"She'd gone? Where?"

"Away to find her homeland, the mythical land of their ancestors from centuries ago. There were stories about a distant land with underwater houses of quiet beauty each with its own garden of green seaweed and red sea anemones, a drowned market square where you could talk with fishes and an undersea church dedicated to St Doris. Above were said to be rocks perfect for sitting on and singing to passing fishermen. It was the fishermen most of all that they yearned for."

"A mythical land? Isn't St Doris Island mythical enough?"

"The ones that stayed said it was foolish, their homeland was but a fantasy and there was nothing out there. They said St Doris Island and the sea was all there was. Of course they believed in the existence of the Turks and Caicos islands and the Bahamas, and some believed in the existence of Cuba too, but to them anything further away was imaginary, just old stories told to while away tropical nights. Perhaps it was the arrival of HMS Higgs that revived the hope in some of them that there might be something more, and that the stories they had been told as merchildren were true."

"There are merchildren?"

"Not very often. A mermaid needs a man. That's why they love fishermen and all seafaring men. Without a man they still yearn to have merbabies, and sometimes the yearning is so strong that a sailor comes to them in their dreams and they get pregnant from sheer desire. But to be truly happy a mermaid needs a man. Without that they gradually become pale and their scales lose their shine. I think that's why, more than any other reason, some of them set sail."

"They made some kind of boat then?"

"A thing of balsa wood and coconut shells like the one we made. A far cry from the legendary vessel their ancestors had arrived in many centuries before. The stories said it was a magical vessel that could move even when the wind was calm and the sails were furled."

"So where was this mythical land of their ancestors supposed to be?"

"Here of course. The mythical drowned land of Lyonesse. That's what I was looking for this morning. Looking for strange eddies that might give away traces of ruined houses, listening for underwater church bells rung by the tides. Looking, most of all, for my lost mermaid."

Captain Kipper's heart was deeply moved. The mistake Alf had made he would not make with Lola. Only rarely does such a thing happen to a man.

The boat's engines continued to get louder as it approached. This was not the friendly chug chug chug of some antiquated engine, but the smooth roar of an immensely powerful diesel driving a boat sharp as a spearhead and the size of a penthouse apartment.

From Myfanwy

Hello again Elegant Elasmobranchs,

Manfred von Marmite has been 'busy.' I don't know what with, but he says he's been 'busy.' He hasn't paid me any attention and sometimes I wonder why I bother being exotic at all.

Anyway, here is a chapter he managed to write in between being 'busy.' Meantime he still won't let me tell you my recipes and if you want Welsh Rabbit you can melt some cheese on top of a bit of toast and *pretend* it's Welsh Rabbit. But you know that, deep down, it's neither Welsh nor Rabbit really.

I'm sending you some sultry kisses, you might as well have them, because I've tried being sultry with him and he just says I'm moody and what's the matter. Nothing, I say. I can hardly say, 'I'm being sultry' because that would ruin the effect.

Sultry XoXoXOOOO,
Myfanwy

22. Union Jack underpants

"IT WAS ON THE HIGH SEAS, MANY YEARS AGO." Edwin Sharck's face set in a frown. "Back then I was captain of an ex-Soviet submarine which the boss had bought, 'off the record' as it were, from a Russian ship breaker. Its name—Stalin—was painted on it in those Russian letters but we renamed her the ~~Sardine~~ Kraken."

"Quite right," Figgis nodded. "Who can be bothered to understand those acrylic letters?"

"Cyrillic," Smithers corrected with a sneer.

"Cyril Icke?" Figgis looked confused. "Is he related to that fellow who thinks the world is run by lizards?"

"Never mind," Smithers said in a voice expressing weariness mingled with contempt.

They were sitting in a corner of the Piskie and Pasty. The locals were gathered far away at the other end of the room, as though there were a poisonous miasma around the three men.

"So we were buccaneers, or as the boss preferred to call us, businessmen of the sea," Sharck resumed. "The boss was with us. We were returning from a successful expedition to Mexico where we had acquired a large consignment of hallucinogenic chillies in exchange for some counterfeit U.S dollars, when..."

"Counterfeit dollars? I didn't know the boss was into that?" Smithers looked surprised.

"Well, he likes to try many things. Diversification. You never know when you will have to abandon something that isn't going so well, so you need tentacles in many pasties, as you might put it."

"Why doesn't he do that now?" asked Figgis. "The quickest way to make money would be to, er, just make it, wouldn't it? Then we wouldn't be having to haul mermaids about the place and chase people with dogs at all hours."

"Well it wasn't one of his best lines. The dollar bill had unfortunately been copied from a picture in a back issue of *International Times* from the hippie era. The picture of George Washington had been replaced by one of Dr Timothy Leary of LSD fame. The pyramid with the eye on top had also got arms and legs and a speech balloon with the injunction to *keep on truckin'*, and the Great Seal of the United States had a beach ball balanced on its nose. Subtle errors, but I'm afraid all too obvious to the trained eye."

Sharck paused. This had started as a simple question from Figgis as to why, on that night in Castle Drog, Sharck had shouted that they had to eliminate the Higgs Bosun at all costs. But now his audience seemed to have forgotten the original question. Short attention spans. It was why the boss needed someone like Sharck, a man not easily diverted, or nothing would ever happen. He stared into the depths of his pint of Cornish bitter, his mind in an imaginary submarine circling somewhere in the dark yellow depths.

The clock at the back of the bar ticked loudly. A long time ago the face had become detached so that it balanced delicately on the spindle that held the hands. Every time the hour hand moved a little the clock face wobbled. Old Ben the former barman had left it that way so that near closing time if a drinker looked up to check the time he might conclude that he had had one too many.

After a while, as if some distant echo of the conversation had returned to the forefront of Figgis's mind, he spoke; "So, er, how does the Higgs Bosun come into all this?"

"Ah," Sharck looked up, forcing his eyes to focus back on reality. "Yes. Well on our route back from Mexico we stopped off in the Bahamas to sample the nightlife and do a little trade. There was an unfortunate incident when I tried to pay for my drinks using some of our special dollar bills. As I was holding out the money to the bartender I heard a voice beside me say, 'I would not take his money, Señor.' I became uncomfortably aware that the man sitting beside me at the bar was dressed in a very sharp white suit and had one gold tooth."

"Do you have a particular aversion to white suits and gold teeth?" Figgis asked.

"No of course not," Sharck returned wearily, "the point is, it was Ramón Pimiento El Picante on whom we had just palmed off nine hundred and ninety-eight thousand nine hundred and ninety-one dollars and ninety-one cents in fake notes—the ninety-one cents were real—in exchange for a boatload of hallucinogenic chillies, street value about four million pounds."

"He probably wasn't very happy, then," Figgis remarked.

Smithers raised his eyes to the ceiling. "About as happy as one of your dogs would be with a nut loaf in the presence of the smell of steak, I would imagine."

"Why not a round million dollars?" Figgis put on his puzzled expression again. There was a sharp intake of breath between Smithers's teeth.

Sharck's gaze reverted to his beer and the imaginary submarine once more, as though the effort of taking his story to the end were more than he could cope with. With a supreme effort he resumed: "Because, obviously, Ramón Pimiento El Picante likes triangular numbers,* and, obviously, nine hundred and ninety-eight thousand nine hundred and ninety-one is the

---

* Footnote: 'Triangular numbers'—According to the Pythagoreans, a mystical sect in the Ancient Greek world, a triangular number is one which makes the form of a triangle. So for example three is one plus two, making a triangle if you place two pebbles underneath one pebble, and six is one plus two plus three. Taking the first triangular number as one, the thirteenth triangular number is 91. The general formula for the nth triangular number is $n(n+1)/2$. If during a toast you chime glasses with all your friends, and you have n friends, then the number of times the glasses will chime will be the nth triangular number. You don't count yourself because chiming one glass with yourself is a bit like the sound of one hand clapping.

one thousand four hundred and thirteenth triangular number, and ninety-one is the thirteenth triangular number, and the number thirteen reminds him of death and hence the festival of Día de los Muertos when he first set eyes on Lola 'Hotstuff' Tabasco."

There was a long pause in which Smithers looked menacingly at Figgis.

Eventually Sharck continued, "He grabbed my lapels and I could see his gold tooth up close. 'You have a leetle debt to settle,' he said. As you can understand I was not that keen to continue the conversation so I twisted out of his grasp and made a run for it. Luckily I lost him in a back alley and then made straight for the ~~Sardine~~ *Kraken*. We set off leaving a lot of our crew members behind, which was justified under the circumstances and of course saved considerably on wages. Unfortunately it also meant that our navigation left a lot to be desired and what was worse the Navy vessel H.M.S *Higgs* came looking for us."

"Why would they do that?" Figgis asked.

"Why wouldn't they?" Smithers responded dismissively. "The pathetic damp squid that is the remains of the British Empire likes to push its tentacles into all kinds of things it imagines it has an interest in."

"A bit like the boss," Figgis ventured, at which point Smithers gave him a violent kick under the table and Figgis spluttered slightly and went a mild shade of puce. Sharck explained, "It turned out the Bahamian government had been asked for assistance in relation to an unfortunate incident at the Governor General's garden party at which some unusual chillies had got mixed up with the tea bags. Several people's trousers fell down revealing Union Jack underpants. A British official called an official of the Bahamian government asking for the assistance of the Royal Bahamian Defence Force but the Bahamian official pointed out that as the matter was totally silly it was plainly an entirely British affair. The British official responded that the ability to be silly was quite possibly why Britain had won the war against fascism, that being an ideology entirely incapable of silliness and therefore ultimately doomed to destruction. The Bahamian official nevertheless felt with all due respect it was more appropriate to ask the captain of H.M.S *Higgs*."

There was another long pause in which Edwin Sharck appeared distracted. Figgis looked uncertainly at Sharck, then at Smithers then back at Sharck again, before venturing in a small voice, "And then?"

"There was a bit of a chase. We lost our bearings somewhere in the Bermuda Triangle and then on the horizon we spotted an island but we had no idea what it was. Since we could no longer see H.M.S *Higgs* the boss ordered that we surface and go ashore in the dinghies. There we stayed for several days, waiting for the heat to die down, using driftwood fires to cook fish and plantains on the beach."

Here Sharck drifted off for a bit, and neither of the others dared interrupt his silent reverie.

Then, "There were mermaids." He stopped again, as though at the memory of something painful.

"They were beautiful, every one."

Another pause.

"We had to. The boss insisted. Never pass up an opportunity. Excellent tourist attraction worth a million in the right hands, he said. He picked one out. She was full of joy, extraordinary. Older than the others but at the same time ageless."

He paused again, and he seemed to be looking at something or nothing beyond the wall.

"To be honest, I didn't want to do it. She seemed totally innocent yet with a beauty that made me afraid. It seemed a crime to touch her. 'So you don't like crime?' the boss said to me. 'So what are you doing here? Perhaps I need someone else in charge of my men? No-one is irreplaceable!' So we surrounded her, pretending to play in the sea, all the time holding a big trawl net under the water, and then together we raised the net. She tried to swim away and I grabbed her but her tail slipped through my hands. The boss just jumped on her and held her round the waist as she thrashed and struggled, and we bound her hands behind her back, then we dragged her bleeding to one of the dinghies. That was when the Higgs Bosun turned up, all alone, walking over the headland towards us."

A note from Professor Neville Twistytrouser

Dear Sirenology Students,
Firstly allow me to explain that Myfanwy is now on an extended holiday. Myfanwy became a little overwrought and Mervyn felt she needed a well-deserved rest, somewhere a long way away, so she is currently vacationing in Tierra del Fuego where apparently other Welsh people live, although they herd goats and speak Spanish as well as Welsh. At any rate they don't, as far as I know, cook goat with cheese.

Mervyn himself is in self-imposed exile in a small shed in at the back of the Co-op in Milton Keynes recovering from over-exposure to Welsh female attentions and unexpected plastic spiders in his tea.

He is writing furiously but he is disorganised, which is why I have sent one of my D.Phil students, Peregrine Pilchard, to camp out at the back of the Co-op in order to pass on to me Milton's fevered outpourings. These I have received in random order in a cardboard box.

I have done my best to organise these into a coherent form although the exact order of the chapters is a little unclear. At any rate, I think this one comes next. To avoid further delay I felt it only right to forward this to you as it is, without the footnotes, cross-references and other scholarly apparatus which I intend to include in the definitive edition, to be published by Coelocanth University Press in due course.

Unfortunately Peregrine got rather drunk on cider which the Co-op had on special, and some of these papers have also been sent to Professor Alphonse Pince-Nez of the Sorbonne. This is regrettable as he has the usual Gallic tendency to interpret everything according to a rather florid post-Structuralist analysis, which given that the starting material is already absurd is unlikely to produce anything other than the usual continental word-salad. If you receive anything from Professor Pince-Nez then you should treat it with the contempt all French philosophy deserves.

Yours in Russell,

Neville Twistytrouser,

Professor of Logical Pescatology and Warden of St Doris College, Oxford

From Stalin

Comrades,

Even though I am an atheist I have been forced to come back from the grave to intervene in what is clearly a capitalist conspiracy to denigrate the achievements of the revolution.

You will notice that in the first draft of this tale the ex-Soviet submarine belonging to the boss was called the Stalin and was then renamed the *Sardine*. A sardine is a little fish, *ochen malinki* (teeny weeny), and clearly it is intended to make fun of me. People like me should be seen as extremely mighty. So I insist that it be changed from Sardine to something expressing the true nature of the far-reaching consequences of my reforms. In this spirit I suggest *Kraken*. You will know of course that I am quite capable of changing history retrospectively. If the author fails to implement this change, which has been agreed by everybody except those

now living in Siberia, I shall initiate poltergeist activity in Melvin's shed as soon as it is approved by Satan, which it will be, or else.
　Uncle Joe
　СТАЛИН

23. El Sueño de la Razón

As Captain Kipper watched from the shore, the strange boat cut its engines and drifted smoothly to the side of the harbour promontory. It was an ocean-going motor yacht, gleaming white and immaculate. The name painted on the side was *El Sueño de la Razón*.

Ramón Pimiento El Picante was a tall man, exuding machismo. Like a pirate he had one gold earring, but he was dressed impeccably in a white suit and his crisp white shirt was open at the collar to reveal the hint of a hairy chest and a gold chain. On his head was a white panama hat with a black band, and his white leather shoes had Cuban heels.

Ramón stepped elegantly from the foredeck onto solid ground and looked around him, his head high. He smiled a big open grin, and even the grey light could not help creating a glint on a gold tooth.

A note from Professeur Alphonse Pince-Nez

Chères Amateurs des Sirènes,
Premièrement, I take grande exception to the remarque de soi-disant 'Professeur' Twistytrouser, que la philosophie Française should be treated avec 'contempt.'

Has he not read mes grandes oeuvres, *Concombres de mer comme métaphore pour des rapports sexuels sous-marins pendant l'ère baroque* (*Sea cucumbers as metaphor for underwater sexual relations in the Baroque era*, Editions Saltimbanques de Mer, Paris 1999), ou peut-être closer to his own psychopathologie, *Knickers tordus—une exploration socioculturelle de l'infériorité-complexe académique en Angleterre postmoderne* (Twisted knickers—a socio-cultural exploration of the academic inferiority-complex in post-modern England, Proceedings of the 13th International Conference on Why the English are not as good as us, vol. XXXI pp.1023-2003)?

Je crois que si le Twistytrouser, or as I shall refer to him, *Le Grand Pantaloon*, had paid plus attention to the matter in hand rather than impugning the productions of his intellectual supérieurs sur le continent, he would have perhaps noticed a lapse in continuité, alors!

How, I ask, did Edwin Sharck know of the conversation between the officials of the Bahamas and the Governor General? This remains to be expliqué! So much for his soi-disant 'scholarly apparatus.' Je crois que it is in his 'scholarly apparatus' that he washes his socks which come out not in pairs!

Et bien, içi le next chapitre, which fortunately for posterity happen to fall into my hands.

Veuillez agréer, Mesdames et Messieurs, les salutations distinguées,

Professeur Alphonse Pince-Nez, Institut des Études des Saltimbanques de Mer, Sorbonne, Paris

From Myfanwy

Hello again Faithful Fishy Folk,
Myfanwy here. I might be still in Patagonia but I know what's going on.

You see, although Marmaduke Montmorency is hiding in a small shed at the back of the Co-op in Milton Keynes, he is still forwarding me the emails. I deduce by this that he really misses me and will soon come to his senses, at which point I shall hop on the first plane from Argentina and burst in upon him with my forgiving heart and Welsh cooking.

Now then, these naughty fellows have got hold of quite a few chapters, I suspect as a result of boxes of manuscript getting mixed up with consignments of Milton Keynes export frozen carp. Just because they have got letters after their names and make a living sitting in armchairs smoking pipes they think they can put footnotes in tiny fonts into my Marmaduke! I mean the university chappies, not the carp obviously. Whoever heard of a carp sitting in an armchair smoking a pipe putting tiny fonts into things? I haven't. Some people are a bit thick in my opinion. Anyway, they can't just insert their tiny fonts wherever they feel like. Not if I have anything to do with it. Once I am back in Europe I shall go round and kick them in their tiny fonts if they don't watch out.

Kisses,
Myfanwy
Casa Aberystwyth, Trelew, Argentina

From His Royal Highness Ruben-Dogsandwich III of Euphoria

Dear Myfanwy,
On those rare occasions when the duties of state permit a moment's light reading, I chanced upon Marmaduke's oeuvre including your note, which for some reason was found wrapping a consignment of Milton Keynes export frozen carp received in the royal kitchens. May I respectfully point out that smoked fish are widely available here, although I'm not sure if pipes are involved. Irrespective of that I wish you well. I also take the opportunity to assure you of continuing good relations between the Palatinate of Euphoria and the United Kingdom, if you would pass this on to Her Majesty, when you have a moment.

Ruben-Dogsandwich III

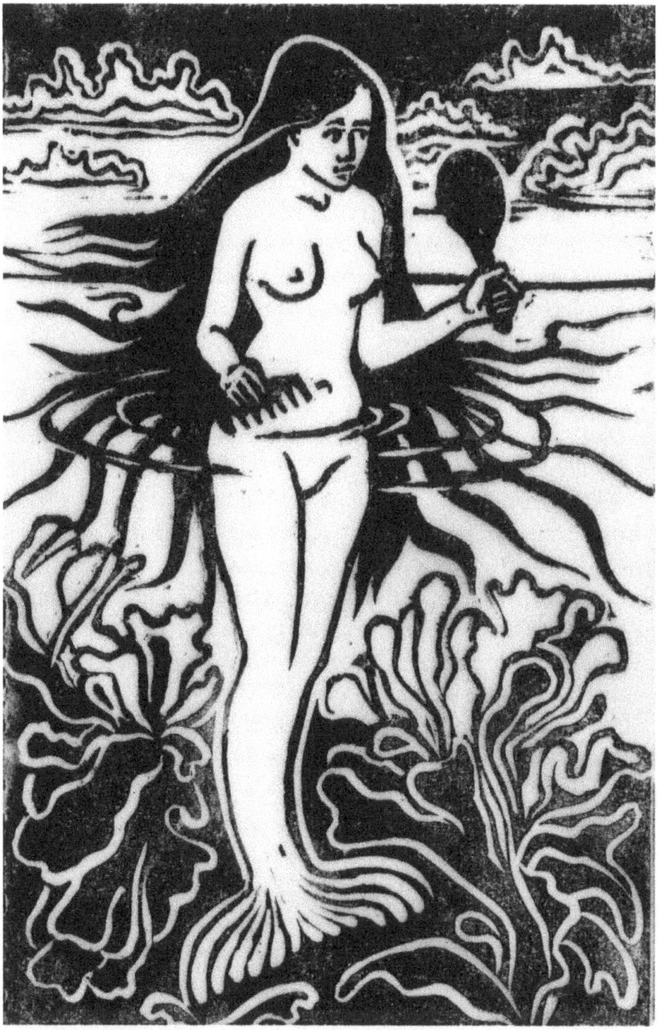

24. The immutable law of the universe

Sharck's beer glass was empty. Smithers looked meaningfully at Figgis, who at first did not understand. Smithers gave him another kick and jerked his thumb in the direction of the bar. It seemed not to matter that Smithers was supposed to be the barman. Figgis limped over to the bar, where Lola was waiting. He wondered how much she could overhear amidst the noise of other conversations.

"Another pint of *Hideous Pigsty*, please," Figgis said. Lola looked at him gently and with a hint of pity as she pulled the pint and handed it to him. No money changed hands as Smithers's friends never paid.

Figgis returned with Edwin Sharck's pint, but Sharck seemed stuck at the point in the story that he had arrived at. He took a few sips of the dark yellow liquid, and whether it was still a submarine he was seeing there or the hazy vision of a mermaid one could not tell. He opened his mouth as if to speak then closed it again at exactly the moment when Figgis piped up, "Who is the boss? Why do we never see him?"

Smithers grabbed him by the lapels and put his face uncomfortably close. Then between clenched teeth, "Just shut up." Figgis went white.

Sharck sighed, not apparently aware of the little drama happening right next to him, or if he was, he didn't care.

Eventually Sharck's eyes refocused with an effort on Figgis and he resumed.

"The Higgs Bosun kept coming, alone, walking steadily towards us. I didn't understand how he expected to do anything all on his own. As far as I could tell he was unarmed, his hands swung by his sides, apparently empty. One of the crew levelled a pistol at him, but he never wavered in his stride. It made no sense.

"'What do you want?' I called out to him. He kept coming until he was close enough to talk without raising his voice, then stopped.

"'You have captured one of the mermaids,' he said. 'I require you to let her go.'

"'Require? Says who?' I said.

"'It is required by the immutable law of the universe,' he replied.

"Some of the crew laughed at this, but I kept a stony face. The boss was behind me, and was not going to let the mermaid go lightly, and as I was his right-hand man, I had to deal with the situation. The sailor with the pistol was still there, pointing it at the Bosun's head. Nobody moved.

"My thoughts whirled. No-one in his right mind would come unarmed and without reinforcements and demand anything of a crew of—er—businessmen of the sea who had a gun. I worried in case this was an ambush. I scanned the edges of the dunes and the headland for any signs of movement. Were there riflemen up there? I could see nothing but sky meeting rock and sand and the gentle waving of tufts of grass.

"The boss was getting impatient. 'Get rid of him,' he said. I hesitated. The sailor with the gun looked at me anxiously for an order, which I did not give. Murder was not part of what any of us had signed up for. In any case, at that moment none of us knew that H.M.S *Higgs* had hit a rock and had sunk with all its weaponry, leaving the crew stranded elsewhere on the island.

"I suppose I was like a dog that won't attack unless the intruder turns and runs. And the whole episode with the mermaid had disturbed me. Something in me knew that what was happening was outside my experience and therefore I did not know how to handle it.

"'Look,' I said, 'we are honest businessmen with a cargo of Mexican chillies. If it's chillies you're after, we can talk. But any mermaid is fair capture. These are not British territorial waters and you have no claim on anything caught here.'

"At this the Bosun reached for his pocket and the crewman with the gun shouted for him to stop. 'Then you may take what is in my pocket yourself,' the Bosun said, and raised both hands away from his sides. I approached carefully and reached into his pocket and withdrew a tattered and very frail piece of cloth.

"'Unfold it,' the Higgs Bosun commanded. It was a piece of stained white linen with a red cross emblazoned across it. At the bottom corner someone had stitched something in English. It read, 'S.Doris Iland claimed for her Glorious Majestie Queen Elizabeth by F-cis. Drake, seafarer 1578.'

"'But that isn't the point,' the Bosun went on, 'a mermaid is an intelligent creature like you. A crime against a mermaid, a crime against any person, is something that follows you wherever you go. It lessens you as a human being. You become filled with lies to justify to yourself what you did, until you are a bag of lies. It becomes less and less possible to be truly human. The clear air of awareness becomes filled with your own gibbering demons. Finally you forget who you are.'

"'Nonsense!' I said. 'A mermaid is a fish.' But I didn't believe it myself. I had seen her face.

"The Bosun went on, 'You know also that a mermaid is beautiful. How do you know beauty when you see it? Only because of the beauty in you. You recognise yourself by yourself. Sell that, and you sell yourself. Deny it and you deny yourself. Imprison it and you imprison yourself. That is why the release of the mermaid is required by the law of the universe, the law you cannot escape.'

"The boss was breathing audibly through his nose and although he was behind me I sensed his impatience. Nevertheless he did nothing and said nothing. The Higgs Bosun started walking towards the dinghy where the mermaid sat covered in nets in a state of quiet melancholy. I felt I was in a dream in which my legs would not move. I turned to watch. The boss seemed transfixed yet burning with anger. Then the Bosun turned to one of the crew and asked for a knife. Unaccountably a knife was handed over, handle first. The Bosun accepted it with a smile, totally lacking in guile or triumph or any other emotion but love, and the sailor smiled back. It seemed our entire reality was replaced by another unfamiliar one as I became aware of the beauty of the palm trees for the first time. The whole scene was bathed in light. Calmly the Bosun cut the bonds from the mermaid's wrists and lifted her gently into the sea, and she swam away."

Smithers snorted. "You're going soft!" he said.

There was a sickening thud as without warning Edwin Sharck's fist hit Smithers in the face so hard that Smithers fell crashing backwards off his stool onto the floor. He picked himself up slowly, his nose bleeding profusely. With one hand holding his nose he grabbed Figgis with the other and shook him violently, then gave him another kick in the shins.

"Why haven't you rounded Higgsy up yet?" Smithers said through his bloody handkerchief. "Useless copper!"

The rest of the pub fell silent. All eyes were on the little group in the corner.

"Assaulting a police officer..." Figgis said weakly and without conviction.

Sharck looked from Figgis to Smithers and back again. Then, with quiet menace, "Smithers is right, Figgis. I'm a bit upset. And the boss is a bit upset. You shape up or you ship out, and the latter could be more than a bit unpleasant. At least we've got the new mermaid. But the boss wants the Bosun out of the way. Understand?"

A note from the Warden of St Doris College, Oxford

Dear Perusers of Piscine Prose,
It is regrettable when a fellow academic, albeit a French one, casts aspersions on one's scholarship before knowing the facts. It will indeed be part of my scholarly apparatus to add a footnote explaining that ex-Soviet submarines of a type similar to that of the *Stalin* (re-named *Kraken* by the as yet unnamed boss of the businessmen of the sea) generally were equipped with listening apparatus enabling them to pick up and decode wireless communications. This explains how Edwin Sharck knew about the incident with the Union Jack underpants.

As for my socks, I would have Professor Pince-Nez know that my washing machine only occasionally loses socks and this is being carefully investigated by the physics department of our esteemed university, to find out if the sock problem is a manifestation of quantum indeterminacy. If it is, then the materialisation of previously unrecorded socks will be very exciting evidence in favour of the 'Many Worlds' theory of quantum mechanics over the Copenhagen interpretation. However I wouldn't expect Professor Pince-Nez, with his boring mass-produced identical socks, beret, string of onions and silly stripy jersey, to understand this.

I remain respectfully yours,
Prof. Neville Twistytrouser
Senior Common Room by the bottle of College Port, St Doris College, Oxford

From Jel E. Fish

Dearest Myf,
So good to hear from you again. I hope the locals are enjoying your Welsh Tango classes. I know you could reach them a thing or two about passion!

Anyway, hang in there Myf—Men, eh!
Hugs,
Jel E. Fish

From Myfanwy
Hello Seaweedy Soulmates,
Well you have to understand that these people in Trelew, Patagonia are actually Welsh. You might think this would be an advantage because a lot of them speak Welsh too, but since I come from Cardiff, after *iechyd da* I don't actually understand a bleddy word. So I get by in Spanglish. ¡Hola! isn't it, look you.

As for the Welsh style of tango, it gets them going but never on a Sunday, as they're very *chapel*.

Anyway, as far as Mervyn Mildew is concerned I am biding my time. Welsh passion is all very well, but it is not to be lightly frittered away. No. My Welsh fritters are worth waiting for, I can tell you.

Now then, Mervyn is doing so well at the moment that I think the future will bring offers pouring in for the film rights. If that happens then I think there should be a bit of ethnic diversity in the casting, don't you? I notice there aren't any Welsh people in it so far, which is a bit of a disappointment. I asked Mervyn about it once and he wouldn't be drawn, except to say that he thinks Alf the Higgs Bosun could definitely be played by a person of colour. He didn't specify which colour, though. Also he has a suspicion that the mermaid herself is a bit dusky. Possibly there will be a clue to this in some future chapter.

Myf
xoxoxo

25. A WOMAN LOVES A MAN IN UNIFORM

LIONEL HAD BELATEDLY GONE IN TO WORK. Someone had left a newspaper on his desk, folded so as to show the front page headline. It was Friday, the day each week's *Pengoggly Post* came out, and there was a photograph of Lionel outside his house, another photograph blown up rather large of a sea anemone in his bath, and an artist's impression of a giant squid. The headline read, "PENGOGGLY SQUID MENACE!" and in smaller capitals underneath, "GIANT SQUID FOUND IN LOCAL MAN'S BATH."

He sat down to read it and almost immediately Mavis brought him a cup of tea, her large chest casting a shadow as she craned over him, her breathing audible.

"Thank you, Mavis," he said weakly and without making eye-contact. He found himself hunched over his desk, feeling invaded.

"By Tracey Truth, junior reporter," the paper continued. "Police had to remove a large marine creature, thought to be a giant squid, from local man Lionel Fortescue's bath in Marine Parade on Wednesday. P. C. Figgis was overheard to say it could give rise to 'thousands of squid,' but when asked directly about a possible squid epidemic on the Cornish coast he refused to be drawn.[*] Sergeant Spriggan later clarified that the matter was *sub judice* and that for legal reasons he could give no further comment at this time, but emphasised that the police had the situation under control and that the public was in no danger.

"When asked for comment an unrepentant Mr Fortescue said, 'In England one may do whatever one likes in one's bath and that

---

[*] For the benefit of non-British readers, Tracey Truth probably misheard *quid* as *squid*. Quid is English slang for a pound money. A feeble joke that gains nothing from being explained.

makes me proud to be British.' When pressed to explain why he had a giant squid in his bath, he said, 'I don't have anything useful to say.' Mr Fortescue is a local accountant. (Editorial comment page 11.)"

Understandably Lionel could not for the moment bear to turn to page 11. He could imagine that whatever was said about him would do his firm no good. He was now associated with the alleged keeping of marine menaces in a cavalier manner, oblivious of public safety.

The rest of the day passed uneventfully, occupied with columns of figures and the occasional consulting of tax manuals dealing with the finer points of European fish policy. Eventually, distracted from the task in hand, he allowed his thoughts to be sidetracked by the more interesting but admittedly somewhat theoretical question as to whether the expense of breeding barnacle geese could be offset against tax by adding them to the maintenance costs of a fishing boat.

It had generally been accepted by monks in the Middle Ages that barnacle geese were born out of barnacles, and were therefore technically fish. This meant that Church Law allowed them to be eaten on Fridays. Lionel felt sure there was a useful ruse in there somewhere. From that his thoughts moved to what he would have for supper tonight, and from there to his mermaid, and whether she was being properly fed.

With this thought any further capacity for useful work left him. He told Mavis she could go home early.

Just as Mavis was putting her coat on the bell rang and she went to open the door. It was Figgis. A startled look crossed his face and he took a deep breath before recovering his customary rather tight-lipped expression.

"Er, Miss ...?"

Mavis towered majestically over the small policeman.

"I do love a man in uniform," she said suddenly and in honeyed tones, "it gives him such an air of authority."

There was a brief pause, in which Figgis seemed momentarily to have forgotten why he had come.

"P.C. Figgis," he ventured, pulling himself up to his full height.

"Mavis," she breathed.

Summoning up a tone of voice suitable to the full dignity of the law, Figgis resumed, "I have come to speak with Mr Lionel Fortescue." He placed his boot in the door.

Lionel saw no reason to hide. "It's fine, you can let him in, Mavis," he said.

Mavis stood there and Figgis squeezed past her rubenesque form.

"You can go home now, thank you Mavis," Lionel said.

Mavis hovered for a moment before closing the door behind her with a long backward glance, whether at Lionel or Figgis was hard to make out exactly. Lionel indicated the empty chair opposite his desk and Figgis sat, wiping a few beads of sweat from his forehead with a handkerchief.

"To come to the point," Figgis began, "you will see from the newspaper that you are a little bit *personally non gratis* at the moment."

"Persona non grata," Lionel corrected.

"As I said. Now at the moment, to put all my cards up one flagpole, it would not really suit me to arrest you. But I could."

"Why would you do that?"

"If it suited me."

Lionel was aware that Figgis was playing some kind of game with him. No doubt he would come to the point in the end. But it occurred to Lionel that if Figgis were trying to get something from him, then he, Lionel, must have something of value that Figgis wanted. This perhaps put Lionel momentarily at an advantage.

Lionel felt oddly calm. In less than a week he was far from the man he had been at the beginning. The irruption of the mermaid had changed his life catastrophically and forever. Of course, in a sense he had a choice. He could stop struggling against events that seemed out of his or anyone else's control and try to forget her. He could try to return to being the comfortable reasonably well-paid accountant who specialised in the tax returns of humble fishermen. But he knew that then something inside him would die.

He could have comfort or he could have his heart's desire—perhaps. He reframed it. He could have comfort or he could devote his life to pursuing his heart's desire, with no certainty of success. However he looked at it, there was no real choice.

This is the key to the enigma of free will. We who choose to see clearly can choose the good, or we can choose the good. There is no other choice possible. But it is still a choice.

Figgis was staring at him impatiently.

"On what ground?" Lionel asked.

"All sorts of things. Keeping a dangerous animal in your bath."

"At some point you'd have to produce the animal."

"And we could probably match the footprints we found at the back of the police station to your shoes. Breaking and entering."

"I didn't break anything."

"Aha! So you admit it? Not a match for the highly-trained police mind are you, Mr so-called Fishface?" He tapped his forehead. "And you upset my dog. That's harassment that is. And it's against the Cruelty to Fierce Dogs Act. Look, the reason doesn't have to stick. But I could arrest you and then I'd have time to work something out that would keep the magistrate happy and you behind bars until the proper court case. Or I could let Fenrir off the leash by accident when you are going home. I am not without ingenuity. I've got certificates, you know."

Lionel said nothing. There were many things he wanted to know, not least about the wellbeing of the mermaid and how to secure her release, but he felt that asking would have provoked nothing but evasion. Better to create a vacuum which Figgis would feel compelled to fill.

The large plastic clock on the wall ticked loudly.

Figgis drummed his fingers on the desk. Lionel leaned back in his chair, his face impassive.

Time went by.

Figgis fidgeted in his chair, his eyes wandering around the room. He tried once or twice to outstare Lionel but found he couldn't actually make eye-contact. Distractedly, as if thinking out loud, he said, "Mavis..."

"Mmm-hmm?" Lionel made one of those encouraging but non-committal noises that therapists make.

Figgis coughed. "That's not what I came about. I was just thinking out loud." He flushed slightly.

"She's unattached, if that's what you're asking."

"I didn't ask."

More silence in which the only sounds were the plastic clock and Figgis's breathing.

Figgis coughed. "The Higgs Bosun," he said at last.

"Yes?"

"Where is he?"

"In the Large Hadron Collider in Switzerland? Or underpinning the entire universe? Why ask me?"

"Don't play games with me!" Figgis was suddenly animated, leaning forward, his hands gripping the arms of the chair.

"I wasn't intending to. But I do have a ping-pong table, as it happens."

Figgis stood up, as menacingly as he knew how. At the same moment Lionel got up and walked over to the far end of the office and pushed back a folding screen, revealing a ping-pong table. He went to the far end of it, small wooden racket and ping-pong ball in hand. His face was as near to Daniel Craig's James Bond face as he could make it. He bounced the ping-pong ball once on the table and caught it in a slight movement, the rest of his body motionless.

Figgis advanced uncertainly. The other racket lay on the ping-pong table, waiting for him.

"What do you want?" Figgis asked. His tight-lipped expression even tighter.

"I want the mermaid."

"And if I win?"

"I don't promise you anything. I might give you Mavis's phone number."

"It's in the phonebook."

"I know."

It felt too late to back down. It felt to Figgis as if his whole manhood was being challenged. As he picked up the racket there was sweat in his palm. If he lost he knew he would not get any information about the Higgs Bosun out of Lionel, and he had a fair idea of what Smithers would do to him.

"Do we have to do this?"

"I didn't ask you to come here."

Figgis hesitated, not moving. Their eyes met. A long time seemed to pass. Then, slowly, Lionel raised his racket and at the same time the ping-pong ball was in the air, like a spaceman doing a moonwalk, travelling upwards then down in a narrow parabola towards the point where inevitably Lionel's racket would hit it. Figgis felt in his gut that moment of impact before it happened.

Pok! Figgis's mind went blank as his racket flailed instinctively for the ball. Somehow he hit it and the ball was in. Before he had time to think it was back again, right at the edge of the table, and he hit it again. Again and again, now to the left, now to the right, always just in. Sweat poured from Figgis while Lionel barely seemed to move, as though in some Zen space removed from stress or panic. One more shot and the ball came whizzing back towards Figgis, he lurched and missed as by some curious spin the ball touched the table and curved away like a cosmic ray particle in a cloud chamber, or like the elusive Higgs Bosun himself. Figgis could stand it no more. He collapsed, breathless in a cold sweat across the table. It was over.

A note from Angelina Jolifish

Dear Myf,
The last chapter ended very thrillingly didn't it! I can imagine, in the film, they will do the ping pong duel all slow motion acrobatics like in *The Matrix*.

I think you should tactfully inform Milton Marzipan that one wields a 'bat' in ping pong not a racquet—just to avoid possible persecution from pedantic ping pong players.

Love and hugs
Angelina Jolifish (a.k.a Jel E. Fish) x

From Professor Neville Twistytrouser

'Bat,' 'paddle' and 'racquet' are all acceptable terms for that thingy that you hit the ping-pong ball with. *Racket* is an acceptable alternative spelling for *racquet*, and *racket* is the older form, being derived from the Flemish *raketsen*. While I have your attention, *pedantic ping pong players* is an excellent alliteration, which made this whole digression enormous fun, at least for us intellectuals if for no-one else.

A WOMAN LOVES A MAN IN UNIFORM

Warning to readers from Myfanwy

Really if these naughty professors think I am going to worry my head about their pedantry and preposterous theorising they have another think coming. If you get bogged down in Professor Pince-Nez's franglais just skip ahead.

Real life goes on around intellectuals, like a river around a wooded island. The little islands with their tangled undergrowth make us wonder what it would be like to be on them, but we never get around to going there.

From Professor Alphonse Pince-Nez

Chères Amis de Mer,
La suggestion that I wear a stripy jumper is absurd as it is objectionable, nor do I carry oignons about on my bicyclette. Like all true intellectuels français I wear a beige polo-neck jumper and smoke gauloises.

As to the signification of the present histoire, indeed Le Grand Pantaloon d'Oxford have not understood that it suffice not merely to add little details in footnotes, but we must undertake a project to engage with the whole oeuvre in its totality both *synchronically* and *diachronically*.

Am I making sense so far? Probably not. Good, I continue.

Et bien, we must approach its 'tout-ensemble' or *Gestalt*, both as pertains to its present sociolinguistic implications and also as it informs us of its own ontological *mythos*. This we can only do from a position of *amour propre*, c'est à dire, we must allow it its existential domain within our own frame of reference, à la même temps acknowledging that our analysis will necessarily be through the distorting lens of our own determining cultural subjectivité.

The types of metonymy that the use of language forces upon us condition our *seeing* and hence the narrative that we are able to extract. If there is an underlying reality (and that is a matter that cannot well be debated since it is *meta-linguistic*) then it will always be subverted by language, and we are prisoners of language *faut de mieux*.

It follows that the meaning of the text will depend on the instrumentality that we use to decode it. The text, *enfin*, is composed of multiple *signifiers* whose *significands* cannot be forced into a definite cognitive space.

I respectfully suggest that the Pantaloon stick this into his pipe and smoke it.

Veuillez agréer, Mesdames et Messieurs, les salutations distinguées,

Professeur Alphonse Pince-Nez, Institut des Études des Saltimbanques de Mer, Sorbonne, Paris

From Professor Neville Twistytrouser

Dear Shoal of Saline Sympathisers,

I think on stylistic grounds this next chapter follows on from the one you received recently from the French Buffoon, in that Milton Marzipan seems gradually to be settling into a more relaxed sentence structure in terms of comma frequency, and also that the text refers to 'Friday afternoon.'

As to Professor Pince-Nez's little academic outburst, it is regrettably exactly what I predicted: a continental word-salad.

A little 'textual deconstruction' of my own reveals that he is saying nothing that has not already been said, and considerably more succinctly at that, by the ancient Greek philosopher Dumptaios.[*] Regrettably nothing much is known about Dumptaios

---

[*] Diels and Krantz, *Die Fragmente der Vorsokratiker* (Berlin, 1960), Dumptaios fragment 1.

himself other than the very brief account in Diogenes,[*] but a good English gloss of the sole surviving fragment of his thought is to be found in Carroll, L.[†]

In any event, Prof. Pince-Nez's promised analysis of the text so far can be reduced to the assertion that it can mean whatever you like—not, I would venture, a very promising start to an academic exercise.

I remain, yours,
Neville Twistytrouser
Third table on the left next to a pint of *Theakston's Old Peculiar*, the Vicky Arms, Oxford

From Myfanwy

Hello Sagacious Sirenophiles,
Just briefly now, this next chapter is about love I think, and whether it is an illness. Tricky. Well, until Melvyn sees fit to call me to his romantic hideaway behind the Co-op I shan't worry about it all that much, and I certainly shan't simply waste my considerable talents. No.

Anyway, got to go now as I've just spotted goucho Dai Gonzalez-Jones over the road at the café and I think it only right to sidle over nonchalantly to say ¡Hola!

I don't want to lose my touch, do I?
kisses,
Myf
xoxoxo
Casa Aberystwyth, Trelew, Argentina

---

[*] Diogenes Laertius, *Lives of the Philosophers*, Humptaeus Dumptaeus.
[†] Carroll L, *Through the Looking Glass* (London 1871), ch.6.

26. How to Diagnose Imaginary Illnesses

ON FRIDAY AFTERNOON Smithers had sent Lola into Pengoggly to buy groceries for Saturday's pub grub and Sunday's roast lunch at the *Piskie and Pasty*.

Lola was feeling distressed, her emotions in turmoil. She wanted to go and find Captain Kipper and throw herself into his arms, but at the same time she didn't want to because she wanted to be sure that the Captain really loved her.

You might think such brief encounters as theirs could not reasonably evoke love, but you would be wrong. Love does not answer to the rational mind. Its fire can be slow-burn, but also it is often instant. Yet sometimes it deceives, Lola knew. She had intended simply to go to the supermarket and buy a bottle of milk of magnesia, because as Lola also knew, sometimes that feeling of love turns out to be indigestion. As she crossed the seafront she could not help noticing the low bright pink building with its friendly sign offering alternative medical help.

"If I have an illness, it is certainly an alternative one," Lola thought.

She went in.

The interior was coloured pale lilac with limed oak skirting boards and doors, and there was the sound of whales playing in the background, calling to each other about where the most tasty fish and krill might be found. The reception desk had a limed oak top and on it was a clear plastic rack with leaflets about all the treatments available for all known and some unknown diseases, also advertisements for health foods such as caffeine-free coffee, fat-free yogurt, chocolate-free chocolate and fresh-air pie to help with weight loss. There were also advertisements for medicine-free pills. Nevertheless none of these things were actually free, even assuming you wanted them. They were all, however, allegedly natural.

In the area behind the desk was a large lady of uncertain age and strangely forbidding aspect, despite her knitted rainbow-coloured shawl and her tent-like dress made of batiked Indian silk.

The lady ignored her until Lola realised she was to ting the little Tibetan bells, which she did.

'Tinggg!' A slightly eerie discord echoed round the room for several seconds.

At once the lady glided over and on her face appeared a disconcerting smile, creating much the same emotional effect as a wisp of black cloud crossing the moon.

"Can I help you?"

"Si, er, yes, I would like to see the doctor. How much is it, as I no have much money?"

The disconcerting smile increased. "Ah, this month we have a special introductory offer! The first consultation is free."

Lola smiled, a genuine, sweet smile. "I should like an appointment very much," she said.

The lady ushered her into the lilac waiting room, where all was plush chairs and sofas with ethnic cushions and mystical magazines on a low coffee table. On one wall was a huge framed photograph of an ecstatic woman swimming with eels, and on another a poster showing a semi-transparent cat sitting upright with a shiny star for a third eye. The cat's collar-tag revealed that his name was Schrödinger, and the caption underneath read, 'Quantum intertwingling with your healed self in a parallel universe.'

Among the magazines on the coffee table was a leaflet which Lola picked up. It read, 'Do you suffer from the Twinge? Do you experience occasional tickles at the back of the neck, especially when wearing itchy jumpers, have an overwhelming belief that the District Council is the cause of all your problems, and feel you don't really want to get out of bed on a Monday morning? You could be suffering from the Twinge. Orthodox medicine doesn't recognise the existence of this important illness, so doctors don't take sufferers seriously. But there is a cure!'

There was more, but Lola had not sat down long when the doctor appeared. He was a small man with dark eyebrows and penetrating eyes. "Dr Fluffycardigan," he said, extending his hand. Lola shook it, and thought it was a little cold. There was something vaguely familiar about Dr Fluffycardigan, which she could not quite place. "Lola Tabasco," she said.

He ushered her into his office, which was dominated by a huge desk in polished walnut. The doctor's chair was of padded black leather and had a large number of levers and controls under it. The patient's chair was soft and enveloping and covered in a pink material. Around the walls were all kinds of posters of inexplicable but colourful geometrical diagrams labelled in various non-Roman alphabets and behind the desk an array of framed certificates, the content of which was impossible to decipher at a distance.

Despite the comfort of the chair Lola felt ill at ease.

"What can I do for you?" ventured the doctor.

She hesitated. "Well, I have a sensation in my chest." She held her right fist between her breasts. "I think it is love."

The doctor's gaze rested on Lola's breasts, and he seemed momentarily hypnotised.

"Love?"

"Si. I think I am in love with Captain Kipper."

The doctor's eyes narrowed and his face tensed, but he recovered himself quickly.

"So you want a cure for love?"

"No, I want to know if it is love or if love is an imaginary illness. Is it just my need for someone to understand and take away my pain? Do you have medicine for this?"

"Ah, you have come to the right place. Treating imaginary illness is our speciality I can assure you. We shall do some tests. Come this way."

Dr Fluffycardigan sat Lola at a desk on which there was a computer screen and a box with two wires coming out of it. On the ends of the wires were handles.

"You hold the handles, and this box here will pick up your vibrations. The software will compare your vibrations with our database of all known imaginary illnesses. What is more it will indicate which of our pills with no medicine in them will be best to treat you. Of course the pills have vibrations in them that interact with your own vibrations to effect a cure."

"Is very impressive!" Lola's eyes widened.

"Yes, indeed. Of course it is not recognised by orthodox medicine which stubbornly refuses to acknowledge anything unless it actually works." His lip curled slightly. "But we find that by selectively remembering all the patients that get better and forgetting about the other ones we get excellent results, which we publish in our scientific journal, *The Journal of the Fluffycardigan Institute*."

Several graphs squiggled across the computer screen at once, and Dr Fluffycardigan stared at them intently. At last he said, "Hmm, you have a blockage in your *rotunda*."

"My *rotunda?*"

"Yes, it is an invisible organ in your chest. It is blocking the flow of energy in your *squiddly channels*."

"Santa Doris! Is it serious?"

"Hopefully not too serious. We'll need to examine your omphalogenic field. If you would lie down on the couch?"

Lola got up and walked over to where there was an examination couch, the latest kind that goes up and down controlled by a button. She lay down. Just above her hanging from the ceiling were a number of bananas on thin strings.

"Ah, we need to examine your omphalogenic field with these detectors. Bananas are very rich in omphalo-magnetic minerals you see. But I'm afraid clothing will interfere with the measurements, so you'll need to undress."

Lola was not too happy with this, but she felt that having got this far she ought to find out why her rotunda was blocking her squiddly channels. She stripped down to her bra and knickers and decided that was as far as she was prepared to go.

The doctor frowned but apparently decided not to push the matter. He pulled a string causing all the bananas to wobble, all the while staring intently at Lola's curvaceous form. This went on for some time, and although Lola felt nothing at all, the doctor appeared rather flushed. Suddenly the door opened and the lady with the disturbing smile walked in without knocking.

"Your next patient is waiting," she said, smiling more disturbingly than ever.

The doctor coughed. "You can get dressed now," he said.

Back at his desk and with Lola back in the pink chair, the doctor became suddenly hurried. "Yes, your rotunda is definitely blocking your squiddly channels. You need to take some alk. pot. parp. squillionth potency twice a day and these tablets of vitamin Gaga with co-enzyme Gonk every day indefinitely. Would you like to pay by direct debit?"

"But she say it is free!"

"Ah, no, the first consultation is free but the medication has to be paid for, you see."

Lola opened her purse then closed it again. Several doubts had crossed her mind.

"I no have money today," she said.

"That's fine, just sign here," he said with a cheesy smile, pushing a form across the desk.

With what dignity she could muster, Lola stood up. "I think about it," she said, and made for the door, with Dr Fluffycardigan following her closely with the form. As she hurried through the waiting room she found the lady with the disturbing smile blocking her way. Suddenly afraid, Lola pushed past and started to run. She hurled herself through the door, causing it to bang violently.

Once on the harbour front she hurtled towards the café, hoping for safety in numbers. But there was something wrong. As she ran she saw that all the tables at the front of *The Frothy Coffee With a Bit of Coffee and Quite a Lot of Milk Café* were occupied by men with big moustaches wearing sombreros. A mariachi band was playing, but the effect of the wind was to distort the sound eerily. The men with sombreros were still yet alert and the atmosphere was one of quiet menace.

Quickly she changed direction and kept running. Glancing back she saw that Dr Fluffycardigan and his disturbing receptionist were no longer to be seen. Straight ahead was a man in an oversized raincoat staring at her. She changed direction again and a moment later she crashed headlong into someone else.

The man wore a white suit and had a gold earring. He had a smile that looked as if it had been fixed there for many years. In that smile a gold tooth flashed in the grey Cornish light.

A note from Professor Alphonse Pince-Nez

Chères Amis des Sirènes,
Here is the next chapitre. There is a certain how you say mix-up with the temps, c'est-à-dire, the chapitre which I now send you follow from the chapitre de ping-pong. Le Pantaloon à send you un autre chapitre which happen peut-être le même afternoon. C'est typical for the soi-disant 'academic' d'Oxford to mix-up his *synchronic* with his *diachronic*.

As to his criticism of the proposed dialectical deconstruction of the text, he fail to understand that it is the possibilité of a life-affirming effusion of interpretations that keeps people like me in *Gauloises* and *vin de la coopérative*, and people like him in

Theakston's Old Peculiar and twisted knickerbockers, no doubt made of scratchy material.

In despite of his blinker view I shall very soon explique the meaning of this whole *roman de poisson* from a psycho-analytical-Marxist perspective.

A bientôt,
Professeur Alphonse Pince-Nez,
Stirring a café-au-lait and dipping a fluorescent green macaroon into it while looking intense, La Durée, Madeleine, Paris

From Myfanwy

Hello You Lot,
I'm a bit busy just now. Keep an eye on those naughty philosophers, won't you?
    kisses,
    Myf
    xoxoxo
    El Bar del Amor, Trelew, Argentina

27. A further history of the Selkies

AFTER THE PING-PONG DEBACLE, FIGGIS returned home a chastened man. He felt hollowed out—his idea of who he was had been severely damaged. He didn't even like himself very much.

Once he arrived home he collapsed onto his bed, still partly clothed, and fell into a disturbed sleep in which Smithers' curled lip appeared and disappeared meaninglessly like that of a deranged Cheshire cat. Then ping-pong balls came at him from all directions for a long time. Eventually the ping-pong balls faded, bouncing several times on the floor before disappearing altogether, and the image of Mavis appeared before him.

"Norman," she said (for that indeed was his name), "Norman, I expected more from you." Later, thinking about this, he found himself unable to tell whether this was a hopeful portent or the opposite.

He woke early feeling sticky and uncomfortable. He showered, the empty feeling persisting in his stomach. Not the kind of empty feeling you can dismiss with egg, sausage, beans and toast, or egg, bacon, fried tomatoes and toast, or with fried tomatoes, mushroom, beans and toast, or indeed with any reasonable permutation of the above—or even porridge with kippers and jam. Had Figgis been better educated or perhaps excessively pretentious he might have described it as an existential crisis, or perhaps ontological insecurity, or even Weltschmerz. But he was not well-educated enough to call it anything other than what it was—emptiness.

Lionel had also gone home to bed. He found himself unable to sleep, adrenaline pumping in his blood. Although he could not explain it, he felt somehow that the tide was beginning to turn in his struggle to get his mermaid back, and perhaps even in the struggle of the people of Kasteldrog and Pengoggly for their beautiful land. Trying to think anything out, though, led to circling thoughts of no use whatever. Instead he turned to the leather-bound volume that he had borrowed from Castle Drog, opening the book at random.

This is what he read:

> During oure sojourn on what at my entreatie my Captain had courteouslie named Seynte Doris Iland, my mermaid and I learned to converse after a fashion in a form of English but with many words from the Kernewek. I confesse that though at times we lacked in the skill of tongues yet we made up for it in kisses. Even so she did teach me something of the story of her people, the which I shall now relate as best I may.
>
> In aunciect times there was a land called Lyonesse, or Lesethow in the Cornish tongue, joined onto what is now Cornwall. It was a land of lakes and forests in which fishy water nymphs flourished, swimming in the fountains, rivers and estuaries and disporting themselves with the peaceful fishermen. There was also a town where the fishermen lived, with houses and a market square and a church withal.
>
> Gradually the land sank, some say because the fishermen ceased to remember Almightie God, others because of the naturall ageing of the world. Whatever had been the cause, and God alone knoweth it, some of the nymphs left Lyonesse forever, to haunt the shores of Saxon lands. Others pined so much for Lyonesse and its good fishermen that they could not be comforted, but remained among the ruins of the sunken town. Sitting on the roofs of drowned houses they spent their

dayes singing aires of such exquisite melancholie that any mortall man hearing it would forget all lesser cares and be drawn to that sound as a lodestone is to the Polar Star.

At length there came a time when the King of Kernow did lose ful many of his finest chieftains to the lure of the Selkies, as mermaids were known in those dayes. A warrior might walk along the shore, perhaps to hear the voice of the Poetick Muse in the sound of waves losing themselves in the sand, or perhaps to find in those sounds his own inner stillnesse. Then the singing of a Selkie longing for a man would draw him to some rock or low promontorie, where he would see that which in this our sublunary world is one of the Mirrors of Paradise, the face and body of a woman.

In such a manner is a Selkie formed, the upper part a comely maiden and the lower part fishe. Thus doth Almightie God arrange this deceitful materiall existence, that we might not be over-enamoured of it and forget that there is a better world as yet unseen. For Paradise is not come by cheaply, but through many travails.

At this point in my Mermaids discourse an urgent question did invade my thoughts, and therefore did I interrupt her to ask whether there be any cure, if a man and mermaid should truly love one another and wish to be together alwayes, other than death?

Lionel stopped reading for a moment, looked up, and almost stopped breathing. He stared at the dimly lit ceiling, his mind momentarily clear of words but filled only with an intense yearning. He sensed that his own story was one in which good would triumph in the end. Yet he knew, too, that endings could be bittersweet. If there was an answer, it was the one thing he most wanted to know. What if there were no answer?

There was nothing to be done but read on, and hope. Sir Henry Herring's book continued:

> At this did my Mermaid hesitate, and put a finger to her lips. Her gaze was loving but intensely serious so that it was hard for me to look upon her eyes. Yet I did, for I would rather be burned to ashes by that intensity than live for a second in the imaginary world that my own eyes would fain wander in.
>
> I felt that in that steady gaze there was a smile, although my mechanickal minde did doubt it. Therefore I left off thinking and placed in my hart a hope, that somehow all would be well. Then we did kisse again, I knowing ful well that a kisse now is worth ten thousand kisses promised but never given.
>
> At length she continued her tale. Many a fine warrior, on finding a Selkie, fell instantly in love, as well he may, for the hart is the lover of Paradise. When it sees beauty it is reminded of the true beauty and aspires to Heaven, as the antick philosopher Plato saith.[*]

---

[*] Plato, Phaedrus 249e

The King was thus much put out, to replace his warriors and chieftains with men of the like metall, for it is alwayes the finest folk and with the cleanest harts, unsullied o'er with scorne and cowardice, who most readily perceive the Selkies and are taken by them. Therefore he assembled in his Great Hall those of his chieftains that remained, and did address them thus:

'Noble chieftains, we have lost full many of our good kinsmen to the Selkies, and our realm will soon lack for the force of arms to keep out the accursèd Saxons. Therefore must we declare war against the Selkies. A bounty of an hundred silver pounds to anyone bringing in a Selkie dead or alive, and if any man can cleanse the coast of all of them, that man shall marry my daughter.'

Now tho' it be contrarie to the tradition of a proper story, the Kings daughter Peryl was not so comely as the brave chieftains might have wished, she having a sauvage temper and a fixèd frowne and moreover a thin bottom, but the lure of inheriting the Kingdom did suffice to have them overlook her something want of charm. 'Huzzah!' cried they as one man, 'Long live the King!'

Then stepped forth one chieftain more wily than the rest, one Sir Squidde Tentakels, who said, 'Noble King, may it not betide that our warriors on approaching a Selkie fall for her charms before he can do aught against her? I beseech your Majestie to inquire of thy Sorcerer some stratagem whereby a Selkie may be prevented to overcome a man by the mere appearance of her face and form.'

Duly the Sorcerer was brought forth and devisèd dark eyeglasses with stained glass opticks, so that all the warriors did look aloof and haughty, albeit they could not see very well.

At first there was a great stumbling about which little affected the Selkies, but in the course of time they became careless and some of our sisters were captured and most cruelly treated. At the same time the fishermen were forbidden to have any intercourse with the Selkies on pain of having their tackle set on fire. Little by little the Selkies became lonely for want of men, and a great lassitude came upon them. Then they did pray to Seynte Doris for to ask what they should do, for they doubted that they could offer any usefull service to the world in their state of despondencie.

As if in answer to their prayers appeared one day a large boat of wondrous form, like an antick galley. This boat sailed without puff of naturall wind, but on the deck was mounted an huge metall sphaere with curved spouts sticking out on its sides and suspended on a great horizontall axle. Underneath the sphaere was a fire tended by members of the crewe, and out of the spouts spewed forth mightie blasts of steam causing the sphaere to rotate with much force. Attached to the axle was also a giant windmill which did turn majestickally causing the boat to sail forward at marvellous speed.

The boat swept into the harbour at Pengoggly and came to rest in a thick cloud of steam. At once many warriors in dark eyeglasses led by Sir Squidde Tentakels rushed to the harbour, tripping over each other, and at the same time the Selkies came up on the seaward side to see what this should portend and whether there be any comely men aboard.

Indeed the crew were comely to the Selkies eyes, being dusky sailors from Africks shores. They told the Selkies that their boat had been made to plans by that philospher of aunciente time, Heron of Alexandria, and by great good fortune they had found the plans in pottery jars in the desert. 'Come with us!' cried all the sailors, 'The Lady Doris hath come to us in a vision, Allah be praised! Great and glorious is He! and sent us here to take you to a new iland far away! We must fain obey or be in peril of our souls, and also we hear that there be easy living in that place. Besides, we see that you are wondrous buxom. So tarry not! Allah u Akbar!'

At this the Selkies did sing for joy, and with an exstasie of strong hands upon wet bodies all the Selkies were hauled onto the deck, their tails sparkling in the sun. Others of the crew, by holding fast to the windmill, held the great axle from turning so as to point one of the sphaers spouts to the landward side. Thus Sir Tentakels men were repulsed by a mighty ejaculation of steam.

Then did that magickal vessel turn and heave into the open sea, the Selkies singing all the while in such an wise as near to break the hart of any man who should hear them.

Needless to say ful many of the dusky sailors fell under the spel of the Selkies on the journey and so when they arrived after a long voyage to Seynte Doris Iland they stayed there and Heron of Alexandrias steam shippe sank to the bottom of the sea and they made necklaces and combs and mirrors from salvaged engine parts.

What became of Sir Squidde Tentakels is lost to the annals of Selkie lore, but we may with good reason believe that Sir Tentakels had to marry Princess Peryl, notwithstanding her fowle temper and thin bottom.

Lionel's emotions had settled. Perhaps the answer to Henry Herring's question was somewhere else in the book, perhaps not. Whether a man and mermaid could be together always, she on the land or he in the sea, he knew not. But at this moment it made no difference. No matter what, he had to get her back.

Sometimes we know the step after the next, sometimes not. But without the next step, nothing.

From Myfanwy

Hello again Salty Sirenophiles,
Now then, I have to tell you that this next chapter is a bit short.
Dai Gonzales-Jones is a bit short, too, but he is quite *muscular*. Now maybe that is not the totality of everything a woman could want, but for a hot-blooded Welsh woman like me who is somewhat languishing, if you see what I mean, it's better than a long Sunday sermon after a Saturday night with more alcohol than

male attention followed by a breakfast of pilchards. There are times, you know, when a passionate embrace goes some distance in compensating for the absence of intelligent conversation and a meeting of *souls*.

That was quite a long sentence, too. Maybe I should be a writer, like Morton Mousehole. I haven't heard much from Morton lately. I hope he's at least building up this story to the thrilling climax it so clearly deserves. I could do with a thrilling climax.

Kisses,
Myf
xoxoxo
Casa Aberystwyth, Trelew, Argentina

A note from Professor Neville Twistytrouser

Dear Fellow Fishy Folk,
I am sitting here on the banks of the Cherwell in Parson's Pleasure, totally naked apart from my straw hat and my pipe as is appropriate in such environs, watching the occasional punt go by laden with undergraduates.

The ladies are sipping champagne with that combination of delicacy and forthrightness required of the denizens of the women's colleges of yore,[*] and the gentlemen (these days like as not from some urban comprehensive) are demonstrating the muscular bravado of those who know how to punt, throwing the wet-smeared pole up to be grasped by the other hand for the next powerful thrust.

It does surprise me that the men do not know they have to take the boat over the rollers and direct the ladies around the path

---

[*] That is, little sips followed by loud ejaculations such as 'Awfully good fizz, Gary! Did you really get it in Lidl?'

so that their modesty will not be affronted by the full splendour of the naked male form. Tch, the young of today are losing all sense of decorum.

Ah, now some fellow in a bowler hat[*] has just informed me that male nudity was abolished here in 1991. Sic transit gloria mundi! I must cover up my glory at once.

Ahem.

So much for creating atmosphere. Also some of my clothes appear to have been stolen by ducks in the meantime.

Now it seems our good friend Alphonse the philosophical fantasist has gone *en grève*[†] as the French are wont to do when displeased with the curliness of their croissants, leaving me to furnish a dignified academic response to this increasingly absurd tale alone.

We may, I think, anticipate Professor Pince-Nez a little here. He will probably say that mermaids stand for the impossibility of achieving one's ultimate desire. That is to say, they represent that which is most alluring (at least for a man), yet because of the fishy tail it is a relationship which it is impossible for a man to consummate. Even if we grant that mermaids may have some so far undocumented genitalia (the form of which would surely challenge a Baroque artist at the height of his or her powers), prolonged entanglement with a mermaid would undoubtedly lead to drowning. So, he will go on to say that mermaids represent the tragedy of the *condition humaine*, or the absurdity of existence or some-such.

For myself, I think that since mermaids don't exist, or to be precise, no convincing evidence of their physical existence has ever been written up in a respectable peer-reviewed journal, the question of the tragedy of the human condition in relation to mermaids does not arise in the first place.

---

[*] No doubt an escaped college servant.
[†] On strike

Well, slightly wanting in sartorial elegance, I shall nevertheless wrap myself in my academic gown and repair to the Lamb and Flag for a jar of Oxford's finest ale, and since I am a don, a considerable leeway will be granted to me, since eccentricity is part, after all, of the job description.

Your friend in Dawkins,
Neville Twistytrouser
University Parks, Oxford

28. The abduction of Lola, and a note on solipsism

RAMÓN PIMIENTO EL PICANTE was a man who knew what belonged to him, although not everyone agreed with his assessment. However, other people's opinions did not concern him. He knew, for example, that he owned Lola 'Hotstuff' Tabasco.

Therefore when she, without meaning to, bumped into him in her flight from Dr Fluffycardigan's holistic clinic, he immediately claimed her as his own, grabbing her arm in a painful grip.

"¡Mi amor!" Ramón delivered this deadpan, like a threat, and his grin was unchanged, like a crocodile's.

"¡Váyase al diablo!" Lola spat, twisting free and backing away from him.

Ramón walked slowly towards her. He looked confident, unhurried. She turned to the man in the oversized raincoat, looking for some support, but he just stood there. Sidney Sinister's gaze, in fact, was on the door of the clinic. He was looking past her, as though the little drama being enacted in front of him concerned him not at all.

Then Lola ran. She was between Ramón and the café, so at first she was running towards *The Frothy Coffee With a Bit of Coffee and Quite a Lot of Milk Café* with its new clientele of motionless Mexicans. In the distance she glimpsed *The Saucy Jellyfish* at anchor in the harbour and made for it at once, skirting the café as best she might. There, standing on the quay was a figure, almost certainly the figure of Captain Kipper himself.

She ran on, and the figure looked up. Hope swelled in her chest. There was no sound of Ramón running after her, and when she glanced back she could see him just standing there, grinning. He was a man certain that what was his would come to him without his having to demean himself by chasing it. That didn't stop Lola running.

The Abduction of Lola, and a note on solipsism

Perhaps it was a wink, or a twitch of his mouth, or perhaps even just a slight alteration in the glint on Ramón's gold tooth, but there must have been a signal. Whatever it was, the moment Lola looked back she ran straight into a huge sombrero-wearing Mexican and stopped dead.

"I theen' I found what you wanted." The big Mexican's grin matched Ramón's as he pulled Lola's wrists roughly behind her. A white Porsche Cayenne with dark tinted windows pulled up and the Mexican bundled her into the back.

With a deepening of the engine note the big car took off along the harbour and towards the town with unnecessary speed.

A note from Professeur Alphonse Pince-Nez

Bonjour Perverse Pogonophores!
Hein! Le Grand Pantaloon have try to guess what is my opinion of this histoire! Also he distract himself with wild surmise concerning the Baroque genitalia! This is not how we analyse les contes sur le Continent. Non, we have a more intimate relation with them than that, I can assure you.

He suggest that les sirènes are metaphor for the pointlessness of human existence. Quelle (how you say) piffle! Non, it is tout-à-fait a more deeper thing. Les sirènes signify, par example, the psychoanalytical confusion between la mer et la mère. Thus, the sea itself represent the Unconscious, as it were the matrix of everything that happen, unless something happen that is not Unconscious, if such a thing were to be possible.

Also, from a Marxist perspective we cannot help noticing that the oppressed peasants représent the oppressed peasants. We shall see, sans doubt, les mauvais, how you say, 'bad guys' collapsed by their own internal contradictions, although whether this will occur through a bloody revolution or merely the collapse of their fiat currency we shall have to see.

For the record, I was not *en grève*. It was merely that I thought the revolution had come and we must to the barricades—alors, it was a false alarm, so here I am back at my table in La Durée munching a madeleine.

A bientôt,
Alphonse Pince-Nez

From Myfanwy

Hello Faithful Fishy Folk,

Pogonophores! I ask you! Pogonophores, in case you were wondering, are little worms that live in tubes and have no mouths and live by absorbing sulphur at the bottom of the sea. Melvin told me that they are all solipsists, which apparently means that each one sees no reason to believe that anyone exists besides itself.

Now that wouldn't suit me at all. Apart from sulphur being a lot worse than Welsh food, I couldn't do with just my own company shut up in a tube. No, I'd have to go out partying once in a while.

I shan't bother you with a description of the next chapter because you can read it for yourself and besides I am going out with Dai Gonzalez-Jones in a minute. Do you think I should kiss on a first date or keep him hanging on a bit? On the other hand, we're not very conversational since my Welsh is rubbish, so there's not a lot else to do, and I must say I could do with a bit of a fumble. Then again, perhaps I shouldn't let myself go too cheaply.

Why doesn't Melvin write to me any more? He must be missing me just a little bit. He doesn't even know how to make tea properly.

It's hard being a woman sometimes.

I think I'll go shoe shopping tomorrow.

Myf xoxo

29. Hallucinogenic tea

Captain Kipper ran.

The woman in the brown cloak revealing a hint of cobalt blue skirt had to be Lola. He had seen her running toward him and then she had been stopped and bundled into a white Porsche van. Lola was in trouble, that was clear.

As he passed the café the heads of the otherwise motionless Mexicans turned to follow him with their eyes. By the time the Captain had reached the front of the clinic Ramón had disappeared, hidden perhaps among the Mexicans, or just away on some other business, and the Porsche, too, was gone.

Captain Kipper ran into the café, running from table to table. The heads turned silently as he dashed from one part of the café to another, but there was no sign of the man in white. Kipper put both hands on one of the tables and leaned in towards three of the coffee drinkers.

"Where be the man in white? The man I saw outside this café just now?"

They looked at him blankly.

"No sabemos, Señor," one of the Mexicans at one of the other tables replied in a growl. The others nodded slightly, their sombreros tipped forward so that their eyes were concealed and all Captain Kipper could see was a café full of moustaches.

"Did 'ee see what happened?" the Captain asked the woman behind the bar, whose name incidentally was Morwenna.

"Don't 'ee involve me in all this," she replied, avoiding eye contact and continuing to stack clean coffee cups on top of the machine. "I be already in enough trouble explaining to these gen'lemen why I can't serve tequila."

Kipper ran out and again scanned the rows of cottages facing the bay for any sign of the Porsche. There was nothing to see.

Turning round, the bright pink concrete slab that was the new clinic filled his vision and he went in.

The large woman of indeterminate age ignored him. "Excuse me miss," he ventured. She nodded her head in the direction of the Tibetan bells while maintaining a stony silence.

Captain Kipper duly tinged the bells together and the eerie discord filled the air for a few moments. As it died away the lady gave her disturbing smile.

"Would you like an appointment to see Dr Fluffycardigan?" she asked.

"No thank 'ee, Miss. Did 'ee see a man in a white suit come in here just now?"

"A man in a white suit?"

"Aye. And a white panama hat."

"A man in a white suit, you say?" The doctor had started to speak even before entering the room. He looked agitated, then his eyes narrowed when he saw that it was Captain Kipper. There was a pause in which nobody moved and there was silence, the kind in which whether there will be violence is entirely unclear. Then, as if the script had suddenly changed without explanation, the doctor spoke. "Lucretia, a cup of tea for our guest?"

The doctor's voice became smooth as molten chocolate and he indicated one of the lilac sofas. "Please, sit down for a moment."

"I can't be hanging about, thanking you sir. I be looking for someone who's gone missing."

"The organic chamomile with added ginseng?" the large woman asked.

"No of course not!" snapped the doctor, then, smiling, "the SPECIAL tea. For our SPECIAL friend Captain Kipper. Perhaps we can help you," he continued, turning back to the Captain, the smile becoming more oleaginous by the moment.

"Well, can you?" Captain Kipper remained standing.

"Please, sit down," insisted the doctor. Reluctantly, the Captain sat, looking out of place in the lilac softness. Lucretia

Hallucinogenic tea

appeared with the tea which was served in thin-walled porcelain cups decorated with hand-painted giant squids devouring ships.

"Well, perhaps you could tell me more about this man in the white suit," the doctor continued. "It seems we're both interested in his whereabouts."

Lucretia poured the tea and handed Captain Kipper the cup. Another cup, already poured, she handed to the doctor. The Captain's tea was orange and smelled piquant. He sniffed it and took a sip. It wasn't particularly pleasant.

"I just saw him from a distance. I think he be the same as came into the harbour this afternoon in that big shiny motor boat."

At this some colour drained from the doctor's face, and Lucretia's cup rattled against its saucer. The Captain took another sip, more out of politeness and habit than for any desire for more tea. He supposed that since herbal infusions were supposed to be good for you there was no reason for them to taste nice. His head swam slightly, which he attributed to not having got his land legs back again, although it was some time since he had last been out at sea. He thought perhaps that at least the tea might help with the feeling of vertigo. Perhaps it was simply that he was unused to sitting in lilac comfy chairs. He took another sip.

"Arr, and suddenly the whole café be full o' Mexicans too." At this the doctor's own cup rattled violently. Captain Kipper found his attention drawn to the storm developing in the doctor's tea as if he were himself sailing in that treacherous yellow ocean. Time slowed and a protuberance of tea rose up and began to break over the side of the doctor's cup, like the giant wave in Hokusai's famous woodcut—the foam-fringed mass of water about to engulf a small fishing boat. The sense of vertigo got worse. Of course the tea was yellow, not blue like in Hokusai's picture. Yellow, not orange like the tea in his own cup, he thought vaguely.

"So you are looking for him?" the doctor resumed his composure with a struggle. His face seemed strangely distorted, even rather hideous.

"Not exactly. I be looking for Lola."

It might have been the Captain's imagination but Lucretia's already disturbing face seemed to tense.

"She was here," the doctor said, "just a few minutes ago. But we've not seen your man in the white suit. Where Lola has gone I don't know, but if I hear anything I'll be sure to let you know. As neighbours we should help one another, don't you think?" He paused, as if weighing up something in his mind. "Now tell me," he went on, his voice at maximum oiliness, "I need to speak with that naval gentleman who has been seen about this town recently about an important matter to his advantage. Do you have any idea where I might find him?"

The doctor's face seemed unnaturally close to his, although nobody had moved, and the doctor's eyes were pools of darkness. Everything the Captain looked at was larger than it should be. Captain Kipper thought of Alf and that Alf would be keeping a low profile somewhere in or near the *Saucy Jellyfish*. He certainly did not trust the doctor but he could not be sure whether what he was thinking he was also saying. His thoughts, like most thoughts most of the time, came and went as they pleased, but his speech —that was the thing he had to try to control. The comfy chair wasn't helping.

With an effort Captain Kipper stood up. "Well I'll be on my way then," he said rather incongruously. Then, collecting himself, "Likewise, if I hear anything that it's right you should hear, you shall hear it."

Captain Kipper felt his legs sway. He felt he might faint. He steadied himself against the arm of the lilac chair.

"Please, you don't look well. You're welcome to sit here until you feel better." The doctor maintained his best oleaginous smile.

The captain fought the feeling of faintness but realised he was going to lose, and had little choice but to sit in the chair again.

"More tea?" Lucretia asked, holding the teapot over his cup. The teapot, too, displayed the remarkable design of a Kraken, a giant squid about to drag a tiny fishing boat down into the sea in its wavy tentacles. On the convexity of the teapot's side the Kraken loomed towards Captain Kipper, its eyes round and empty. When you look into the eyes of a horse or a dog you may see something resembling a soul, an animating presence. In the eyes of a goat, though, you see nothing comprehensible. The Kraken's eyes were like that. The Captain looked away and found himself staring into the doctor's face. The doctor's eyes were like that too.

Captain Kipper's hand moved in a gesture intended to stop the pouring of more tea, but the hand seemed to wave ineffectually as more orange tea poured into his cup. Even the smell of it was nauseating. He remained still, but the room moved.

"So, you were saying?" the doctor resumed, "You were telling me, I think, that Alf, the Higgs Bosun, is hanging out at Lionel Fortescue's place?"

"No, I never said that!" Captain Kipper replied. Then he realised he might have been tricked. "Or maybe I did. I don't rightly recall that part o' the conversation. What's your interest in Alf, anyway?"

"As I say, I have some information to his advantage."

"Well then, you can tell it to me and I'll pass it on when I see him—whenever that may be."

"Ah, no. That's not possible I'm afraid. A highly confidential matter. Let's just say it concerns the whereabouts of something or someone he is looking for."

Captain Kipper tried to stand again, and managed to bring himself to his feet. The effort was very uncomfortable, but it cleared his head a little, and that felt good. "As for me, I be looking for one Lola Tabasco as has been kidnapped by that man in the white suit I told 'ee of. When I find her, shall I tell you where to find him or shall I tell him where to find you?"

As the Captain guessed, this last hit the mark. The remains of the doctor's smile were sustained only by a supreme effort and he turned a whiter shade of pale. "Please don't trouble yourself on my account," he said, looking momentarily as ill as the Captain felt.

"Arr, maybe not." Captain Kipper walked towards the door as fast as he felt able without falling over. "And this place be an architectural monstrosity," he muttered.

"All plans approved by the Council," the doctor rejoined testily.

"Arr, the Council be to blame, no doubt."

"I'd be careful if I were you," the doctor shouted after him as he reached the door. "Blaming the Council is the first sign of The Twinge. You're ill, you know. You mark my words! The Twinge!"

When Captain Kipper finally made it through the front door he found the harbour-side all but deserted. The café was empty and closed, the Mexicans gone. The sun was approaching the horizon in a hazy grey oval.

From Myfanwy

Well now my little fishcakes, my emotions are all a bit confused just at the moment.

First of all, Dai Gonzalez-Jones took me out to a really fantastic party where I drank a lot of really excellent Argentine wine but still managed to dance and he whirled me round the dance floor like a top and everyone started clapping so we must have made a fine couple and later in the slow dances he held me tight to his muscular body and I gave his buttock a little squeeze by accident as it were. Then he took me home and I let him kiss me but I said I was tired and had to go to bed right away so I didn't invite him in, although I was sorely tempted I can tell you. He growled but he did go away after a bit of a fumble in the porch.

At the same time Melvin has started sending me his manuscripts before they get into the hands of those saucy philosophers. (I mean, baroque genitalia? Is that what goes through your head when you have a university education? Something should be done about it.) This obviously means he is thinking about me and it won't be long before he realises he can't do without me. So I can't decide whether to keep myself pure, or not and lie about it. Tricky.

Anyway, I'd better start doing my job, and that is to type up what he has sent me and send it on to you, with the warning that this next chapter involves the effects of mind-bending ingredients. Most people's minds are bent already without making it worse, so don't try it.

If those naughty philosophers want something to chew on, here is Myfanwy's thought for the day:

Reality is an illusion caused by lack of orgasms. Discuss.

love,

Myf

xoxoxo

From Neville Twistytrouser

Dear 'Fishcakes' (ha ha) as the young lady will have it,
Well, there's a challenge.

I must say we do get a bit carried away by things that seem somewhat trivial when viewed in better states of mind, such as, say, after a pint or two of *Theakston's Old Peculiar*. As to orgasms, hmm, thinking back to when I was an undergraduate, er, anyway the psychoanalyst Wilhelm Reich thought that we didn't get enough and if we did we would give off orgone energy, which apparently is a blue light. I'm not sure that's right, but if it is right then it makes one wonder what goes on in the average speeding police car. Hmm.

Just thinking round the problem while refilling my pipe with some rough shag.

Well now, when we're having an orgasm, if memory serves, we're hardly there at all, but at the same time there more intensely. Something like that.

I think I'll stagger over to the bar and get another pint. Helps clear the mind more or less completely I find. Yes. Words get all mixed up, which is all right, because they just get in the way of understanding anyway. The only problem is trying to write down what it is one has understood afterwards. Probably that's the answer to Myfanwy's conundrum too, if only I could remember what it was we were talking about. Oh dear my gown is slipping revealing a bit too much I fear.

The landlord's ordered a cab for me? But I was only just starting on my third pint! Oh I see.

Ah well, *sic transit* etcetera!

Neville

30. Useless are the Thoughts of Mortal Men

NOT KNOWING WHERE TO GO, Captain Kipper started walking, at first at random, then in a more systematic fashion, up one street and down the next, working his way up the hillside with its rows of pastel-coloured terraced cottages all facing the little harbour and occasionally interrupted by oddly positioned larger houses.

What did he expect to see? He had glimpsed the white Porsche—that was really his only clue, unless he bumped into a lone Mexican and could perhaps extract some information from him by violence. But the Captain was not by nature a violent man. Were there times when violence was justified? Or would violence breed more violence, in a whirlpool that would suck the sweet essence out of the participants? Even so, he thought, sometimes it was necessary to stand and say, enough!

The colours of the town faded as one by one the streetlights came on. A band of pale glistening grey receded gently across the sea towards the patch of brightness in the clouds that marked where the sun had set, the rest of the ocean becoming dark like a late Rothko. In front of that great stillness rose a cage of steel girders, arisen suddenly in the last day or so, the skeleton of the planned hotel punctuated by a grid of lights.

Captain Kipper found his attention drawn to that oppressive spectacle—to its own unrepentant beauty—the kind of beauty that belongs perhaps in an oil refinery at night, but not in a sleepy Cornish village by the sea. That metal web threatened him and he felt as if he could become trapped in it. He thought of Lionel's mermaid, and of her impending incarceration in the amusement arcade that was to be part of the development. He thought of Lionel's brave stand at the planning office, and the uselessness of resistance. Most of all he thought of Lola.

Suddenly there was a large white car in someone's drive—but it was one of those oversized Minis. Then he saw the shadow of a

Mexican in a sombrero on a wall—but it was just the effect of a streetlight shining on a bush. The mist was clearing and stars began to appear in the sky above the top of the town and they moved in swirls as if Van Gogh had painted them.

As he walked, despair gripped him. By not acting when he had had the chance he had lost Lola. To him in that moment Lola was everything, better than a huge catch of fish in the night, their scales shining in the moonlight. Better than his boat, the *Saucy Jellyfish*, fresh from the dry dock, free of barnacles, with its seaworthiness certificate and a fresh coat of blue paint. Better than fish, chips and mushy peas in a harbour-side café served with a pint of *Hideous Pigsty* Cornish Best Bitter. Better, in fact, than anything imaginable is the love of a good woman.

Sometimes it seems that our destiny slips through our fingers through lack of courage. Did we imagine that dreaming could achieve anything?

Captain Kipper felt he had failed. The moment had passed when taking a tiny risk would have changed everything. If only the gods or the saints or someone had warned him in advance, he might have been prepared. But it was only he who hadn't been quite there when the moment presented itself, by the church at Ankarrek that night. The confusion had been all in his own doubts, and the truth, in Lola's face.

Then, at the top of the town where the street lamps stopped, the hazy shadow of one bush upon another formed itself into the likeness of a man's face. A man Captain Kipper had recently met. Looked at directly, it was hardly there, just two pools of darkness suggesting eyes, but a glance to either side showed a face looking remarkably like that of Dr Fluffycardigan. It seemed to speak, although there was no sound except the semblance of a meaning in the Captain's head.

"Nothing can stop me," it said.

"Who are you?" Captain Kipper asked out loud.

Useless are the Thoughts of Mortal Men

"You know who I am. When I dream I roam about. I have tentacles everywhere. I control everything. Nothing can stop me."

The dream doctor seemed very pleased with itself. By some trick of vision it grew larger, until it became one with the darkness. "Nothing can stop me," it said a third time. Then it disappeared.

"I read in a book once that whatever be said three times be true," the Captain thought, and shivered.

His despair and his remorse were worse by far than the nausea induced by the doctor's tea, a nausea that made the whole world seem worth very little. Then it seemed to Captain Kipper that the Kasteldrog chorus appeared, although why and from where he did not know. From the top of the tower of Pengoggly's church a little group of men and women spoke clearly into the still night air:

"Do you not know, in your seaweedy mind,
How Aerfen has charted out your fate,
Directed currents, waves and winds and storms
To bring your story to its proper end?
Useless are the thoughts of mortal men
And not to be believed. Useless too
Your wish to change one moment of what's gone.
Remorse is bitter medicine, let it go
Once it has cured you, and disbelieve despair:
It is your work to hold the light within."

The Captain walked on through the night, finding nothing in Pengoggly, but he kept going, all the way to Ankarrek, to where he had been so close to saying to Lola, yes.

Yes, Lola. No to doubts. Lola. Yes.

Of course there was no-one there. The spot where they had met, and said, and failed to say, was empty, just an almost black clearing in the trees lit only by the stars. He stayed there a long while, thinking nothing. Then he edged his way towards the door of the church, feeling along the walls until he found the latch in the wooden door. It opened, as churches in remote places sometimes do. The creaking of the door alarmed him in the silence. Blackness enveloped him as he entered, walking slowly until he bumped into a pew, then felt his way to the front. He sat, and found to his faint surprise that looking up he could see the carving of Saint Doris fighting the giant squid. The squid was barely a shadow, a darker stain in his visual field, but Saint Doris herself with her retinue of sea slugs seemed to glow. Where the light came from he could not tell.

Although an unbeliever, he started to pray. He didn't exactly know how this was done. Was it wrong to pray if you didn't believe? Is it wrong to hope for the last bus, if you don't know whether it will come? As he knew no prayers, he simply looked up at Saint Doris and tried to let his thoughts settle. He could not pray for himself, that felt wrong. You cannot ask a saint to do your work for you, nor assume that you are of any importance. The right question is, what should I do? And then, how should I do it? Saint Doris, if you can hear me, what is the right thing for me to do?

Whether it is a saint answering you or something in yourself, you need to know what the problem is in as much detail as possible. You need to have done your utmost to solve it, to have struggled with it. Then, only when sufficient work has been done, when the rational mind has failed in all its efforts, you let the mind relax, give up trying too hard, and perhaps the whole answer will rise before you. It is best if you give up your self-will to fate and to that still small voice within. What is the right thing for me to do?

The glow around Saint Doris seemed to grow brighter, but no answer came. Even so, a great calm came upon the Captain, as though a heavy responsibility had been lifted from him. In that moment, strangely, he felt joy warming some secret place within him. Then it seemed to him that in the periphery of his vision appeared a fish.

He turned to look at it, and there was nothing there. Yet when he relaxed his vision and looked straight ahead, somewhere at the extreme right of his field of view it was there again. A flat speckled fish with both eyes on one side of its head.

Captain Kipper stood up and bowed respectfully to the altar and then to Saint Doris, then turned to walk out of the church. The fish followed him, not quite invisibly.

From Myfanwy

Well my Squidgy Jellyfishes, I have to tell you that this next chapter is very exciting, because some important details about mermaids will be revealed. You will also find out who Lionel's mermaid is and who Nellie is. There is the most wonderful information about Yorkshire tea as well.

You know, sometimes I think that Marvin Marmalade is really inspired, and it's not just Aerfen, the Celtic goddess of fate who is guiding his pen, but the poetic muse as well. I love an artist, don't you? It fairly makes my heart go pit-a-pat.

Ah me!

Now if I could make one man out of the physical passion of Dai Gonzalez-Jones and the artistic genius of Marvin, that would be a man!

As for Dai, he exudes machismo. He exudes it so much that dark-eyed Rhiannon Aguerre-Evans is round him like a moth round a light-bulb. Mind you, she's got appalling dress sense, what there is of it. I mean there's not a lot of actual material between the hem of her skirt and her neckline. Legs all the way up to her fanny-pelmet. An open pastry case containing a filling, if you follow my word-play.* I don't think discerning men fall for that sort of thing, do they?

Enough of that. Marvin sent me this next chapter to pass on to you so there's hope yet. It's pure poetry.

Kisses,
Myf
xoxoxo

A note from Professor Alphonse Pince-Nez

Chères Amants des Sirènes,
C'est drôle, n'est-que pas, que Professeur Twistytrouser find himself in the predicament after the ducks steal his clothing and he is wrapped mostly in his academic gown! Alors, the academic gown have a purpose after all, that is to cover up the learned nakedness, je crois!

Well, I must be generous to my worthy opponent, pedestrianly quotidian though his opinions are généralement!

La philosophie française plumb the depths of a more exciting obscurity! Voila! If no-one can understand it then it will take many years to discuss what have possibly been said. It is creatively suggestive, like swimming through the sea swarming with fishes without a particular destination. This will provide work for the writers in intellectual journals of the *nouvelle vague*† to explain it all, preferably equally floridly so that the whole process become self-sustaining.

The Thought of Alphonse Pince-Nez—I can see it now. Then there will be *Pince-Nez Made A Little Bit Simple* for the wider audience. It will still be incomprehensible but the writing will be bigger and

---

* For the benefit of non-British readers, this is an untranslatable pun in which a word denoting the described baked goods is also a colloquial term for a lady of the night.
† The new vagueness.

there will be a lot of pictures. Then I hope a TV show in which I expound my ideas in brief and resonant *paroles* against sunny backgrounds around the world. I must remember to mention Pythagoras so that I can go to both Greece and Italy, and if anyone know of a philosopher in Barbados please write me on a postcard.

Mais, on with the game! La Myfanwy propose un problème profond, c'est-à-dire, whether reality is an illusion caused by lack of orgasms. Provocative, non?

Well, we should have to decide whether *reality* is to be understood as the *for itself*, or whether the *in itself* is prior. Then again, phenomenology is precisely the relation between the *in itself* and the *for itself*. Also, for the *for itself* the *in itself* is existentially the sum total of all of its possible phenomenological manifestations, and its 'essence' so-called is no more than this projected totality. But what is the *for itself* but the sum of these phenomenological manifestations in their condition of *being manifest*? Or is it something else?

But before we get too involved with that (and in any case I need another café-au-lait and a madeleine), we should definitely discuss the entire history of sexuality, from whatever unusual salaciousness we can make up about the Iron Age Beaker people based on potsherds found in grave burials, through to the adventures of Madame Kinky in Surbiton. Bien sûr! Normal is defined by that which it exclude and in any case it give one a *frisson*.

Nevertheless the condition of *orgasm* is precisely when the *for itself* gives up itself to a more intense *being* and is therefore ontologically both void and full at the same time. This is the paradox.

My apologies that this is not quite as obscure as I would wish, but I shall work on it some more. I think the book will be a great success as long as it have a lurid cover.

A bientôt!
Alphonse

31. Follow Your Soul

OF COURSE FISH DO NOT TALK. But its two eyes, both on the same side of its head, stared at Captain Kipper from the periphery of his vision and he could still sense the fish as he walked back towards Pengoggly. As he entered the town he turned towards the harbour, and the fish disappeared. When he turned around it was there again, not directly visible, but definitely there. So he kept walking so as to keep the sense of the fish always present, and the route led him towards the police station. It was clear to him that he should not go to the police station but to Nellie's next door.

Nellie opened the door in her dressing gown. It was about four in the morning, but she did not frown and when she saw it was Captain Kipper she smiled and let him in at once.

Nellie's dressing gown was white, decorated with leaping dolphins in bright blue. She opened the door wider for Captain Kipper to step in. He noticed that her bare feet were wet, and indeed there was a trail of water behind her. Also her feet looked almost silvery, which he attributed to the effect of moonlight, although had he thought about it he would have realised that it was a moonless night.

"Sorry to have interrupted your bath at this hour," he said, not sure why anyone would bath at four in the morning.

"Think nothing of it," she said. "I'll make some tea."

"Not herb tea, please. It does something to me head."

"No. Proper Yorkshire tea from the tea plantations of Yorkshire."

The room seemed preternaturally bright. It had seemed bright when he had been here before with Lionel in their failed attempt to rescue the mermaid from the police station, but now the brightness seemed more intense. Yet it was not a painful brightness. It was like the blissful brightness you would expect at the heaven end of the tunnel if all those stories about near-death experiences turn out to be true.

Nellie poured the tea and it was indeed good strong tea, the kind, as it is said, that your spoon might stand up in. Legend has it that when they bring in the first tea harvest they brew the early leaves in a giant blue and white Wedgwood teapot decorated with classical scenes of naked men in flat caps and demurely draped women with whippets, made in the days when Queen Victoria was still Empress of Yorkshire. They brew it until it is so strong that it gains the paradoxical properties of a thixotropic liquid, such that it acts as a solid when something lands on it with sufficient force, and they pour it into a teacup the size of a small swimming pool. Then a fine Yorkshire lass in the first blush of youth, chosen for her well-rounded physique, has to run across in bare feet from one side to the other dressed only in a sufficiently large tea towel. She is then crowned Queen of Yorkshire for a day.[*] But I digress.

Captain Kipper knew that the doctor's tea had messed with his mind, but in Nellie's presence the badness all seemed to turn into something quite different. Even if you are a coffee person and don't much like tea, there is something altogether healing in one person making a cup of tea for another. It has to do with being told to sit down by someone who actually cares about you, and it has to do with the time while the kettle is coming to the boil when it is not necessary to do or even say anything. Captain Kipper felt his despair transform itself into acceptance. Not the kind of acceptance that will do nothing, but the kind that understands that worry is wasted emotion.

As the Captain sank gratefully into Nellie's armchair there was a strange noise from another room, hard to describe, perhaps like a cat miaowing under water, if such a thing were possible.

---

[*] Source: *Arbuthnot Mangelwurzel's Compendium of Curious English Customs*, Cheese Rolling Press, Tingewick, Buckinghamshire 1898, pp236-44.

"Is your cat all right?" the Captain asked.

"Perfectly," Nellie replied, "although he has a complicated condition. But he's actually all right. More or less."

There were no more words as Nellie poured, just the liquid tinkling of tea entering cups. The clear brown liquid flowed out of the spout of a more homely teapot than the doctor's. It was reassuringly round, and its white surface was decorated in blue with the charming motif of a sailor cavorting with a mermaid, the same that also graced the wallpaper. The cups were also white with happy-looking fishes, jellyfish and sea anemones on them. As the tea settled in the cup the first wisp of steam inhaled through his nose seemed to the Captain the most comforting thing he'd ever experienced.

"So," said Nellie, changing the subject, "Tell me all about it."

"About what?"

"Nobody turns up at my house at four in the morning if there's nothing to tell," she smiled.

"Arr, well, it's about Lola."

Slowly, as now there was no rush, the Captain told Nellie everything, how they had gone to Kasteldrog but failed to rescue Lionel's mermaid (he thought of her as Lionel's, although of course Lionel did not own her), and how Lionel had tried to stop the development of the harbour, with its garish alternative medical centre, the skeletal framework for the big hotel, and the planned aquarium attraction with the mermaid to be the centrepiece. He told of Lola, how he truly loved Lola, and how he had missed his chance of saving her. Then he told of watching the big shiny boat come into the harbour, about Ramón Pimiento El Picante and his crew of Mexicans, and about Lola's abduction. Finally he talked about his regret and despair, and about what had happened at St Doris's church.

If ever you try to pray, and you experience an unusual state of inner peace, and especially if you then almost but not quite see a flat fish with both eyes on one side of its head in the periphery of your vision, it is generally best not to talk about it. But the Captain sensed that Nellie was one of the few people in the world that you could safely say these things to.

"It all makes sense," Nellie said.

"Including the fish? The fish makes sense?"

"The dark night of the sole," Nellie explained.

"Oh."

The underwater miaowing started again, and Nellie excused herself and ran into the next room. In her haste she failed to push the door fully closed, and it swung open of itself. To his surprise Captain Kipper saw Nellie cradling a creature that seemed in the process of turning from a cat to a catfish and back again. The thing was clearly agitated, and Nellie was doing her best to calm it, stroking its dorsal fin as its front paws turned to fins and back, and its mouth, wide with miaowing, changed between furry and shiny wet. Nellie, too, was a little upset, and her ankles looked distinctly scaly and her feet a little finny around the toes.

"I didn't mean for you to see this," Nellie said, as the creature calmed down and turned back into a fish. She kissed it and put it back in its aquarium, and it settled contently to the bottom. Nellie's feet became more feet-like and she smiled again. "I'll have to ask you to say nothing about this," she said quietly, "but now I'll have to tell you my secret."

This was the most astonishing thing that the Captain had ever seen. Was it still the doctor's herbal tea playing with with his mind? But there was something clear and undreamy about his perceptions now. There is an indefinable difference between the hallucinations of dreams and the waking state, and the trickery of it is that one can only appreciate it when awake. He could not be sure, of course, that he was as awake as it is possible to be, but he knew that he was not dreaming, even though the fish was still there, somewhere at the edge of his sight.

"Arr, they do say a true friend is a secret's grave,"* he said. "I'm listening."

"There's no use pretending to you any more," she said, "I am, or was, a mermaid."

Nellie closed the door behind her and came back into the room and sat down. "Once upon a time a big ship was wrecked on St Doris Island, and we mermaids became friendly with the sailors as we always do. We spent the days swimming with them in the warm sea, and nights cooking fish on the beach and drinking coconut juice and palm wine. We kissed and caressed and were kissed and were caressed. We brought each other to loving ecstasies and then did it all over again."

She paused, a faraway look in her eyes, before resuming.

"After a while the sailors became listless and sad. 'Is it something we have done?' we asked. 'No, you've done nothing wrong,' they said, 'but we need to be doing something, making something, achieving something, otherwise we cannot take pride in being men. We need to return to the Navy.' Then they started occupying their time making a raft and became happy again. Of course eventually the day came when the raft was finished and they realised they would have to use it. They put on their brave faces. After one last night of passion they bid us farewell, kissing us violently before pushing the raft into the sea."

Nellie sat cradling her teacup, a single tear glinting on her cheek.

"Of course we missed them terribly. We used to sing each night, each one of us making up new songs about love and about the sailors we had lost. A long time went by, but the memory did not fade, and our songs and poems only increased our longing. Some of us began to think we might follow—build our own raft and each find her own sailor. We thought they might have gone back to the land of men which tradition has it is next to

---

* Possible source: Al Ghazali, On Brotherhood, book XV of the Ihya

Lesethow, that is, Lyonesse, the legendary sunken kingdom of our ancestors."

"A risky thing to do, following a story like that with no guarantee of success," the Captain remarked.

"Yes. Many said that it was nothing more than a myth, and in any case very far even if we had a map, and that we were foolish to try as there would be nothing there. 'Where's your evidence?' they said. But a few of us were not put off, because we said, our passion is so strong there has to be an answer, and if there isn't then it's a good enough myth to live and die by. We made a boat made from many palm trees, with a sail made from the fibres of banana trees and with ropes made of our plaited hair. It was hard work, but love and longing helped us do it."

"The journey must have been hard."

"It was. The waves lashed us and the currents were against us at first and we made very poor headway. As we went further out to sea it was cold at times and the fish became harder to catch, too. All began to pine for the safety and familiarity of St Doris Island, where there are plentiful fish and coconuts and warm breezes. The memory of our sailors faded and the difficulties of the journey became more real. Many began to doubt that Lesethow was a real place after all, or that it was somewhere else and we were going the wrong way. One by one our friends deserted us, saying we were mad, and they swam back to the island."

"'Ee say 'us,'" remarked the Captain. "How many of you made it all the way?"

"Just two."

"Arr," said the Captain thoughtfully. "Then the other one must be Lionel's mermaid, if I may call her that?"

"Yes, just us two."

"Why just two? What was different about the two of you that you made it all the way?"

"For me, it was not just love for a day or a season. My sailor was different. Someone you might meet just once in a lifetime. I knew this from the moment I first saw him."

She sat, still cradling her cup of tea, not drinking.

"I was playing in the sea when I saw a group of sailors approach the shore in little boats from a large submarine. At first I was overjoyed to see real sailors, and I leaped and cavorted in the water to catch their attention. The men surrounded me in the shallows, and I smiled at them playfully. But what I didn't see was that they had a net hidden under the water, and at a signal from the man they called the boss, a small mean-looking man, they had me caught. I cried out, but all my sisters were over the other side of the ridge."

She paused, then went on, "The men started dragging me towards one of their boats. But then—then something amazing happened. A man came over the ridge and kept walking. He told them they had to let me go. One of the pirates pointed a gun at him, but he did not stop. A man, so full of kindness, so full of courage."

There was a long pause. The Captain sipped his tea quietly, watching her face, listening. Now the tears started to run silently down both Nellie's cheeks and she did not attempt to brush them away. "It's hard to explain. He was so full of love they were terrified. The boss was furious, you could see it in his whole body, but the sailors let me go."

"And the man?"

"He must simply have walked back. I met him on the other side. I was totally in love. His name was Alf, from HMS Higgs that was wrecked on the island."

Captain Kipper raised an eyebrow.

"So," he said, "'ee came here because of love for Alf, the Higgs Bosun. Do 'ee not know that he be here? We picked him up in Lionel's Morris Minor right after we left you, that night when

Lionel tried to rescue the mermaid from the police station next door!"

"Yes. I've watched him from the harbour. He didn't see me."

"He be looking for something *or someone* of great value to him, that he told me. Might that someone be you?"

"I don't know."

"And your legs? What about your legs?"

"If a mermaid loves a man then her fishy tail can turn to legs by day, but her legs turn back into a tail by night. Only if she is certain that she is loved by a man then she can have legs by night. Then, if she loves and her love is returned, she can have legs all the time and live safely on the land. In any other state she will always pine for the sea and may turn back into a mermaid at any time."

"Well I can find Alf for you and bring him here! Nothing simpler!"

"No, it's not yet time. He must search for me a little longer. You see, much as my heart yearns for him, a man must prove his love. Yes, he saved me once, and we frolicked together and kissed and loved until he left. But he did leave. You must not say anything about what you have learned tonight."

"Well, I have given me word, 'ee can count on it. But I have more questions. The pirates' boss—did 'ee catch his name?"

Nellie frowned. "There was a man by the name of Sharck who gave the orders. But the small man who told Sharck what to do, Sharck called him Dr Squidtentacles."

"Arr," The Captain frowned. "I've heard that name afore. He be the one as disappeared after Lucretia Fumble died o' the Twinge! And Lucretia, come to think of it, be not such a common name!"

There was a puzzle here, and things were beginning to look connected. But there was something else he wanted to know.

"The other mermaid—what gave her the courage to come with you all the way?"

Nellie suddenly looked overwhelmingly sad.

A MERMAID IN THE BATH

"The other mermaid is my daughter."

She paused again, and took a deep breath.

"Not having loved a man or been loved by one, she had a fishy tail by both day and night. She took to the sea, living in Lesethow in the drowned village.

"I used to go to her at dusk and swim and we used to talk. After a short while she grew to that age when a mermaid yearns for a man. 'You need a man,' I'd say. 'Don't talk about it,' she'd say. Then one day she wasn't there. Sometimes a young mermaid gets legs for a short time and goes along the shore looking. But she never came back."

"Then the mermaid that was in Lionel's bath was her?"

"That's what I believe," Nellie said quietly.

From Myfanwy

Hello Sea Urchins,

Well that was a bit sad, wasn't it?

Here is another chapter. Now of course I'm wondering what Sidney Sinister has to do with all this. I expect the pace will hot up fairly soon.

Talking of hotting up, I was getting all excited because Dai was going to take me to the pictures tonight, and they're showing one of those chick flicks. You know, girl gets boy, girl loses boy, girl gets boy again. It's American with Spanish subtitles. I know men hate them and would much rather go to one of those movies where there is some random violence and then a car chase and then an explosion, repeat ad nauseam until the dust settles and the bloke gets to kiss the girl right at the end, unless of course she's been bumped off in the meantime. Pointless. Anyway, if a man takes you to a chick flick it can only be because he wants a bit of a grope. Which I was looking forward to.

Then Dai sent Conchita from the bar to tell me that he can't take me to the pictures tonight as his mother is ill. Then I saw Dai going off with that Rhiannon. I am not a happy woman right now.

I think that Mervyn is sitting in his shed surrounded by unwashed laundry and dirty coffee cups and he is living on takeaways. I think he might think of me if only he weren't so wrapped up in his work.

I am going to consume this jug of Welsh Sangria very slowly until I fall asleep, all on my own.

A wilty kiss,
Myf
xo

A note from Neville Twistytrouser

Dear Seaweedy Chums,

I hope you will forgive this more familiar greeting, but we've been through a lot together and I can hardly pretend to have behaved in an entirely respectable manner lately, so there's no point in my being stuffy.

I must thank my noble French colleague Professor Pince-Nez for his intention of generosity toward me, however clumsily expressed! Naturally I agree that the academic gown sometimes serves to cover a certain academic nakedness, just as a prolix and sesquipedalian style can sometimes veil a lack of substance in the writings of certain continental intellectuals.

But let us not quibble! Just so long as the good professor's book has plenty of illustrations, preferably large ones, I shall buy a copy. Naturally I shall pretend that it will be for the learned essay of Professor Pince-Nez, whereas you will all guess that I shall read not a word of it (except the chapter on Madame Kinky) but look at the pictures. Well you may think what you like, but I know you will all be peeking at it in the bookshop while cultivating an air of learnèd disinterest.

As for Myfanwy's question, I definitely understood it in the pub but now I have forgotten it. Who knows whether I'll ever find it again?

ta-ta for now,
Neville

Another note from Myfanwy

Hello again Elegant Echinoidea (Sea Urchins),
I didn't sleep well last night and this morning I have the most thumping headache.

I dreamed that Aerfen the Celtic goddess of fate had a message for Milton Mowbray, and that he had missed out something important about fish from the next chapter, so I sent him a text message about my intuition. To my joy he replied! But only to say that I should add this sentence to the end of chapter 32:

"Pointless though the gesture was, Lionel pulled the fish from his pocket and slid it under the door."

I thought he might be a bit more grateful but that's all he wrote.

Anyway I have dutifully added it to the text.
Myfanwy
x

32. Snooping around at night

WHILE THE CAPTAIN HAD BEEN WANDERING THE NIGHT, Lionel also had not slept. When the sky was blackest he got dressed, took a large fish from the freezer, and crept out.

The Morris Minor started first time and he drove as quietly as he could manage up through the town and onto the main road, but instead of taking the turning to Kasteldrog he drove up to Ankarrek and parked there. He must have missed the Captain, for neither of them saw the other.

He paused in front of St Doris's church. Looking up towards the relief of St Doris over the door he could see little but he knew it was there. It comforted him somehow. He took a deep breath and walked on towards Kasteldrog along narrow footpaths, guided only by a flashlight.

He had no plan, just a burning desire.

Meanwhile Sidney Sinister had not been idle. He too was on this day a creature of the night. Earlier he had sat outside the café nursing a cappuccino, a conspicuous figure in his loose brown raincoat among the brightly coloured Mexicans. Then he had strolled over to Dr Fluffycardigan's clinic intending to pose as a patient, just at the moment Lola happened to burst out of it. He had caught a glimpse of Lucretia and the doctor and decided that was enough information for now.

The abduction of Lola as far as he knew had nothing to do with his client and so nothing to do with him. Someone else's problem.

Then he had returned to the café, ordered another cappuccino, and sat down. Eventually the mariachi band packed up their instruments and left, and gradually in twos and threes the Mexicans departed too, disappearing back into the belly of the large shiny white ship moored at the end of the harbour. He was alone, but still sat with his notebook open, perhaps hoping to be mistaken for a poet.

At last, without looking up, he noticed two figures emerge from the clinic, and he heard them lock it up. He waited until they were out of sight, and then a bit longer. Then he got up and strolled as nonchalantly as possible around the back of the builders' hoardings to a place he had previously noticed where the boards were not properly nailed in place. He felt in his pocket for his large Swiss Army knife and unfolded the jemmy that was part of it, applied it to the gap in the boards and pushed his whole weight against it. There was a splintering sound and a gap appeared just wide enough for Sidney Sinister to squeeze through. He was happy to see that the boards sprang almost back into place, so that the gap was not obvious.

Then, stepping over boards, breeze blocks and cement buckets he made his way to the back of the bright pink building, to the door that would in due course connect it to the hotel. There he found, as he expected, a temporary door secured by a small padlock, which he broke using his Swiss Army knife chain cutter tool. He was in.

Sidney Sinister was nothing if not professional. Before entering he covered his shoes with plastic covers of the kind used in operating theatres. He put on gloves. He walked carefully, switching on no lights but using a small flashlight from yet another pocket. The third eye in the image of Schrödinger the cat glowed from the wall, an effect Sinister attributed to luminous paint, and he was not perturbed. From the waiting room he entered Dr Fluffycardigan's office and moved around to the doctor's side of the desk, taking care not to disturb the bananas suspended over the couch, and with his gloved hand eased open each desk drawer in turn, lifting and replacing papers with the minimum disturbance. At last he found what he was looking for, photographed the papers using his Minox spy camera, and put them back.

Snooping around at night

Gentle reader, my privileged position as writer allows me to reveal to you what Sidney Sinister found:

Marine, Fire and Unstable Jelly Insurance Company

To: Ms Plokamia Kalamari
Kraken and Kraken Solicitors

Dear Ms Kalamari,
Re: *the estate of the late Lady Lucretia Fumble*
Thank you for your letter regarding the claim on the life insurance policy taken out on the late Lady Lucretia Fumble. We note that you claim that the deceased died of the Twinge. Our medical adviser informs us there is no such disease. May we draw your attention to paragraph 55.13(c) of the policy document which specifically excludes claims for imaginary diseases.

Additionally, paragraph 101.94(f) makes it explicit that we are not obliged to pay out on people who merely think they are dead, as opposed to people who are actually dead.

Furthermore, should you wish to pursue this claim then we would require a sight of Lady Lucretia Fumble's entire medical record in order to trawl through for any evidence that she suffered from the Twinge prior to taking out the policy, which would of course invalidate any claim.

I am sure you can see that trying to get any money out of us is doomed to failure so you might as well give up now.

Respectfully yours,
[squiggle]
Ebenezer Haggis
for Marine, Fire and Unstable Jelly plc.

Letter from Ms Plokamia Kalamari
Kraken and Kraken Solicitors
Specialists in Probate and more or less Anything involving large sums of Money

To: Ebenezer Haggis
Marine, Fire and Unstable Jelly Insurance Company

Dear Mr Haggis,
Re: *the estate of the late Lady Lucretia Fumble*
We are advised that the Twinge is a genuine medical condition as documented in, for example, Fluffycardigan, *Diagnosis and treatment of Mondayphobic urticaria* ('the Twinge'), Journal of the Fluffycardigan Institute.

On a separate matter you will recall that you were persuaded by another client of ours, Cephalopod Entertainments, to have one of their fruit machines installed in your foyer to enhance your image as a company that sometimes pays out. The payments on this machine are considerably overdue.

Your contention that you never wanted a fruit machine in the first place is irrelevant given that the order for it is signed by one Athelstan Dogbiscuit acting *in loco* of your company, so you are liable according to the principle of *respondeat superior*. The fact that Mr Dogbiscuit no longer works for your company and is or may be *loco* in another sense is therefore beside the point.

Our client advises that unless this matter is settled without further delay he will have no choice but to come and remove said fruit machine. You will find in paragraph 193.99(z) of the hire agreement that Cephalopod Entertainments are not responsible for any damage to your property caused during the removal of a Cephalopod fruit machine, such damage not infrequently being non-negligible.

I look forward to receiving your early remittance.

Respectfully yours,
[squiggle]
Kraken and Kraken

Sidney Sinister also found a copy of the will of Lucretia Fumble donating a very large portion of her estate to 'Dr Squidtentacles, who was so kind to me in my last illness.'

It was all fitting into place. Lucretia Fumble, wife of Lord Fumble, had faked her own death. Her death certificate had been written by Dr Squidtentacles. And there could be little doubt that Dr Squidtentacles was the man now masquerading as Dr Fluffycardigan.

As carefully as he had entered he left, replacing the broken padlock with a new one on his way out, and easing the boards back into place before walking home. As soon as dawn broke it would be time for Sidney Sinister to make a phone call.

Meanwhile Lionel walked on, several miles through the woods, the track to Kasteldrog sometimes being crossed by paths almost as wide that led to dead ends blocked with fallen branches.

After a long time Kasteldrog village appeared, marked only by the light of an occasional street lamp trying to penetrate the branches of a tree. Lionel pressed on up what passed for the main street, past the *Piskie and Pasty* and onwards until Castle Drog itself appeared as a black rectangle where the stars were not.

Lionel knew of course that the alsatians, Ragnarok and Fenrir, might be loose in the grounds. His ping-pong victory over Figgis was no guarantee of anything. He decided he didn't care. His comfortable life as a humble accountant living in a cottage with a sea view had once been all he could have desired, but now the thought of living there without his mermaid made him feel empty.

The iron gates were unlocked as before. He pushed one of them open carefully, then stepped off the gravel path and onto the lawn. All he could hear as he walked over the soft grass was the slight whisper of wind in trees. The way was interrupted occasionally by topiary bushes which he circumvented by feel. He knew he was getting close to the house by the blackness gradually enveloping him, blotting out more and more stars.

At length he found the side entrance through the conservatory, and once again made his way past the caressing fronds and tendrils of hothouse plants.

This time knowing the way, he passed quickly and quietly along the corridor and up through the servants' staircase to the hidden passage. There was the door with its thin crack.

There was light from a dim bulb in the centre of the room. The mermaid was reclining awkwardly against the wall of the aquarium, apparently asleep. Algae was growing up the sides of the thick glass and the water looked as if it hadn't been changed. Most of all he noticed her hair, the hair that had so dazzled him when he had first seen her in his bath, glorious, wavy, alive with rivers of seaweed and little crabs. Now it was straight, straggled. Her back was exquisitely beautiful as always, curved like an Ingres, like an Eric Gill, like a Henry Moore, like nothing any artist has ever managed. This is why real artists never stop, because they can never match this beauty and they can never stop trying. Yet this time that curve was also a slump, an expression of hopelessness, something beyond melancholy. Lionel felt his eyes fill.

He tried the door but it would not move. He pushed harder but it still would not give. Someone had fastened it from the other side.

He ran at the door with his shoulder and his shoulder stung with pain. Then he tried to brace himself on the opposite wall and kicked as hard as he could. There was no result other than a loud bang. Several more attempts resulted in nothing but more noise.

The fish had thawed and was wet and limp in his trouser pocket.

His mission was pointless, he knew that. Therefore there was no point in trying to do anything sensible. He cried out in the darkness. He called her beautiful, marvellous. He told her he would never give up trying to set her free. He told her he loved her.

He stopped, breathless, wiping away the tears from his eyes so that he could see again. There was nothing more to be done. At last he looked again through the crack in the door.

She had turned. He could see her face, an expressionless look that nevertheless expressed everything, beyond despair, beyond pain, beyond happiness. For this timeless moment her face was the face of a goddess, implacable, objective, terrifying, wonderful. Then the moment passed, and she was a trapped mermaid once again.

Of course she could not see him, only hear him crying out from behind the door. Yet something was from that moment altogether different.

Pointless though the gesture was, Lionel pulled the fish from his pocket and slid it under the door.

From Myfanwy

Hello again Salty Sirenophiles,
How can Milton Marmalade write so beautifully about the anguish of hopeless love and yet send me away to the Welsh bit of Argentina? Me who asked him if he wanted a cup of tea every

quarter of an hour and regaled him with anecdotes about sheep to keep his spirits up? 'Quiet,' he'd say. 'I'm trying to write.'

Well I knew that didn't I? I was just trying to cheer him up. Not appreciated, I am.

I hope he doesn't go all existential and write a sad ending, or one of those endings where the whole thing is unresolved and you're left sort of dangling. I think when that happens you should ask for your money back. Writers like him need someone like me to remind them that great art doesn't have to be gloomy.

Anyway, the next chapter's quite short.

Thankfully the Professors are on holiday, suffering the extreme stress of thinking profound thoughts while drinking *Hook Norton Ale* and vin rouge respectively.

a kiss
Myfanwy
xo

33. "Nothing can stop me"

LIONEL, WORN OUT, had walked back from Kasteldrog to Ankarrek, retrieved the little Morris and driven back to 7 Marine Parade and his bed, where he had slept little. Before dawn he heard a soft tapping on his front door. There he found Captain Kipper, and let him in.

"Arr! Such a night!" the Captain said.

Lionel in a daze went to make tea. The Captain said nothing about his visit to Nellie, for he had been told so much that he was not to pass on. Instead he confined himself to telling about Lola's abduction, and about his visit to Dr Fluffycardigan and the receptionist called Lucretia, and how Dr Fluffycardigan was very interested to know about Ramón but not so keen for Ramón to know about him, and about the Twinge.

The tea began to bring Lionel back to life, and they sat, thinking.

"Dr Squidtentacles wrote a death certificate with the Twinge on it just before he disappeared," Lionel said.

"Arr, and it were Lucretia Fumble's death certificate, too. Might that Lucretia and this be one and the same? And I'm thinking Dr Fluffycardigan might be none other than Dr Squidtentacles himself."

Lionel looked puzzled. "How does any of that help us?" he asked.

"Well," the Captain continued, "as I were walking in the night I had a vision, an hallucination you might say. It seemed to me that it were the doctor, and he were saying, 'nothing can stop me.' Three times he said it."

"That's not evidence that would stand up in court. It's not really evidence of anything."

"Arr, but I be convinced in me own mind that Dr Squidtentacles be the evil genius behind this whole thing, the hotel, the pink medicine centre, the motorway through Kasteldrog, the mermaid aquarium—the whole lot. If we want to rescue your mermaid, he's the man we have to deal with."

"And Lola?"

"Ramón has got Lola, but I don't know where."

"On his boat would be the most likely I'd say."

"Arr. And there's me searching high and low in the town. Why didn't I think of that? Must've been that pesky herb tea fuddled me brain."

"So... what next?"

"Let's go find Alf. Then we go for the doctor and the Mexican. Are ye with me?"

"Do we have a plan? Won't we need help?"

"The villagers. Let's see who'll volunteer!"

"What are we going to do?"

"I don't rightly know. Mebbe the villagers will turn up with agricultural implements and burning torches like in the horror movies. Who can tell? We have to do something or it'll be too late!"

From Myfanwy

Well my little Barnacles, this next chapter is about a woman who is languishing a bit because she is deserving more love than she is getting, a situation that I can very much sympathise with. It is very difficult when you are full of passion and it's all seething inside you, if you know what I mean. Well hats off to her for taking a bit of initiative.

There are some doctors in this chapter as well, which is very boring I know, but apparently it's important for the plot. Bring on the love scene, is what I say.

"Nothing can stop me"

Dai came knocking on my door this morning and I didn't answer. In fact I was in bed with the covers over my head. He left a little note saying sorry he had to go and see his mother last night. Probably Rhiannon didn't let him have his way with her which is why he's back onto me, is my guess. Well he can stick his note.
Myf
xo

34. High Noon at the Pink Clinic

IT WAS A SUNNY SATURDAY MORNING and Mavis decided to stroll down to the harbour for a coffee and a doughnut. She also knew that PC Figgis was wont to park his patrol car nearby and sit down at the café on a Saturday morning, under the excuse of community policing. Mavis was dressed for the occasion: casual, so that it didn't look too obvious that she was trying to attract attention, but at the same time with well-chosen clashing colours and a plunging neckline. A girl has to make the best of her assets, and Mavis knew that her assets were considerable. It just needed the right man to appreciate them.

On her way she passed the supermarket car park and noticed the sunlight glinting on a row of black Jaguar saloons.

As she approached the café she found the noise from the building site deafening and there was dust everywhere. She thought about turning back but was surprised to see the café was full.

Curious, she stopped and saw that at every table was a man, and sometimes a woman, in a dark suit. Every one of them looked grim-faced and mean, and they stayed there even though the dust got into the coffee and between their teeth. There among them was an aristocratic old man who looked somehow familiar, talking to a man in an oversized raincoat.

The aristocrat was Lord Fumble.

Mavis decided to stay and watch. She bought a piece of chocolate tiffin and a large latte in a takeaway cup with a lid to keep out the dust and sat down as close as she could to Fumble, since she loved a bit of gossip. The men and women in suits barely moved, all eyes on the front door of the pink clinic opposite, and a light breeze started to come up off the sea. The dust formed brightly lit swirls as the sun burned between the steel girders. An hour went by and everyone including Mavis waited. The opening time of the pink clinic approached.

Then Mavis's patience was rewarded. A police car screeched to a halt, stirring up the dust even more, and Figgis stepped out.

"What's all this then?" he asked loudly to no-one in particular, looking around. Then he spotted Sidney Sinister.

"Might I ask the meaning of this?" Figgis enquired. He stood on tiptoe so that his face could be uncomfortably close to Sidney Sinister's, and tried to look authoritative.

"You might," Sinister responded, "but client confidentiality forbids."

"I don't see any harm," Lord Fumble interjected. "The game's up, and it's out of the law's hands anyway." He turned to Figgis. "We are the General Medical Council, of which I am a lay member, and we've come for Dr Squidtentacles, alias Fluffycardigan, for being generally wacky and bringing the profession into disrepute with bananas. The docs also don't like people going around inventing new diseases, since the job's hard enough already. Plus he ran off with my wife, which is what's really cooked his goose."

"If he has broken the law then it is very much my business." Figgis said, his his jaw set firm.

"Don't worry," Fumble replied, patting Figgis on the shoulder, "We're going to take him back to London and show him the instruments and when he confesses we'll turn him over to the secular arm."

Figgis fumed but said nothing.

Mavis was not so distracted by all this that she did not notice something odd. At the next table one of the men in dark clothing was also wearing a sombrero, a detail that had somehow escaped the normally vigilant eye of Sidney Sinister. The man extracted a mobile phone from under his black and white poncho.

"I theen' I found the other thing you looking for, boss," he said into the phone. There was an inaudible reply and the man put the phone away and sat back, grinning broadly. Then he reached across and put his hand on Mavis's knee.

"What a fine woman like you do in a place like thees?" he asked, his smile showing even more teeth and his eyes bright.

Mavis coloured slightly, taken aback at this sudden invasion of her personal space. Even so, a hand on the knee has some merit if you are feeling under-appreciated. Frowning, she removed the hand firmly but followed this with an ambiguous smile.

"My name is Pedro. Like the English say, a hand on the knee is worth one on the bush!"

Mavis didn't know quite how to take this, and she felt a little threatened, but on the other hand she noticed that Pedro was not at all bad looking. His appearance that is. His morals might be another matter. Which could also be interesting.

"Mavis," she said introducing herself. "I think you'll find that the expression is, 'a bird in the hand is worth two in the bush,'" she added primly.

Pedro looked confused for a moment, then: "I don' know what birds got to do with it, but if you stick with me, one in the bush ees plenty. You will no be disappointed." He slid over to the empty chair next to Mavis, put his hand round her waist and gave her a squeeze. Mavis was surprised to feel a surge of energy go through her body as though something had been released that had long been dormant, and she breathed a little harder.

While the man with the poncho might have escaped Sidney Sinister's attention he had not escaped the policeman's. Figgis had no interest in Mexicans one way or the other, but the presence of this man with his arm around Mavis's waist aroused his indignation.

"Is this man bothering you, madam?" he enquired.

"I'm all right, officer," she said, not sure yet whether she was, but very keen to find out.

Figgis fumed inwardly for the second time that morning, wondering whether he could detain the Mexican on a pretext and thus save Mavis from danger and so become a hero.

"Do you have a permit for that sombrero?" he asked, counting on the foreigner's ignorance of English law.

"I no need any permit, señor, as my hat is a special hat. This hat is blessed by the Pope when he come to Mexico, as I was there for the Papal blessing of the crowds and the Papal blessing fall on my hat. This hat, señor, has diplomatic immunity and answers to no-one, no even you, supreme sir."

"So, you would obstruct an officer in the course of his duty? I shall have to ask you to accompany me to the station!"

"Ah, but my hat refuse. I wish to help you, but I can do nothing if my hat refuse."

Figgis was losing the battle of wits and was about to reach for the handcuffs when a brown Morris Minor with a bit of rust behind the headlamps drew up and Lionel, Alf and Captain Kipper stepped out. Moments later a white Porsche Cayenne appeared from the other direction and stopped near the clinic, its engine still running, followed by a crowd of Mexicans on foot, dressed in brightly-coloured ponchos with the mariachi band bringing up the rear.

The Captain made for the Porsche and banged on the heavily tinted front window. It opened lazily with an electric hum, and Ramón Pimiento el Picante turned slowly to face him, his usual grin intact.

"What have you done with Lola?" the Captain demanded.

"Ees none of your business," Ramón replied. "Besides, I am busy."

"It's very much my business!" the Captain shouted, "Come out and we'll talk about it, man to man!"

At the sound of shouting Figgis saw his opportunity to extract himself with dignity from his losing confrontation with Pedro. "Now then, now then, what's all this then?" he said.

"This man has kidnapped Lola Tabasco! I demand you search his van and then his boat!"

"And who might this Lola Tabasco be?"

"The barmaid at the *Piskie and Pasty*. She's been taken against her will!"

Ramón did not move from his seat in the front of the Porsche Cayenne.

Meanwhile Pedro was luring Mavis towards the Porsche. "How about we go for a little drive in my car?" he was saying, careful that Ramón did not overhear. He opened the back door and ushered Mavis into one of the plush seats with a gentle hand on her bottom. Then he got in beside her and closed the door just as Figgis saw what was happening.

"Step outside the car, sir," Figgis tapped loudly on the back window, then getting no response addressed the same to Ramón.

Ramón ignored him. Figgis sputtered in fury and got onto his mobile phone for Sergeant Spriggan to come and assist him. "Bring the dogs, too! These people have no respect for the law! It's a revolution I tell you!"—at which the Mexicans all shouted, "¡Viva la revolución!" and threw their sombreros in the air.

Just at that moment a black Bentley Continental saloon appeared on the road from the top of the village to the harbour. All heads turned to look, and everyone fell silent. There were two figures in the car: a man and a woman. As the car descended the hill it slowed, then stopped and did a rapid three-point turn.

"¡Ees him! ¡Ees Squidtentacles!" shouted Pedro from the back of Ramón's Porsche. Ramón gunned the engine and took off at speed. Mavis was thrown back in her seat and Pedro seized the opportunity to thrust his arms around her ample form in a protective gesture. At once Lord Fumble and all the black-suited men and women rushed out of the café and ran towards the supermarket car park. At the same time Figgis jumped into his patrol car and the wheel-spin left black streaks of rubber on the road as he started after the Porsche, turning on the blue lights for a more dramatic effect, his chest heaving with passion.

Lionel, Alf and the Captain got into the Morris Minor and followed, and as they passed the car park they were joined by a line of black Jaguars. Every time there was a widening of the road the little Morris was overtaken by one of the black saloons. A 918cc, 27.5 horse-power engine is more than sufficient in a place of remote country tranquility and sleepy harbourside pubs, but it is not enough to keep up with a modern turbocharged two litre. Finally they were overtaken by Spriggan, who had gone down to the harbour, found no-one there other than the barista in the café, and turned around, siren blazing, horn sounding and the two alsatians with their heads hanging out of half-open back windows barking furiously. The little Morris was left behind.

"What do we do now?" asked Lionel.

"We keep going," the Captain responded.

"That's right," added Alf. "As the preacher says, 'the race is not to the swift, nor the battle to the strong.'"[*]

"Well I don't understand that at all," said Lionel.

Nevertheless he drove on.

From Myfanwy

Hello again fellow Lovers of Littoral Literature,

Here's the next chapter, sent to me by Marvin Mildew himself. He said 'thank you for your efforts' which has cheered me up no end. I think he really loves me after all, although I might be over-interpreting.

I won't say any more about Marvin or I'll get all upset.

---

[*] Ecclesiastes 9:11

A MERMAID IN THE BATH

This little chapter includes about as much of a car chase as you're likely to get. I am really looking forward to the love scenes, but all we get in this chapter is Alf and Nellie holding hands, and we don't get to hear what happens between Mavis and Pedro, which is a bit disappointing. Really if this story doesn't hot up a bit I'm going to start reading one of those bodice-ripping historical novels.

He gripped her in his strong English arms. "I could not leave you to the mercies of that ruffian Sir Dai," he said. "I shall challenge him to a duel on the morrow and shall certainly do him in. I have not slept for thinking of you, and have ridden day and night to fetch you back to my estate at Milton Keynes and your rightful place by my side."

"O Sir Marvin!" the Lady Myfanwy's bosom heaved. "You have invaded my castle and now you have invaded my heart!"

His dark eyes stared into her very soul and their lips touched. He pressed her in a fierce kiss.

"This bodice is too tight and I fear I might swoon. Unlace me quickly I prithee!" she gasped.

She felt the urgency of his desire as his rough hands struggled with her laces. "You should have just pulled the ends" she breathed ...

Do bosoms always have to heave? It's the corsets that cause it. You don't see much bosom heaving these days probably because of soft underwear. That's the price of progress I suppose.

Kisses,
Myfanwy
xoxoxo

35. A CAR CHASE AND A MEETING OF SOULS

IT WAS OBVIOUS that the black Bentley was heading for Kasteldrog.

Had Figgis considered the matter he could have used his local knowledge to arrive there by a back route and catch Dr Squidtentacles in a pincer movement. However, Figgis had no occasion to arrest the doctor. It also had not occurred to him (as he had not been told) that Dr Squidtentacles was his mysterious boss, since everything had been done through Edwin Sharck and Smithers. No, Figgis was simply after the Porsche with the intention of extracting Mavis and reasserting his authority as Pengoggly's guardian of the law.

Meanwhile the Mexicans had all boarded the local bus, hanging out of the windows and shouting, "Viva la revolución!" while the mariachi band played at full volume in the aisle.

"¡Follow those cars!" one of the Mexicans instructed the driver.

"Sorry moi lover, this is the bus to Penzance." The bus slowed and stopped to let an old lady on.

"¡You no stop! ¡Follow the cars!" shouted the Mexican.

The driver ignored him and continued down the main road, as the line of Jaguars disappeared up the side road to Kasteldrog followed by Spriggan's patrol car with the dogs howling just under a semitone out of tune with the siren.

"¡You do what we say!" The Mexican drew a small revolver.

The old lady was Nellie. In her gentlest voice she told the driver, "I think he means it, dear."

"¡Si! ¡We means it!"

The driver looked up and the revolver was in front of her face. Her eyes widened, she turned white, did the fastest three point turn anyone has ever seen a fully laden bus do, and turned up the minor road to Kasteldrog accompanied by more enthusiastic shouts of "¡Viva la revolución!" To emphasise the whole *joie-de-*

vivre of the moment the Mexican shot a hole in the roof of the bus, causing the driver to press unexpectedly hard on the accelerator pedal, the jolt causing the mariachi band suddenly to change key from G to A without changing the accidentals. The music became surprisingly modal and not altogether unpleasant, although not very Mexican. The bus lurched on down a road never intended for such a vehicle, bumping from grass verge to grass verge.

Some distance behind, the little Morris kept going.

As the Morris reached Castle Drog itself the three friends could see the traffic jam that had formed outside. The bus was now empty and in front of it was Spriggan's patrol car, apparently trapped, but Spriggan and the dogs had gone. A knot of black Jaguar saloons was blocking the road, one by one squeezing past the half-open gate. The Bentley was nowhere to be seen, but the white Porsche was parked in front of the house with Figgis's police car parked across it to block any attempt at exit. In the distance the Mexicans could be seen, ponchos billowing, running like a swarm of butterflies across the lawn, the mariachi band following as best they could with their instruments. But there was someone else who caught Alf's eye.

Nellie.

Lionel reversed down the road and backed the Morris into the car park in front of the *Piskie and Pasty*, thinking that if a swift getaway were to be needed then strategy might count more than horsepower. "The readiness is all,'[*] he thought, quoting Shakespeare. Alf jumped out and the others followed.

"It can't be..." Alf faltered.

He ran to where Nellie was standing by the bus, she looking as calm as an anemone in a rock pool. Their eyes met.

---

[*] *Hamlet* Act V, scene ii, line 237.

A Car Chase and a Meeting of Souls

Alf did not know what to do. His mind was telling him, "it can't be, it's a normal woman, she has legs." His heart was telling him, "it's Nellie, my mermaid, beyond a doubt."

He stood there for what felt like a long time, seemingly paralysed. Lionel started to say something. "Hush," Alf said in a whisper. Nellie looked at him with her gentle gaze, saying not a word, waiting.

The running Mexicans and the roaring of diesel engines faded out of importance, a psychedelic hum in the background of a much deeper moment. Somewhere in the distance the barking of dogs could be heard, and men shouting. Lionel tensed, but he knew that the time for action was not yet. When the hand of fate writes, everything must happen in due order.

At last Alf spoke. "Nellie," he said.

She smiled, the kind of smile that is seen on the faces of medieval saints and bodhisattvas. The archaic smile of the pre-Classical Greeks, before they became clever. The kind of smile that knows what heaven is, that invites one who sees it to join it.

"Alf," she said. "Yes, it's me."

But the time for embracing was not yet. They joined hands briefly, a connection that had to stand for so much more. Then Alf said, "I have to go. My friends need me."

"Of course."

"When shall I see you again?"

"You will see me again, don't worry," she replied, letting go his hand. Her eyes were saying, go, you have work to do.

From Myfanwy

Well now my Driftwood Dreamers,
I am much happier now because Martin Murgatroyd is sending the manuscripts directly to me and not through the professors. I don't

know how the professors ever got hold of them and I can only assume that some interfering PhD student is hiding in the bins behind the Co-op in Milton Keynes and intercepting Milton's inspired outpourings. This means that Milton values my help so much that he ventures out to the post box in order to post them himself, most likely just before sunrise when the PhD student is still asleep on a pile of date-expired vegetables.

The poor dear is so lost in his creative genius that he probably goes out in his dressing gown and bedroom slippers, it wouldn't surprise me. Whether he eats a proper breakfast I don't know either.

Anyway, this is a longer chapter in which quite a lot of things happen, and joy of joys we hear more about Mavis and Pedro, although no bodice-ripping I'm sad to say.

As regards Pedro's moustache, my spellchecker puts a little red line under the word 'tickly' no matter how I type it. 'Tickly' is a perfectly good English word I'll have you know, and even if it isn't, everyone knows what it means, and that's all you can reasonably expect of a word isn't it?

Half way through Milton addresses himself to you with the words 'gentle reader... .' Who does he think he is, Jane Austen? Anyway I hope they put her picture on the banknotes as it's about time we had a woman on there. Mind you the Queen is on all of them isn't she? Talking of Jane Austen, that would have been a good name for a car in the heyday of the British Motor Corporation, instead of the Austin Cambridge, like. Then the Morris Oxford would have been Jane Morris. As you no doubt know, Jane Morris was the muse of the Pre-Raphaelites. It must be nice being a muse and getting all that male attention.

Goodness, this Argentine wine is good! I'm feeling quite inspired now. Perhaps I'll write that bodice-ripper myself and then I can ask Milton to help me with it while I snuggle up to him. Once I'm back in England. And I'm not living in a shed at the back of the Co-op. He'll have to get a proper house.

love and kisses,
Myf
xoxoxoxoxoxoxoxoxoxo

36. Dr Squidtentacles escapes

"JUST DISTRACT THEM AS LONG AS YOU CAN. It's the GMC after me. They've nothing against you, you'll be fine."

Dr Squidtentacles omitted to mention the Mexicans, not a small matter when you consider that it was Edwin Sharck who had had to run from Ramón Pimiento el Picante in a bar in the Bahamas over the small matter of nine hundred and ninety-eight thousand nine hundred and ninety-one counterfeit dollars paid for a consignment of hallucinogenic chillies. The doctor went on, "Lucretia, you'd better stay here. It's not safe to be around me right now."

Lucretia just stood there, saying nothing, her face unreadable.

"What about the mermaid?" Sharck asked.

"What about her?"

"She ate the fish!" interjected Smithers.

"What the blazes are you talking about? Of course mermaids eat fish! Cretin!"

Sharck drew a deep breath. "The fish appeared on the floor near the blocked servants' door. We don't know how it got there. Someone must've pushed it under the door."

"And your point is? Apart from the fact that you probably let Fortescue get in again, which merely proves your total incompetence!"

"The point is," Edwin Sharck spoke slowly as if to a person of limited understanding, "it was on the floor. And she ate it."

Dr Squidtentacles paused to take this in, but he still didn't get it. He stared at Sharck menacingly.

Sharck spelled it out. "She. Must. Have. Got. Out. Of. The. Tank."

"But she doesn't have legs!" Lucretia exclaimed.

"But she did."

Dr Squintentacles escapes

Dr Squidtentacles was in no mood to discuss the imponderable of a mermaid being able to walk across a wooden floor. "Whatever. Smithers, you drive the Bentley to wherever you like, and make sure they all follow you. I'll take the Land Rover. Sharck, get the cage. The mermaid's coming with me."

Lucretia looked ominous but said nothing.

As Sharck ran to get the cage the doctor grabbed a chair and swung it at the glass tank. The mermaid flinched and shielded her face. At the first swing a huge crack appeared in the wall of the tank and at the second it shattered into thousands of fragments, water spilling everywhere. The mermaid could do nothing to defend herself, and Sharck and the doctor dragged her into the the cage.

"Careful! Don't damage the goods too much!" shouted the doctor.

The mermaid was covered in cuts and bleeding. She found she could not cry out, and her mouth opened soundlessly. Salt water tears streamed down her cheeks.

The three men heaved the cage out of the back of the building and into the Land Rover that was waiting there, and Lucretia followed. Sounds reached them of revving engines, shouts, the barking of dogs and a strangely out-of-tune mariachi band. Dr Squidtentacles leaped into the driver's seat.

"This is but a temporary setback!" he shouted. "You'll see! I have planning permission! Nothing can stop me!"

Lucretia ran round to the other side and attempted to get in but the doctor pushed her out forcefully and moved off, the passenger door still open.

"You bastard!" Lucretia cried.

"No time for farewells now my love!" shouted the doctor as he sped off through the grounds, putting ruts in the lawns and toppling vases as he went, heading on out over the fields towards the coast.

The three friends ran across the lawn. The last of the mariachi band was a little ahead of them, following the rest of the Mexicans who had got mixed up with the swarm of black-suited doctors. Lord Fumble was in their midst, all running towards the left side of the house. Across to the right Lionel could see Sergeant Spriggan holding the leads of two frantic alsatians, looking around and clearly wondering what to do next. Figgis was next to him, guarding the Porsche although no-one was in it. Ramón was nowhere to be seen.

Under cover of the general confusion Pedro had taken Mavis around to the right of the house and found a walled rose garden, badly neglected but all the more romantic for that. Somehow he had acquired one of the band's instruments, a small vihuela. He took off his poncho and folded it neatly on a lichen-encrusted stone bench and invited Mavis to sit on it. The sounds of shouting and barking were barely perceptible here, and seemed irrelevant. The wind susurrated in the trees just beyond the walls and the sun warmed the weathered bricks. The song of birds could be heard.

The vihuela he began plucking gently, and a melancholy but beautiful tune began to emerge from it.

"Ees a sad tune, but we must have sad tunes. Melancolía is no an illness but a longing. This song say even bad boys and girls is worthy of love."[*]

Mavis sat entranced. She was so far out of her comfort zone that she didn't care any more, and gave herself to the moment with a strange mixture of fear and tranquility.

"This song," he continued while still plucking a background melody, "is called 'Mavis mi amor.' I translate for you the words. It say, 'Mavis although I am a very bad boy I seen you eating

---

[*] Melancholia: sometimes confused with depression, it is simply life in a minor key. From the Greek for black bile (μέλαινα χολή), one of the four humours or four temperaments of ancient Greek and Roman medicine.

chocolate cake in the café and my heart melt like the chocolate on your cake on a hot day. If I could be the chocolate on your cake you would lick me off and we should both be happy. Surely we are all sinners but we all deserve some love.'"

The words didn't seem naturally to fit the rhythm of the tune and Mavis had the distinct impression that Pedro was making the whole thing up on the spot, but somehow he managed to squeeze all the words in, with sentences spilling over the ends of song lines in ways that stretched the rules of prosody to their limits.

"Te he visto comiendo torta de chocolate en el café... Ay ay ay... Mavis mi amor!" he sang, and a lot more besides. He seemed quite inspired, although he was probably not good enough for a recording contract. Mavis started to revise her aversion to moustaches, and wondered whether a kiss would be tickly.

There we must leave them for the moment and return to the action at the house.

Ramón had found his way through the conservatory and along the corridor, just as Lionel had the previous night, followed by a crowd of Mexicans and doctors. But instead of taking the servants' way in he took the main staircase and went straight into what had once been the grand salon. Meanwhile another group of Mexicans had become detached from the main crowd and formed a small knot in the grounds just as Lionel, Alf and the Captain caught up with them. There appeared to be some kind of altercation going at the centre of the group, with shouts of 'let us go, you morons!' The black Bentley was parked nearby.

The three friends agreed that Alf and the Captain should stay to find out who might be at the centre while Lionel followed the main crowd going into the house.

The Mexicans and doctors followed close behind Ramón, squeezing into the big room in twos and threes. Lionel heard Ramón shouting angrily and the crowd inside turned around, causing a crush at the doorway. The Mexicans pushed past the doctors, Ramón following with unaccustomed speed, violently elbowing straggling doctors out of the way as he went.

Lord Fumble raised his voice authoritatively, "Come on chaps and chapesses! Do keep up!"

Then the doctors turned and jostled the Mexicans, and the whole crowd flowed down the staircase like a jellyfish on a theme park water slide.

As the last of the doctors left the big room Lionel glanced in to see what they had seen. There was no-one, only a large smashed aquarium and shards of glass spread over a parquet floor flooded with water. There were traces of fresh blood. A tightness formed in Lionel's chest. He started to run back outside.

Pedro, meanwhile, was closing in on Mavis with practised ease. Slowly slowly is the way. Lead, but let the woman feel she is in control. Not logical of course, but we are talking about the seduction of women here. It is not a logical process. He finished his song and sat down close beside her, but leaving a little gap. That gap, he knew, is like the gap between magnets held slightly apart. He leaned in as if to land a kiss on her cheek and Mavis leaned back instinctively, then Pedro moved his face away, smiling mischievously. Mavis was by now in a state of high tension. She leaned in towards him but Pedro kept his distance. "You should understand I am no a pushover!" he said. "I don' give myself away cheap." She laughed.

But we must return to the front of the house or I shall not be able to keep up with the events there. Gentle reader, it is hard not to get muddled up when everything is happening at once.

Sergeant Spriggan by now was getting bored. "Why'd you drag me out here?" he asked Figgis. "This is a waste of time. None of this has anything to do with us."

"But this is where we brought the mermaid," Figgis reminded him.

"So? Sharck hasn't called us and Smithers hasn't called us, and in any case we're outnumbered. Best keep out of it. If a bunch of

Mexicans want to run around this godforsaken stately home playing Schoenberg on folk instruments then I presume that is their privilege. English law permits everything that isn't expressly forbidden, and if you can find me a statute against doctors boogying to atonal music then I'd like to see it. Meanwhile I'm going home." With that Spriggan dragged the dogs back out of the grounds and towards his patrol car, which could now get out since the Jaguars were all parked on the lawn.

The bus driver meanwhile had decided that enough was enough, and had driven out of Kasteldrog and was by now well on the way to Penzance.

Figgis realised at this point that staying by the Porsche was not achieving anything. He also did not want to get involved in a scene that was entirely outside his control. Since Mavis could have gone either way it made no difference where he started to look, so he started off round the right hand side of the house, away from the confusion. As he rounded the corner he heard the faint strains of a vihuela, playing not Schoenberg but rather something that could be recognised as a tune.

Mavis, meanwhile, had moved subtly nearer Pedro. By shifting her weight a little her hips could touch his without her appearing to have done anything. Pedro was good at detecting physical signs but he pretended not to notice. She leaned closer and he leaned back. "Naughty! You theen' I kiss on a first date?" he said. Mavis felt as if she might explode. She punched him on the arm.

Meanwhile Lionel followed the crowd back outside the house and rejoined Alf and the Captain. Lionel's face was tense.

The knot of Ramón's men had surrounded two gringos. As Ramón emerged from the conservatory he saw this and his walk slowed to a leisurely pace, his cuban heels clicking on the paving. There was now no rush. The crowd parted like the Red Sea for him and his face resumed its accustomed grin. The sun glinted on his gold tooth. There he found Smithers and Edwin Sharck looking distinctly uncomfortable.

"We meet again." Ramón spoke slowly and with mild menace. Mild menace is more effective that the other kind, because it suggests that much worse is to come. "There ees the small matter of two million and twenty-seven thousand and ninety-one dollars you owe me. Time for you to pay."

"Two million and twenty-seven thousand and ninety-one dollars? But it was nine hundred and ninety-eight thousand nine hundred and ninety-one dollars and ninety-eight cents!"

"Interest for the time you have had my money and I have not. Ees the two thousand and thirteenth triangular number, and thirteen is a lucky number."

"That's a hundred and two point six two and a bit percent!"

"Exactly. You see how generous I am! If you had the same loan from a payday loan company you would pay four thousand percent. Lucky for you I am no a greedy villain, just a businessman, like yourself." His eyes narrowed with silent laughter. One of the Mexicans grabbed Sharck from behind in a painful arm-lock and threatened his throat with a knife.

"It's not me! It's the boss!" Sharck spluttered. "I don't have the money, he has it!"

Ramón stared at Sharck, not moving a muscle, his thoughts unreadable but probably centring on what kinds of physical pain to inflict.

It has been said that time is what stops everything happening at once. Sometimes, though, it does anyway. At some point in all this a large band of locals turned up from the direction of the *Piskie and Pasty*, armed with agricultural implements and a ram (the wooly kind rather than a medieval siege machine). Seeing the three friends, Danzel approached Lionel. "Arr," he said, "we be ready. We didn't bring flaming torches because it be daylight. Also we couldn't bring a combine harvester because Cornwall be too rocky. But we got some spades, sheep shearing clippers and a few trowels. I hope that's all right."

Lionel put a hand up for silence. The distant sound of a vanishing Land Rover could be heard, for anyone listening. Ramón's attention was on Sharck, and he noticed nothing.

"Looks like the boss isn't here," whispered the Captain.

Lionel turned to Danzel. "Thanks for coming!" he said, "but there's nothing to be done here. If they start to leave, can you distract them for a while without causing any actual violence?"

"Arr, we can do that!"

Lionel turned to the others. "Back to the car!"

He reasoned that the mermaid was almost certainly with Dr Squidtentacles, who had made a run for it in the direction of Pengoggly. It was time to go back to the harbour as quickly and quietly as possible.

Meanwhile Danzel and the locals prepared an area on the front lawn in preparation for a staging of Aristophanes's lost play, 'Carry On Socrates,' brought to Cornwall in ancient times by Nobblinnees on a Phoenician trading ship. This involved large amounts of cheap kitchenware for Xantippe to throw at Socrates on purpose and other characters by accident, some very risqué double entendres rendered into English from the Greek via the Cornish language (the precise translation of which having caused several tribal wars among speakers of different Cornish dialects), and a lot of scantily-clad young ladies running about to no obvious purpose.

From Myfanwy

Hello again Winsome Whelks,
I am very excited to send you the next chapter which tells more about Mavis and Pedro. Merton Mooncalf has written a cracker

here. If the young men reading this (and older ones for that matter) pay attention they will learn quite a lot about how to inflame a woman's heart.

You might wonder whether what Pedro does is just tricks to fool a woman and you might think the world would be better off without tricks. But then you might just as well say that fine cookery is just tricks and after all it's just food.

Give me romance and good cooking over a clumsy fumble and a takeaway any day. Now if only Merton could put into practice what he writes...

Dai sent another bunch of flowers and a note saying meet me at the Tea House at four o'clock. I might go since I am feeling in a forgiving mood.

a kiss,
Myf
xo

37. A Lesson in Seduction

Before we go chasing off with Lionel to the harbour, you will want to know what happened to Mavis.

The walls of the garden were covered with neglected espaliers of pear and damson trees laden with fruit. The fruit was not quite ripe for plucking. Mavis, too, had been neglected but she too was not quite ripe for plucking. Bees hummed among overgrown roses which lazed wantonly across the paths. Mavis's heart hummed and her body, which was pleasantly plump rather than overgrown, lazed not quite wantonly on the stone bench softened by Pedro's poncho, her head in his lap.

Pedro, meanwhile, sang songs of increasing lewdness, but with a gentle melody and in any case in Spanish. Mavis understood the melody but did not understand Spanish. That does not mean that she did not understand lewdness. A girl must be allowed to understand things when it is in her interest to do so, not before.

Then Pedro stopped playing and singing, and for a moment became serious. "Mavis," he said, "life is short. You know that soon I shall have to go back to Mexico. Yet never have I met a woman like you. I am thinking, should we let such a moment go by? Is it right that a woman as deserving of passion as you should let a man such as me, so well-qualified to satisfy you in every way, slip through her fingers? When the oceans separate us, will you regret what did not happen?"

Mavis blushed but said nothing. Her body tensed a little but she did not move.

"Remember," Pedro went on, "how you said, a bird in the bush is better than a hand on the knee?"

"Maybe not satisfy me in every way," Mavis said wistfully, as if only to herself. She sighed a deep sigh. A moment's pleasure but not a lifetime of domestic gentleness. Life is quite impossible sometimes. Then, to Pedro, "Maybe."

A lesser man might have hesitated. Is that a yes or a no? What if I think it's a yes and it's a no? I will be rejected! Then a crack will appear in the sky and a giant finger will point at me as the most inadequate man in creation whom no woman in her right mind would ever want and I shall be shrivelled up like a worm in the fires of the Day of Wrath. But Pedro was not such a man.

He put down the vihuela and then he took off his sombrero. He stood up, replacing himself with the sombrero as a cushion for her head. Then he kneeled over her, his face inches from her chest.

"Mavis," he said. In the art of seduction it is not what is said that is important, but the boldness and timing of it. He started to breathe his hot breath on her shoulder and moved to the base of her neck. He played with a lock of her hair that had come loose and his face came closer to hers. Mavis tried not to move but her body disobeyed her and involuntarily her back arched. His hand moved behind her head, touching her hair at the nape of her neck. Mavis trembled. Suddenly and without warning she lurched upward, her lips crashing into his with such force his lips were bruised, her arms encircling him without her asking them to do so. Her thoughts all vanished and the fire that she had first felt in the café when he had put his arm round her waist took over entirely.

Pedro was only slightly taken aback by the results of his carefully practised alchemy, since after all this was the intended effect, like a chemistry teacher demonstrating that sodium burns in water but has put a little more in than he meant to.

He put his other hand deftly around her, just at the turning point where the incurve of the lower back meets the out-curve at the top of the buttocks. A touch which is suggestive without being prematurely invasive. Mavis relaxed into his arms as he placed himself on top of her.

At that moment Figgis found the doorway into the rose garden. He stood and stared, his shoulders tense and his arms stiff by his sides, unsure what to do. Then he coughed loudly. Mavis and Pedro's eyes turned towards the source of the sound while remaining locked in embrace.

"So!" Figgis said.

"So!" Pedro replied. Mavis blushed.

"Unhand that lady!" Figgis blurted out. Since he had never been in such a situation before his vocabulary was necessarily borrowed from novels.

"¿Por qué? We are having a quiet time alone. You should leave, according to the rules of British decorum."

"British decorum!" Figgis exploded. "You know nothing of British decorum!"

At this point Mavis made a rapid mental calculation.

"Pedro was just showing me the kiss of life," she explained. "I am the designated first-aider at work."

Figgis looked stunned, and after a brief pause: "That's not how they taught it to us at Hendon."*

"Many things they did not teach you," Pedro observed.

Figgis was not fooled. Indeed, Figgis reflected, the art of seduction was not taught at school either—a serious omission which had no doubt blighted the lives of many young men, struggling for the rest of their lives with only GCSEs and university degrees to show for it. Why, you could be a professor at Oxford and still not know how to do it, looking instead for answers in dusty libraries, cultivating unkempt hair and wearing tweed jackets with elbow patches.

While Figgis had not graduated from Hendon summa cum laude, and in general was not the finest intellect in the Cornwall Constabulary, at this moment his mind opened to a rare perception. That is, he created a gap of a hair's breadth between

---

*Hendon Police College.

his desire to contradict Mavis's claim to be participating in cardio-pulmonary resuscitation training, and his actually voicing it.

Why he maintained silence, you may surmise, was for the same reason that Mavis had made her implausible explanation for her entwinement with Pedro. Dear reader, you may guess it.

Mavis struggled to get up, and Pedro slipped off her and gallantly helped her to her feet, dusting her off solicitously. Then he punched out the dent in his sombrero and put it on, his back straight and his face unsmiling. Mavis smiled bashfully at Figgis.

Figgis coughed, then said, "Well that all seems to be in order. However, since you are now finished, perhaps I can offer Mavis a lift back to Pengoggly? I should be happy to transport you in the patrol car."

"But señor, we have not yet practised the special manoeuvre!"

"Special manoeuvre?"

"Si. For reviving sensibility in one overcome by existential ennui, as those crazy French philosophers say."

"I have not come across this on-you-wee and it's probably illegal. You can't do that here."

"No, ees French for the fed-up-ness that result from the meaninglessness of the human life."

"Why do they call it on-you-wee then?"

"It sound more clever that way."

Figgis saw no reason to suppose that his life, and by extension human life in general, was meaningless. If he was fed up it was because he did not know how to go about securing the affections of Mavis. And if any special manoeuvre were to be performed, he wanted to be the one to perform it. Anyway, he determined to do his best with the situation as he found it.

"Mavis?" he said, making eye-contact and gesturing towards the door out of the garden.

There was a pause in which Figgis anticipated defeat. Even so he did not let it show in his posture. While a sinking feeling formed in his chest, so familiar from schooldays when every girl he asked out turned out to be washing her hair that particular night, he kept upright and looking at her, although the urge to look at the ground was strong.

Mavis hesitated, blushed, and turned to Pedro.

"Thank you for a most instructive lesson. I shall not forget it." She sighed. Then she kissed him lightly on the cheek and walked rapidly towards the door out of the garden, not looking at Figgis and not looking back.

Figgis bowed towards Pedro. "Perhaps some other time Mr Pedro would explain to me the secrets of Mexican resuscitation?"

Pedro frowned, then his good humour returned. For men like him there is always another day. "Ah señor, it requires application! You must become a different man. You will have many failures. The secret is not to repeat them!"

Figgis turned and walked swiftly towards Mavis, catching up with her at the door of the garden.

From Myfanwy

I think Figgis may yet win Mavis's heart. Although Pedro was quite exciting, wasn't he?

    Myf

    x

From the Warden of St Doris College, Oxford

Dear Philosophical Chums,

Luckily for me my DPhil student (not PhD—that's what they do at universities that were founded less than nine hundred years ago) is still able to scan Morton Mongoose's scribble using some kind of 'app' on his mobile phone thingy every time Morton goes out for a sandwich. This is quite important because of the definitive edition with footnotes which I shall prepare in due course. Morton seems quite unaware that he signed an agreement with Coelocanth University Press when they gave him the money for the lease on the shed.

Anyway, as you can imagine I am mightily amused at the last chapter suggesting that French existentialism is simply a fancy way of having a mope!

Snort!

I think it's probably really a bit more complicated than that.

But not much!

Ha ha!

As for Oxford dons wearing tweed jackets with elbow patches, well, guilty as charged.

If there exists a treatise on Mexican resuscitation please would somebody send me the reference? Sadly I couldn't find it in the Bodleian Library index.

ttfn,
Neville Twistytrouser

38. Being out of Time

ALF WAS ALREADY HEADING OUT of the castle grounds, having understood the same thing that Lionel had. As he ran towards the *Piskie and Pasty* there was Nellie, still waiting.

As Lionel and the Captain ran past towards the car, Alf stopped. He tried to say something, but no words came. Although they were both old, Nellie's beauty had not diminished. Where there had once been a young woman's smooth skin and the kind of harmonious face that heaven uses to confound unbelievers, now there was wisdom, gentleness, acceptance—qualities that transcend mere youth for those with eyes to see. Even so there was anxiety too.

"Alf, this is about the other mermaid, isn't it?" she said.
"Yes."

Nellie looked into Alf's eyes. That moment lasted forever, but in some direction other than time. "We must hurry," she said.

With that she ran with the others and sat beside Alf in the back of the Morris.

When they reached Pengoggly they found the Land Rover parked and unoccupied, its back door hanging open, and a thin trail of water and blood leading to the shingle beach where the little boats rested. The shingle had been disturbed in a line towards the water, the rest of the trail hidden behind a large fishing boat. Beyond the fishing boat as they ran they could see nothing but a still sea glaring under a merciless sun.

Meanwhile a hum had developed quite unnoticed by Lionel and the others. Now, though, it was evident. If they thought of it as near, it was not very loud. But if they thought of it as coming from beyond the fishing boat it was the sound of something very big indeed.

Now there was a dense shadow in the water just outside the harbour, getting larger.

Then an ear-splitting scream, a woman's scream, reached them from the other side of the fishing boat.

A note from Prof. Alphonse Pince-Nez

Cheres Amateurs d'Amour,
Ah! The interchangeability of curves!

You will read in ce chapitre suivant a concept tres interessant. C'est à dire, the shapes of an abstract sculpture may peut-être stand interchangeably for different parts of the anatomy, et aussi the shapes of the parts of the anatomy may stand as metaphor for each other. In this way an armpit can stimulate the desire.

I shall have to write a chapitre on the geometry of desire and insert it in my magnum opus.

A bientôt,
Alphonse

39. How not to do seduction

WE MUST NOW GO BACK IN TIME A LITTLE to find out what happened to Lola.

Ramón was a man who was attractive to women. That of course was why Lola had become involved with him in the first place. He had a certain machismo, a quality scorned by feminists but loved by women—a contradiction at the heart of so many problems.

Consider a man who habitually walks with slightly round shoulders, who believes that he was not as handsome as his classmates at school, and who imagines that muscular development such as he does not possess is essential to attracting a really desirable woman. Perhaps he was also not very good at games and is not very rich. Such a description might have fitted Lionel at the beginning of our tale.

Now consider another type of man, a man who has been convinced since childhood that he is not only the apple of his mother's eye but also of the whole world, who was able to beat any of his classmates to a pulp if he so desired, and who naturally attracted the deference of his peers, whether through fear or desire to be one of his gang. Such a man walks tall and stimulates desire in the opposite sex in ways over which they have no control. Of course this is unfair. Is it possible to attract a good woman without being bad?

A woman may say, oh no, those things don't affect me, I look for finer qualities than that in a man. Equally, a man may say, I am not affected by the sight of pert breasts and well-formed thighs. Perhaps someone believes them. Those more immediate qualities, at any rate, are what spark attraction, no matter that they fade in importance later on.

Anyway, to resume our tale, Lola found herself locked up in Ramón's executive suite on his yacht, *El Sueño de la Razón*. The furnishings were opulent in the American manner, so visibly expensive as to be utterly lacking in refinement. There were no icons made out of tissue paper or flying hearts made of painted tin. What was not polished wood was done in cream, from the walls and curtains to the deep pile rug and the thick quilted bedspread. The only concession to human feeling was a small painted Madonna surrounded by sun rays over the bed. There was a dressing table with a bottle of tequila and two shot glasses on one side, and on the other, a bottle of champagne in a silver bucket, two thin-stemmed glasses on a silver tray and a box of chocolates tied up with a large red bow.

Why would he go to such trouble to get her back? Surely he had not come all the way from Mexico just for her? Lola was not as young as she had once been, and pretty women are plentiful in Mexico. Perhaps, though, it was a matter of reputation—whatever is taken from Ramón must be returned to Ramón, because Ramón is Ramón.

Lola opened a wardrobe and found a number of revealing but opulent dresses in her size and a dozen pairs of women's shoes, some encrusted with diamonds and all with expensive designer labels, also in her size.

The inside of the wardrobe door had a mirror. In it she saw a woman with a determined face, the hint of a wrinkle at the corner of each eye, and pale lips. She frowned, took a red lipstick from her purse and applied it.

Then she picked out one of the dresses, a deep blue number, and held it against her. She had curves in all the right places, although her tummy was a little wider than it had once been. "I still got it," she whispered to herself, as if doubting it.

She lingered there for a while. Then putting the dress back, she threw the wardrobe door shut and sat forcefully on the edge of the bed which, because it was a water bed, wobbled unexpectedly under her weight. The lipstick fell from her hand onto the bed and thence to the floor, unnoticed.

She sat there for a short time, thinking. Then she walked over to the dressing table and pulled the ribbon off the box of chocolates, opened it, and studied the contents for a while, eventually picking one out and eating it.

All but one of the Mexicans had gone with Ramón chasing after Dr Squidtentacles, leaving José her sole jailer. José had volunteered for the job, and Ramón had accepted the offer with a shrug. After a short while José came to check on her. He stared through the round window in the door. I shall translate for you the conversation that followed.

"So you like spying on women?"

"I'm just checking on you."

"Want a chocolate?"

"They are Señor Ramón's chocolates."

"Well he left them for me, so now they're my chocolates. He won't know if I gave one to you or ate two myself."

"You are just trying to trick me into opening the door."

"I'm just bored and lonely. So are you. I have tequila too."

"Señor Ramón will not like it if his tequila is gone."

"Well, suit yourself."

Some time went by. José leaned against the door looking out across the harbour. The opposite side of the harbour had a little row of terrace houses, each one painted a different pastel shade from the next. Just as in Mexico, people liked painting things. Unlike in Mexico the colours were gentle. At the end of the row jutting out into the sea was a dark brown rock. Just as there would have been in Mexico there was a church on the rock, unlike in Mexico the church was grey. But the sky at least was blue today.

Lola paced the room wondering what to do. She picked up the red ribbon from the chocolate box and idly twisted it through her fingers. Then, turning her back on the door she held up her hair away from her neck and started to rearrange it with the ribbon. José turned and studied Lola's neck through the window.

It was a very fine neck. Her raised arms revealed graceful armpits. Had he known more about Cornwall he might have thought of the curves of a Hepworth sculpture, curves that might or might not belong somewhere or other on a woman's body. The landscape of desire is full of interchangeable surfaces.

"So you *are* spying on me!" Lola turned her head round far enough to make eye-contact with José, that ambiguous look over a rounded shoulder that is in Vermeer's *Girl with a pearl earring*.

"I have my job to do," José responded.

Lola sighed. "Ramón is very *macho*," she said, as if to herself, "but I wish he was more sensitive. Sometimes a girl needs a man who is sensitive."

"What do you mean, sensitive?" José asked. "I am sensitive but I am not a cry-baby. No real man is a cry-baby."

"I mean, a man who is sensitive to beauty, who maybe writes poetry sometimes, who can be gentle when he needs to be."

José paused for a moment. "I write a little poetry," he said.

"Really?" Lola sounded enthusiastic. "Do you remember any of it?"

José looked bashful. "Maybe it's not very good."

"Let's hear it anyway. It will be good if it comes from your soul. I am no critic—I shall judge it on the quality of your soul."

José coughed and shyly brought out a very folded scrap of paper from his pocket. He unfolded it, looked from the paper to Lola and back again. His hand shook a little.

"I studied Shakespeare in English classes," he said. "It's a sonnet. In English."

He coughed once more, then took a deep breath:

"Were I allowed with you to fall in love,
Roll up my sleeve and show my heart upon it,
With gentle verses I your heart should move
And weave for you my love into a sonnet.

How not to do seduction

> What makes me hesitate to give you posies
> Of little verses—do I fear disdain?
> If you'll take flowers, I should make them roses,
> If you reject them, I should take the pain.
>
> So, I should praise at first your shining eyes
> And then your face, O! Where should I begin?
> And when you smile, the Gates of Paradise
> Would open then, and I should walk within.
>
> Allowed or not, there's nothing I can do
> Except to risk, and tell you, I love you."

He stopped and looked up with an anguished expression. There was a stunned silence.

"This is the moment," José thought, "when Lola will fall into my arms. At least she will when I open the door. Or not." That pause between one event and the unseen next, when exactly nothing was happening, would be burned on his memory forever.

"It's in iambic pentameters," he explained, although no explanation had been asked for.

Lola sighed, smiling. At last, picking her words as though she were sorting through a pile of cherries not all of which were good to eat, she said, "You're very sweet."

There was another pause, in which José's hope and fear formed a tangled knot in his stomach.

"I think we should have a drink," Lola said. She poured a generous double of tequila into each of the shot glasses and offered one to José from the other side of the window. Her smile remained.

José unlocked the cabin door, rattling the key awkwardly. As he entered Lola handed him the glass. She raised hers, entwining her right arm with his as she raised it to her lips, taking a sip. He did the same, taking a gulp.

"You will say nothing of this to Ramón," she said. "Until we are in Mexico we must act as though none of this ever happened." José sat down on the edge of the bed and nodded. Then he emptied his glass.

She held his hand and pulled him up. Linking arms with José she walked towards the door. "Let's take a stroll. I should like to see the sea again. The sea is so romantic."

"But you must return to the cabin before Ramón gets back!" José insisted.

Lola smiled at him and he was at once devastated. They walked out onto the deck. Lola rested her arms on the rail and looked out towards the row of pastel coloured houses and at the lonely church on the rock where the land ended. José did the same, standing as close to her as he could, sensing her warmth. Tentatively he put an arm around her waist, and she did not move away. José felt paradise open up inside him and all his thoughts were replaced by the wordless humming of angels.

At length Lola suggested to José that he should return to his duties. She promised to return to the cabin but begged a few more minutes just to look at the sea and the sky. "The seagulls remind me that I was once free," she said. José turned, hoping for a kiss on the lips, but she fended him off gently. "Not now," she whispered.

Reluctantly, but still full of a peace that burned, José walked off towards the rear deck where he could watch for his master's return. Perhaps he had forgotten that tomorrow has a way of never coming.

As Lola lingered there she saw a shadow in the water. The shadow was approaching the harbour and increasing in size. Down on the shingle a man was dragging something towards the sea.

How not to do seduction

From Professor Neville Twistytrouser

Hello again philosophical chums,
Well my continental colleague is interested in the geometry of desire, I mean, who isn't? No doubt he will make a continental mélange out of it. In my opinion a continental mélange is hardly the stuff of serious philosophy. Nevertheless it can go nicely with a bit of custard, perhaps with some of those chocolate sprinkles on top.

What is perhaps more profound in this chapter, albeit only as a brief footnote, is the idea that tomorrow never comes. Which of course it doesn't, because when it arrives it is today, and tomorrow is another day, as the saying goes. So today is the only day when anything can actually happen. If you want to explore the geometry of desire or merely indulge in a mélange, with or without sprinkles, now is the day to do it.
ttfn,
Neville

40. The Fight on the Beach

AT THE SOUND OF THE SCREAM, Lionel, the Captain, Alf and Nellie all ran towards the shore. As they rounded the fishing boat they saw two figures struggling with each other.

One was a man in a dark suit, and the other was a woman in a blue dress and a brown shawl. There was something else too: a cage, and something in the cage, like a huge fish.

Captain Kipper shouted, "Lola!" at the same time as Lionel saw the cage, and his heart stopped for one beat.

As they got closer to the water's edge the man in the dark suit was joined by more men clad in skin-tight black uniforms, arriving seemingly out of nowhere. All the uniforms carried the silvery insignia of a squid on each shoulder. They overpowered Lola, still struggling, tied her up and dragged her into a small black boat marked with the same design. Captain Kipper got to them first, and flung himself into the boat, lunging out at the men as they attempted to pin him down.

A hired hand is motivated by money, which he can get elsewhere if he has to. The Captain was motivated by love for Lola, who could not be got anywhere else. Captain Kipper's fury was at that moment equal to the force of several ordinary men, and they knew it.

The man in the dark suit stood aside and watched, dusting down his sleeves which had become rumpled in the struggle with Lola.

Lionel rushed onto the cage as more minions closed in on him. The mermaid curled up under his feet in terror. As the minions rushed in one by one, Lionel felt blind fury turn into a strange calm. The odds against him were overwhelming. Any thought of victory or defeat left him. Everything was happening so fast that there was no time for thought at all.

The Fight on the Beach

He gave himself up to the moment. The rudiments of judo moves he had learned a long time ago came and went, and his body invented its own moves as fast as his attackers came for him. Time moved slowly for him. Thinking was replaced by simple being, and he watched dispassionately as his fighting body held off his flailing attackers. He did not hate them. He was like Cuchulain fighting the invulnerable tide, and for a moment, impossibly, it ebbed. It was as though all the minions paused for breath at the same time.

Dr Squidtentacles looked at them, unmoving but with a fierce glint in his eye. Perhaps the minions experienced that mental struggle, never seriously explored in James Bond movies, between on the one hand, obedience to the boss, and on the other, the certainty that in the end they will all be destroyed. It always happens. Yet they never change sides.

The doctor's glance was enough for them now and they piled in once more, but Lionel's fists and feet inflicted blow after blow on them as one by one they went reeling back in pain.

Nellie and Alf were the last to reach the fray, being older than the other two. Even so they piled in, Alf putting a neck lock on one of the men attacking the Captain. Nellie headed straight for the cage like a woman possessed and felled one of Lionel's attackers in a deft judo move. The minions hesitated again, as if some power they did not understand were about to engulf them. No-one expects to be attacked by an old lady unless she is backed by cavalry or at least cover from snipers. The hesitation did not last long. No cavalry or snipers appeared, and the minions, being what they are, reverted to unthinking violence.

At last the Captain was overcome with a low punch to the stomach that doubled him over. One of the minions sat on him while another sat on his legs and yet others tied his flailing feet and hands. They left him in the boat with Lola, bound by ropes. They pushed Alf violently out and he rolled painfully onto the shingle. Then they pushed the boat out to sea and two of the black-clad men leapt in.

Alf stood up. None of the men could bear to look him in the eyes and instinctively backed away from him even as they hit out. He walked toward the cage, where Lionel and Nellie were still fending off their attackers. Alf put his hand up as if asking for silence, and strangely the men obeyed and for a moment all fighting stopped.

"What's in all this for you?" Alf asked them. He made eye-contact with each of them as he spoke. The men looked at each other.

"Are you happy?" he asked them. Again they looked at each other as though someone else might have the answer. They hesitated again. None of this was in the script.

This dangerous moment, in which something strange and new might have been brought to birth, ended suddenly. Alf was felled by a blow from behind, then held and bound and thrown into another boat, a black motorboat sporting the same silvery squid insignia.

Nellie resumed the fight as if she had absorbed legendary and impossible Chinese fighting techniques, crouching ready, surrounded by felled black-suited minions. They came on, one after another. After a while some of the men realised that it was no fun being beaten one at a time, although it would probably make good cinema, so they all rushed her at once, and at last Nellie was down. She too was bound and thrown into the black motorboat alongside Alf. The boat sped off towards the shadow in the sea.

That left Lionel, still standing on the cage, his face calm and alert.

Again there was an ebb in the tide of violence. Tense black uniformed men waited for some signal as to their next move. They could overpower Lionel between them, but no-one wanted to go in first.

The Fight on the Beach

Finally Dr Squidtentacles walked slowly into the circle.

"What's mine is mine," he said calmly, but with an edge of menace. "What are you waiting for?" Then he shot a look at one of the men—he didn't care which one—and the man edged forward. Then another followed. The circle closed.

Meanwhile the boat carrying Lola and the Captain started out to sea, with one man guarding the front and the other steering with the outboard motor. The boat approached the growing watery stain. The hum was now very loud, and directly over the shadow a thin spike broke the surface.

Lola was at the prow end and she turned to make eye-contact with her guard. He leered at her. She smiled back. Suddenly and without warning she thrust her whole weight at him and he fell headlong into the water. A split second later the Captain heaved himself towards the other minion, causing him to jerk the tiller so that the boat spun away from the overboard man. The minion pulled a knife, but Captain Kipper fell on top of him. The man's arm was flattened against the floor of the boat. Lola stood as best she could, standing in a boat with her feet tied not being easy, and hopped, partly crouching, until she was able to jump onto the man's wrist. The knife fell from his hand, she bent and with her teeth grasped the handle. Then with further contortions she set to work on the ropes binding the Captain's hands. With a sawing motion gradually the fibres frayed, until the last few were broken by the Captain himself. The man writhed under the Captain's weight.

Now the Captain set upon his captor and each was at the other's throat. Soon, though, the man turned and bucked under him, dropping the Captain overboard, his feet still bound. The knife was still between Lola's teeth but the man wrenched it from her and kicked her hard in the stomach so that she fell in agony back into the prow. Grabbing the tiller he turned the boat again. The last Lola saw of the Captain was of him trying to swim, weighed down by his clothes, his legs thrashing up and down like a mermaid's tail and his arms waving. Soon she lost sight of him altogether, his body swallowed by the waves.

At last Lionel was overcome. The minions threw him off the cage and pinned him down.

Then others lifted the cage and dropped it into a third boat and Dr Squidtentacles stepped in with the air of a man confident of victory. The black boat joined the other two roaring out to sea.

They left Lionel alone on the shore, bruised and in pain.

As he watched, the three boats approached the shadow. The thin spike rose up. A dark turret appeared under it, looming into the sky. Finally the monstrous body of a nuclear submarine broke the surface of the sea, dwarfing the boats that rocked like bath toys. Water sluiced off its sides in apparent slow motion. Written on the side was its name—KRAKEN—and the sign of the giant squid, glowing white against the dark grey hull and high as a house.

More black-suited minions appeared from a hatch in the submarine, small dots moving about on its roof. Ropes, nets and ladders were lowered over the side. The other minions crawled from the boats like ants, pulling their captives with them. Then one by one they disappeared into the belly of the submarine, closing the hatch after them. The *Kraken* went down until nothing was left except a dark smudge moving out to sea.

From Myfanwy

Hello again Judicious Jellyfish,
Well the date with Dai Gonzales-Jones was a washout because every time some long-legged young woman passed by the teahouse his head swivelled and I had to repeat whatever it was I

was saying. After I while I went to the ladies loo, climbed out of the back window and went home. Men. Feh!

Molten Molecule is obviously in a creative frenzy because he is sending the manuscripts to me to type up thick and fast and I can hardly keep up. The stamps are put on wonky and sometimes I have to pay extra at the post office because he hasn't bothered to weigh the package. Needless to say he doesn't trouble to thank me for my pains. I should be used to it by now.

A kiss,
Myfanwy

41. The First Thing to Do is to Pray

Lionel watched that smudge disappear. His heart was empty. There was not even despair. The sun beat everything into a whiteness.

Then there was anguish. He had been shown something approaching love—a woman's love—or at any rate a mermaid's. That she was a mythological creature made no difference. It is the emotion in a woman's face a man falls in love with, whatever the initial attractions of breasts and thighs, or as in this case, millions of tiny shiny scales.

It had not been said, but it had been there, in her eyes.

His anguish was the loss of something inestimably precious, something that, once sensed, no man or woman can do without. Lionel felt as if a huge wave were about to engulf him and drown him in the dark waters then toss him out onto the sand to dry like driftwood. Perhaps he would carry on his old trade as before. That had not been living, but he had not known anything else. To know is hard to bear.

The wave came and he was still standing. He watched as his emotions writhed like beached creatures of the deep after a tsunami.

He had done everything possible—he had not run away or faltered, he had not considered his own safety, he had not failed for want of trying. He was clean inside. But to stay in that state of grace he knew he had to continue. The struggle goes on. He stood there for what seemed a long time.

Lionel had not seen Captain Kipper fall into the sea, focussed as he had been on protecting the cage in which the mermaid had cowered in a mixture of hope and terror. He thought that all his friends were now beneath the sea in the *Kraken*.

Meanwhile the Captain had not yet succumbed to the waves. He swam like a clumsy mermaid since with his feet tied he had no other option. Many times his head sank beneath the waves and he felt as though he would certainly drown. Then out of the corner of his eye he saw a fish, a fish that followed him smoothly irrespective of the violent movement of the water. The fish that he had seen that night when, under the influence of the wrong kind of tea he had stumbled towards Nellie's house. Unbeliever though he was, he gave up a little prayer to St Doris, although at that moment he expected nothing and hoped nothing. What the prayer consisted of he would not have been able to say. Even so, the half-seen fish gave him courage, or at least persistence, and he continued, not knowing what would happen.

Suddenly his head hit something hard, and again. He reached out to protect himself and found his hands touching the rough granite surface of a sea wall. Blood ran from a wound in his forehead but he hardly noticed. His hands fumbled for something to hold onto as the sea flung him backwards and forwards like a piece of flotsam. Then his fingers found a gap in the masonry and he wedged them in and started to lift himself a little out of the waves. He could not climb, but he could at least hold his head above water. He was at the harbour wall but far from the shore.

His breath came in gasps, and he waited for enough strength to return for him to move. Then he stretched one arm in the direction of the shore and found another finger-hold. Letting go with his other hand, he let the water carry the weight of his body, and pulled. The cold numbed him and he could no longer feel his feet. His hands too were barely his. It would be so easy to sleep now and die.

He closed his eyes for a moment and there, in the corner of his vision, yet luminous as in an aquarium, was the fish. With an effort he opened his eyes and repeated the manoeuvre with his hands, edging perhaps a foot closer to the shore. Still the thing seemed impossible. Still he continued, but each time with less progress than before.

"Lionel!" A voice heard only in Lionel's head. How curious to hear your name spoken in your head, yet from out there, yet not from out there. Lionel stood in amazement as if in a dream. He had no theory, no thought about it. He widened his gaze and then he saw.

"Captain!" This time the voice was real, in the air, and it came from Lionel's mouth. Lionel heard it in wonder, felt his body running up the shore to harbour level, along the harbour wall to the *Saucy Jellyfish*, grabbing a rope from the deck, unwinding it as he ran, then turning it twice around a bollard directly above where the Captain held onto his life by his fingertips, and dropping the end down into the sea.

"Captain!" Again Lionel shouted, and the Captain looked up and grabbed the rope first with one hand then the other, moving slowly as if to make sure that his hands were obeying him. "Hold on!"

Holding on was all the Captain could do. He could no longer move.

Faster than thought, for indeed thought is slow, Lionel ran back to the shore and untied one of the rowing boats, dragged it into the water and jumped in, setting the oars into the rowlocks and pulling. "Let your body do the driving" was what Alf had said back then, when he had tried to drive the little Morris in the dark, crashing the tyres against the muddy banks. Now Lionel's body knew what to do, and it did it with precision and speed.

The little boat bobbed next to the harbour wall and Lionel could not see how to pull the Captain into it without capsizing. "You have to climb up the rope!" he shouted, "Just a little way."

There was a pause in which nothing happened, then with an effort the Captain moved one hand above the other on the rope and pulled. His body rose from the water no more than a foot.

"Again!"

Another foot up. The Captain's waist was above the water.

"Bend your legs!"

The First Thing to Do is to Pray

Then Lionel bent into the water, grabbed the Captain round the knees and hauled his bound feet into the boat, tipping it dangerously and pushing it out away from the harbour wall, the Captain still clinging to the rope. Lionel took the oars again and pulled until the boat was almost under the Captain's body. Then he grabbed him by the waist and pulled the rest of him in together with several gallons of seawater. "Let go!" Lionel ordered, and Captain Kipper dropped heavily. For a moment his open hands remained in the air, as if offering thanks to St Doris, or perhaps because he was so cold he no longer knew what his body was doing.

The kettle whistled on the camping gas stove as the *Saucy Jellyfish* rocked gently. Lionel made two mugs of tea and handed one to the Captain, who sat with a blanket over his shoulders. At first he could barely feel the mug but slowly the warmth of the tea had its magical effect. Tea and true friendship.

"We must set sail, now!" Captain Kipper said as soon as he had stopped shivering enough to say anything.

"You're only just out of the sea!"

"Arr, but our friends be in that submarine, and we must do something."

"But do what?"

"That I don't know. But the great thing is to begin it now."

Lionel paused, confused. "What should I do first? Untie the boat?"

"No," said the Captain decidedly, "the first thing to do is to pray."

Lionel was startled. He looked at the Captain for a moment, then decided to say nothing. He knelt down and put his hands together in the way he remembered from primary school assembly, half closing his eyes. Then he looked at the Captain to see what he would pray for, but the Captain was silent for a long pause. Then noticing Lionel's confusion, the Captain spoke.

"I have learned a few things in the last few days. The most important is friendship. The next is that I know nothing. Then, that it be not my place to say what should happen, but to trust in fish. And if there be a Saint Doris, or something or someone that we choose to call Saint Doris, well... what do I know?"

"Saint Doris... ." Lionel looked doubtful. "And when we pray, what do we pray for?"

"We pray for nothing. It be not our place to do otherwise."

Lionel did not understand, but the two of them knelt in silent prayer.

Then slowly, because the Captain was still barely able to move, they started to prepare the *Saucy Jellyfish*. The Captain started the engine and Lionel unwound the ropes from the bollards. At last the little fishing boat was headed out to sea.

At first there was nothing but the sun beating down on the flat water. The Captain still looked unsteady and the boat passed very close to a bright yellow buoy. Lionel called out, "Aren't we supposed to avoid those?"

"Mebbe. But I know these waters and she'll pass right over those rocks. Nothing to worry about."

They kept going, having no direction and seeing nothing.

Then, unexpectedly, the black conning tower of the atomic submarine broke the surface. The *Saucy Jellyfish* rocked like a toy boat as the dark mass of the *Kraken* heaved up from the deep, shrugging off a million gallons of sea.

From Myfanwy

Hello again Mermen and Mermaids,
After all that frenzy I have heard nothing of Melodious Mackerel for a while. Then yesterday I got a note scrawled on a box of Co-

op 99 tea sent from England (postmarked Milton Keynes) saying he's busy writing the thrilling climax, which is requiring all his skill to accomplish, and signed 'MM.'

I am hoping for a happy ending of course, but the presence of a Greek chorus, even if they are Cornish, is a little worrying.

He sent me a gift! Even though it's only a packet of tea.

I do hope he's all right.

Love and kisses,

Myfanwy

42. What to do when you have nothing left

LIONEL GLANCED BACKWARDS and noticed a few tiny figures down on the shore, then more appearing from the town, and yet others lining the railings along the harbour wall. He could make out the sombreros of the large group of Mexicans mingling with a dark patch of doctors. Lord Fumble could be seen standing next to Ramón Pimiento el Picante. Sidney Sinister was there too. Finally the motley group of Cornish men and women arrived, still wearing the ancient Greek garb of the play, *Carry on Socrates*. Parked outside the *Frothy coffee café* he could see Figgis's patrol car. A large shapely woman hovered nearby, almost certainly his secretary Mavis, and next to her, Pedro, his arm around her waist. Somewhere a young woman pressed through the crowd, Tracy Truth of the Pengoggly Press, her pencil and battered notebook in her pocket and a camera around her neck. There also, pushing their way to the front were Smithers and Edwin Sharck closely followed by Lucretia Fumble, her face a picture of fury.

There was an awed silence, broken only by the cries of seagulls and the swirl of water splashing against the two vessels. Then the hatch of the *Kraken* opened and Dr Squidtentacles stepped out. A loud murmur went up from the crowd.

The doctor raised his hands in a gesture for silence.

Edwin Sharck shouted out from the railings: "Do we have a deal or not?" at the same time as Lucretia was shouting something incoherent and unrepeatable.

The doctor strained to hear, and Sharck shouted again. Then Squidtentacles picked up a megaphone. "Of course we have a deal. Nothing can stop us! We still have planning permission!"

Loud cries of "No!" went up from the players, and Dr Squidtentacles laughed into the megaphone. "You want to stop progress, but where were you when the planning application was there for all to see in the planning office? Have you no respect for the proper way things are done? This will bring prosperity and jobs to Pengoggly, but no, you want everything to stay the same! I tell you nothing ever stays the same!"

Somehow Ramón Pimiento el Picante had acquired a megaphone too. "If you have all thees prosperity, then where ees my money?"

At this all the Mexicans shouted as one, "Give us the money! Give us the money!"

"Ha! You want money for your illegal chillies? Dr Squidtentacles does not give money to criminals! Figgis, arrest that man!"

Figgis was skulking at the back of the crowd, trying to avoid being seen. Smithers elbowed his way violently back through the mass of people towards the patrol car until he found him. "You heard!" he said, grabbing Figgis by the neck of his shirt. Figgis went a shade of puce.

Sergeant Spriggan had turned up together with the dogs and looked on, momentarily stunned. "The Mexican hasn't done anything wrong on Cornish soil, as far as I can see," he said slowly, anticipating perhaps that arresting a man with a large following of mean-looking men in sombreros might not be without problems.

Figgis held Smithers' gaze with a steely eye. Slowly Smithers released his grasp and Figgis straightened his collar. Figgis said and did nothing else. After a pause Smithers retreated into the crowd with a scowl. Mavis saw everything and gave a quiet sigh. Pedro looked on, realising that his day was not yet won.

"You'll be struck off!" This time the cry came from Lord Fumble, and all the dark-suited doctors cried in unison, "Struck off! Struck off!"

"Struck off yourself!" Squidtentacles' megaphone crackled. "Do you imagine I care? The public does not care as long as I tell them things they want to believe. I simply give people what they want."

"Struck off! Struck off!" the doctors continued ever louder, as the Mexicans, not to be outdone, tried to drown them out with a chorus of "Give us the money! Give us the money!"

Amongst all the shouting, Morwenna from the Frothy Coffee Café (whom you may or may not remember from chapter 29) decided that having the largest crowd ever gathered at one time round the harbour was an excellent opportunity to do a bit of business. As it was a hot day she prepared a large quantity of iced tea sweetened with copious amounts of sugar, using a special consignment of herbal tea that she had got cheaply, but which was unfortunately undrinkable in any other form.

Thus a great noise began, louder and louder, overwhelming the gentle splash of the waves against the boats. If you had been there you might have heard it as a hideous din. Yet to Lionel, empty of both hope and strategy, it was like a sound poem flying into the hot summer air, a fugue of the two chants—"Struck off!" "Give us the money!"—interweaving in different time signatures, punctuated by megaphone exchanges in the bass line. Then there were the growls of the two police dogs, Fenrir and Ragnarok. Weaving in and out of all the cacophony one could make out a sweeter melody, "Iced tea? Only a pound. Thank 'ee. Iced tea? Only a pound. Thank 'ee." Then, as in any sufficiently modern composition, the top line inarticulate, irregular, anguished, made by the piercing cries of the gulls. It meant precisely nothing, although to Lionel it also had a strange beauty.

Then one of the players sounded a gong, and the crowd for a moment lapsed into a startled silence. Into the quiet air the Cornish men and women spoke as one. Even the gulls seemed to listen as they wheeled above.

> "Imagination is the way of mortal men
> Wishing the world were other than it is,
> Pulled here and there by unimportant things,
> Missing the wonder of each simple hour.
> Imaginary are our days, passing like dreams,

Schemes left like weed upon the wrack-strewn shore.
O to see truth! Alas we are too full
Of useless thoughts. Only the humble man
Reduced to nothing by fate and heaven's will
Can come again into reality
And change defeat to glorious victory."

"Ha ha ha ha!" shouted Dr Squidtentacles. "You and your ancient notions! Market forces are the engines of prosperity! Sell dreams and spectacle! That's what I'm bringing you—something to distract you from your tedious lives!"

"Why are you telling us all this?" shouted Danzel from the chorus.

"Because you need to be shaken out of your stubborn resistance! You need to stop struggling against me! You need to understand that I cannot be beaten! I'll bring you wealth and pleasure if only you'll cease your futile objections!"

As he spoke the engines of the *Kraken* hummed ominously. Dr Squidtentacles turned up his megaphone and pointed it at Lionel, who still stood, staring up from the deck of the *Saucy Jellyfish*.

"I have won, puny sea worm! Nothing can stop me! I shall bring the *Kraken* into Pengoggly harbour and my men will make sure all my works are completed!" the doctor shouted. "My captives—Nellie, The Higgs Bosun and Lola—will be turned over to the police to be charged with public affray. You, Mr Fishface, will be arrested for attempted theft of my property. Then we can begin to make Pengoggly into a theme park that will bring tourists by the thousand!"

"Your property?" shouted Lionel.

"The mermaid of course!"

The *Kraken* seemed a little nearer to the *Saucy Jellyfish* than before, edging towards the harbour with the little fishing boat in the way.

Meanwhile Ramón was losing patience. The Mexicans piled into the shiny white boat, standing on the sides of the deck and hanging onto the railings. Someone brought up rifles and automatic weapons from below and the boat bristled with armed men. The mariachi band were aboard too, and started up with an uncharacteristically martial tune, something like a Latino version of Beethoven's fifth with heavy metal overtones. Ramón himself took the wheel, and *El Sueño de la Razón* powered out of the harbour and around the back of the *Kraken*.

Not to seem idle, the doctors started to argue amongst themselves that they should do something. A few hotheads said they should take immediate action to dismantle the pink alternative health clinic, others that they should write stiff letters to the press, and yet others that they should wait and see what the government told them to do, not wishing to jeopardise getting MBEs later on for services to making the government look good.

Lionel watched all this, his mind free from thought. The roar of the crowd rose up again, now joined by the *Kraken*'s din, the mariachi band and all, and he remained calm. He did not understand the Captain's new-found faith, yet in some deeper part of himself he accepted that his own resources had run out and there was nothing left but to wait patiently for what might come.

From Myfanwy

Hello again Faithful Fishy Fans,

Wait patiently? I think I've been more than patient waiting for any more thanks from that Mildew Marmalade for all my efforts in sending out the outpourings of his inspired soul. That's exactly the trouble, isn't it? Just because he's inspired he expects the whole universe, or in the present case, me, to put up with him. Just a little word of gratitude is all I want. I like to feel appreciated. Who doesn't?

Anyway, I've given up altogether on Dai Gonzales-Jones because a woman needs someone who is reasonably attentive as well as desperately handsome. Or attentive and passably good-looking. Or at least not a total scruff.

But enough of my moaning. I have no idea how Lionel is going to get out of this. A little man in a fishing boat standing up to a nuclear-powered submarine. I just hope Mildew hasn't run out of inspiration or this story is as doomed as the *Saucy Jellyfish* appears to be.

I am blowing you, faithful readers, a few wan kisses,
Myf
x...o...x...O...x...o

43. The vision of St Doris

MEANWHILE THE HERBAL TEA was beginning to have its effect. Morwenna was not to have known that it was contaminated with some of Ramón's chillies, which accounted not only for its piquant taste but also for strange apparitions that now affected the crowd.

As the Kraken drifted threateningly towards the Saucy Jellyfish, Danzel gave a shout, pointing towards the horizon. Everyone on the shore stared. At first all that could be seen was the blinding haze of sun on the sea. Then there was a form made of sunlight and vapour. Just as a picture can form in clouds, it resolved into something temporarily definite.

Once more the crowd including all the Mexicans and the mariachi band fell silent, leaving only the loud hum of the Kraken and the engines of El Sueño de la Razón ploughing the sea on the other side. The Kraken continued to drift closer to the little fishing boat. Lionel and the Captain could not see the vision because of the bulk of the submarine looming over them, and Dr Squidtentacles could not see it either, so intent was he on dominating the crowd. It was the Greek chorus that gave it a name.

"Saint Doris!"

The doctor turned. "There's nothing there! You're deluded!"

"You don't see because you have no eyes for the truth!" shouted Danzel from the shore.

It seemed to many in the crowd that the saint rode on a scallop shell drawn by huge spotted sea slugs, their fringes waving with the grace of angels, the saint herself full of light and majesty. Some saw only a vague glowing form, but for a few even the face of the saint became visible in glimpses—impassive, serene, implacable.

The Vision of St Doris

"Get out of my way, Fishface! I shall crush you!" shouted the doctor, not understanding why the fishing boat was still there, not understanding why Captain Kipper had not turned the *Saucy Jellyfish* around and headed for safety, not understanding why Lionel still stood there doing nothing. The doctor barked an order down the hatch. There was an unheard reply from below which seemed to enrage him, and he shouted again to some invisible minion below. The hum of the *Kraken*'s engines deepened, the huge vessel now turned its prow directly towards the *Saucy Jellyfish* and its speed increased. The little fishing boat was about to be pinned between the *Kraken* and the harbour wall.

Captain Kipper blanched but held steady on the wheel. Lionel made eye-contact with him, his face expressing a question he did not need to say out loud.

"We hold firm," was the answer.

Now the Mexicans began to shoot, with rounds of automatic fire clattering against the hull of the *Kraken* from the other side. The doctor dived for cover down the hatch, shouting through the megaphone as he went, "Get out of the way Fishface! I am not responsible for what will happen to you! You will be crushed! You are nothing I tell you. Nothing!"

There were shouts from *El Sueño de la Razón* as several bullets ricocheted off the impenetrable side of the *Kraken* and back onto the shiny yacht, denting its hull in an ugly line. More and louder shouts followed as some of the bullets hit the Mexicans too, and several of them fell into the water. The mariachi band played several bars of Schoenberg, and a bullet grazed the shoulder of Ramón himself. At a barked order all shooting ceased and lifeboats were lowered.

At this the doctor re-emerged and stood on the top of the *Kraken*, laughing hysterically. "Fools!" he shouted, before again disappearing below.

The periscope of the submarine now turned on Lionel, and the *Kraken* gathered pace. There were only a few yards between the looming prow of the submarine and the fishing boat. Lionel felt faint and looked at the Captain. The Captain set his jaw and did not move.

Lionel's fear was total. It engulfed him. Then something, he knew not what or how, let him fall through it as though the fear were a sea of nameless trouble and he was not the sea. He gave himself up to fate. There was nowhere to go and nothing to do. He felt himself to be that nothing.

With a sickening impact the *Kraken* hit the side of the *Saucy Jellyfish*. It rocked violently and there was a splintering of wood as part of the deck rail gave way. The boat tipped at an increasing angle. Lionel found himself hanging onto what remained of the rail to avoid sliding across the deck and into the sea the other side. Captain Kipper held fast to the wheel, his feet in water that swirled up onto the deck.

"Don't worry!" shouted the Captain. In part of Lionel's mind this seemed an absurd, almost humorous thing to say, but there was no use or time for worry. As happens in a catastrophe, time changes. The mind, clean of every unnecessary thought, functions with extraordinary speed, taking in every detail, responding calmly. Moments go by, one by one, in no hurry. Yet each moment calls forth its proper response, without argument or debate. The gap between necessity and action disappears.

Yet that action was still to hold fast and do nothing.

The *Kraken* ploughed on, pushing the little fishing boat towards the harbour wall as if to crush it like an egg.

From Myfanwy

Well my Nihilistic Nematodes, it looks like the end for Lionel. I don't see how he can get out of this at all. I think Mordred Mollusc

The Vision of St Doris

has totally lost the plot and his mind has been overtaken by what those naughty philosophers will probably call *Angsty* or something German-sounding like that. Anyway, the next chapter is a poetical interlude, which makes it worse, because I'm sort of in love with the mermaid, and with Lionel, and I really think Mordred should go against the tide of what I call Modern Moping and write a happy ending.

—sigh—
Myf
x

From Professor Neville Twistytrouser

Hello Philosophical Chums,
The words my continental friends use are *Angst* and *Weltschmerz* since these words sound more respectable than Modern Moping. Mope not! We live on the "fairest isle, all isles excelling,"[*] and even when we do not stand on it with our feet yet still we hold it in our hearts, and will have no truck with moping! A walk by the river preferably ending at a country pub and a jar of *Hook Norton* Ale will cure most things.

On with the story, I say. The next bit is indeed somewhat poetical.

Neville

---

[*] John Dryden (1631–1700), Song of Venus, from Henry Purcell's opera King Arthur.

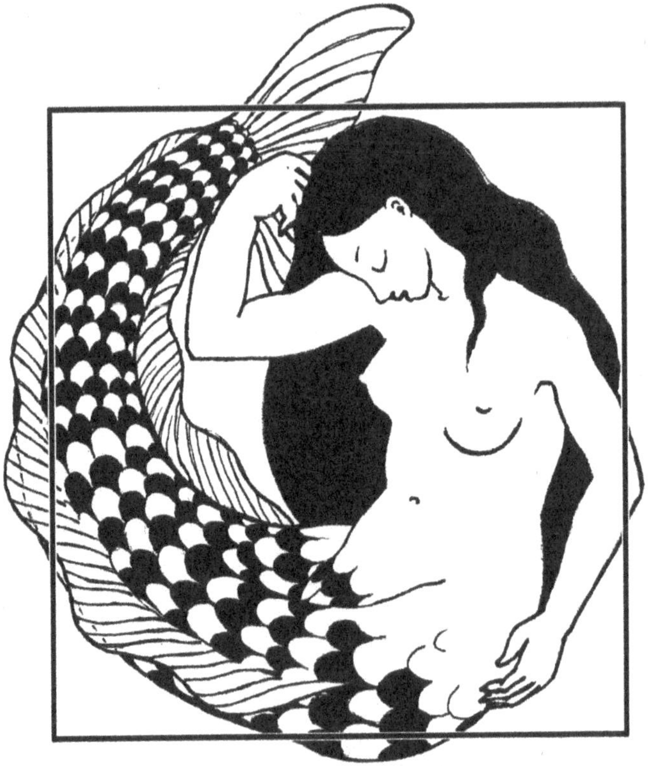

44. The mermaid's sleep

IN HER IRON CAGE deep in the bowels of the *Kraken* our mermaid sleeps. Yet her sleep is not like our sleep—or in a way it is, but our own sleep is something we do not properly understand.

In our own dream we see her face—placid, her eyes closed under heavy lids, her lips barely parted. She has the trace of a smile. Her breath whispers as her breasts gently rise and fall. The cold iron bars indent the flesh of her back as she lies there, curled up, and her sparkling tail flicks occasionally as if dreaming a dream all its own.

How can this be? Despite all that she has endured, her sleep is the sleep of the just. In that sleep there are no thoughts, no images, almost nothing that can be remembered later. In deepest sleep we, like the mermaids, return to the nameless origin. A love so total that we are lost in it. Later only a trace of that endlessness will remain, as a reminder, a fragment of lost treasure, as something almost altogether forgotten on coming into that state we call "waking."

Our waking is the dream until we learn to carry that endless nothing in the heart.

She murmurs—perhaps now she is moving towards the everyday state through the dream world, that world of shadows and imagination. Perhaps now she is calling out to Lionel, the man who fell in love with her. Perhaps she is also calling on the saints and angels. Her fishy tail sometimes looks for all the world like two legs close together.

45. Inside the Kraken

THE INSIDE OF THE KRAKEN was a confusion of machinery. Banks of grey cabinets encrusted with switches and dials lined a labyrinth of narrow corridors. There was a continuous hum interrupted by mechanical noises, some near, some farther away. Then there were loud whirring sounds, surging and diminishing, that sounded wrong, like an engine in distress. Metal tubes shot down the corridors in rigid lines before bending abruptly into some other passageway. Tangles of dusty cables hung from the roof in swags. Occupying these spaces were crowds of black-uniformed minions, some leaning against the walls, staring vacantly, others furiously busy.

No-one seemed to be in charge.

Those engaged in busy tasks jostled against one another, getting in each other's way, yet they barely spoke to one another. It was as if each were in a world of his own. Every now and then one of them barked an order and a few of the others would stop and change what they were doing, only to return to their previous activity a few moments later as if nothing had happened.

Suddenly and with a horrible juddering the deck lurched upward. Minions fell onto railings, onto machinery, into each other. Somewhere deep inside the submarine the mermaid's cage slid from one end of the deck to the other until it crashed onto a minion's leg, pinning it to a steel girder. The minion pushed the cage away and then for no reason aimed a kick at the mermaid, disfiguring her thigh with a bruise of blood and torn scales and at the same time hurting his foot on the bars. She cried, softly. He limped away, cursing.

A barrage of barked orders came through the tannoy in a stream, but no-one could understand anything except the curse words.

"What do we do?"
"We're supposed to fight to the death."
"Why?"
"Because we're minions, and that's what minions do."
"I want to be a real person and go home."
"There is no home. This submarine is all there is."
"That's not true. There's Cornwall isn't there? We were in St Doris Island once."
"That is a fantasy. The past does not exist. There is space and time. Shadows. It means nothing."
"Let's go home."
"We can't"
"Why not?"
"We have no home."
"Oh."
"We're not real people anyway."
"What are we then?"
"The Higgs Bosun asked us if we were happy. I'm not."
"Someone bashed him over the head before he could explain the alternative."
"That's right. Let's go and ask him what to do."
"I'd have shot him on St Doris Island."
"Let's not bother to ask him. It's pointless. A comforting fantasy that there might be an answer, that's all it is."
"Well I'm going."
"Face up to reality. This is all there is. There is no path in the sky."

Even so a handful of minions walked to where Alf, Nellie and Lola were imprisoned in a small cell behind bars. The minions knew they had a question, and they stood there for a while, trying to articulate it. Lola curled her lip and Nellie looked nervous. Alf had a calm expression, close to compassion.

Eventually a minion spoke up: "There has to be something better than this."

"Yes," Alf said, simply.
"What should we do to find it?"
"You must first become real."
"How?"
"Understand that this is all there is."
"But…"
"There is no path in the sky."[*]
"But…"
"Understand that this this contains everything."
"That can't be all. What else?"
"You must learn to disbelieve all your anger. In fact you must learn to disbelieve all your thoughts."

The minions looked at each other, puzzled, as though they did not know where to start. As if hearing their unasked question, Alf said, "You have to start now. There is no other time available to you."

Then Alf lapsed into silence, and the minions all started talking at once, about how difficult it was, how surely it was right to be angry when things did not go your own way, about the injustice in the world, about how suppressing anger can make you ill, and many other things besides. They bombarded him with more questions, but no further entreaties would get anything more from him.

Then for some reason hard to understand one of them took the key from a hook on the wall and unlocked the cage. Alf turned to the other two with his finger to his lips. "You must become nothing," he whispered.

They went out silently while the minions argued among themselves, apparently not noticing Alf and the others at all. Only the minion who had unlocked them saw. It occurred to him for the first time that he had no name.

---

[*] Buddha, *Dhammapada*

They walked swiftly but without thought, or as little as they could manage, looking for the mermaid. The minions seemed distracted, some in arguing with each other, others with obsessional tasks involving the controls of the submarine. Rarely a minion would challenge them, and Alf would agree with whatever was said, show deference, smile or look downcast according to whatever was expected, and create as little disturbance as possible in the minion's mind. Mostly the minions seemed reassured by the presence of the nameless one, who followed Alf like a puppy.

The farther they went into the metal labyrinth the more confusing it became. Meanwhile the floor was tilting at a gradually increasing angle. There was no more time, and no choice but to ask.

"The mermaid!" Alf barked to one of the minions. "The boss wants the mermaid taken out of the *Kraken* immediately!" The nameless minion nodded. The one addressed pointed down the corridor. "It's not my job. Ask someone else."

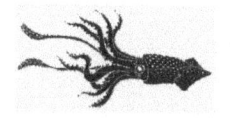

From Prof. Alphonse Pince-Nez

Chères Amateurs de Sirènes,
Well what do you make of that, hein? A lot of talk of Nothing—i.e, *le Néant*. Très interessant, n'est-ce pas? I shall immediately write a 500-page book about Nothing.
 Â bientôt,
 Alphonse

From Professor Neville Twistytrouser

Ha ha! Enough said.
  Neville

46. The missing mermaid

WITH A GRINDING OF METAL the submarine loomed up, seeming vaster than before, water streaming off the newly-revealed underside of the prow. Then the Kraken slowed and started to list ominously, pushing the Saucy Jellyfish towards the harbour wall.

"Arr, she be hitting those rocks! Even a submarine be no match for Cornwall granite!"

With the inevitability of Newton's First Law of Motion the Saucy Jellyfish continued to drift away from the Kraken, righting itself as it did so, and the little yellow buoy to which they had earlier sailed so close scraped round the side of the fishing boat, reappearing on the other side next to the submarine. The Kraken slowed to a standstill, its prow now towering above the fishing boat, showering the deck with seawater, and the list towards the harbour wall increased.

As Lionel watched, four figures emerged from a hatch at the top of the Kraken. Rope ladders unrolled down the side, and the figures started to clamber down. Captain Kipper steered up to the Kraken, and the Saucy Jellyfish's boat bumpers nudged the Kraken's dark grey hull.

There was Lola, coming down first. Then the nameless minion. Then Alf with Nellie following, Alf ready to catch her should she fall, yet Nellie seemed hardly less sprightly than any of them. But no mermaid.

"Where's the mermaid?" Lionel shouted.

At first Alf was too far away to hear against the crashing of the waves and the noise of the Kraken's straining engines.

"Where's the mermaid?" again, louder.

"Dear, we couldn't find her," Nellie said as her foot touched the deck of the Saucy Jellyfish. Her face was a mask of controlled anguish. Alf nodded.

Lola was in tears. "It's a labyrinth in there. No-one would tell us where she was. We went everywhere. We even had a plan to find Dr Squidtentacles and make him give her up, but we couldn't find him either. It's hopeless."

Lionel looked at the Captain as if the Captain would have an answer.

"It's like we did before," Captain Kipper said. "You have to start. You only know that you have to start."

Lionel turned to Alf. "That's the way it is, Lionel. From the moment the mermaid arrived in your bath you had something to accomplish. I have a feeling that only you can do it. We cannot help you any more."

"How is he going to do it if we couldn't?" Lola cried. Her distress was enough to show how much they had tried.

All the Captain's inner turmoil about whether Lola really loved him was gone in that moment. It didn't matter. All that mattered was the woman in front of him. Without thinking he walked over to her and held both her hands in his.

"He'll find a way, I know it," he said, looking into her eyes. Doubter though he was, his faith just then was unshakeable.

It was the right thing said at the right time, and the message was for Lionel as much as it was for Lola. Without another word Lionel stepped onto the rope ladder and started to climb. Out of the corner of his eye he saw Alf hugging Nellie tenderly, she frozen in anguish.

From Myfanwy

Well now Sweet Shrimps,
I'm busy typing up the manuscript of the next chapter, which is really thrilling, because Lionel finds the evil Dr Squidtentacles in his lair. Ooh, I mustn't give too much away.

And another thing, which is really really exciting, well a bit, I'm trying to stay calm, is that Marzipan Mountebank has written me an actual letter! And he says I'm to come back to England at once, because he's run out of postage stamps to send all this stuff to Argentina. What he really means is he misses me and my inimitable Welsh cooking and most of all my Welsh exoticness. Well who wouldn't?

Even geniuses have normal human needs, you know, and I'm the one to rescue him from his pile of unwashed socks, amongst other things.

Well I must get back to typing Marzipan's words. The keys are getting red hot.

mwah! mwah! mwah!

Myfanwy

47. The Song

"If the others couldn't find Dr Squidtentacles," thought Lionel as he ascended the ladder, "how can I?" He banished this thought as unnecessary, and his mind became clear, like the sea on a calm day. When one has no power and no plan but only the necessity to go on, thought is useless, he thought. Then he banished that thought as well. Not that it went away, just that it swam in that sea like one of a number of unconsidered fish.

He entered the hatch and descended into the body of the *Kraken*. There were the minions doing their various tasks, seemingly oblivious of the impending sinking of the submarine. They seemed not to notice him at all. Without a map or direction Lionel simply walked on past dangling cables and humming machinery, the peace in his mind strangely undisturbed by the intense longing in his heart.

"My mermaid," he thought: not that he believed he possessed her, more that she possessed him. The thought was but the echo of an unshakeable feeling of certainty, though certainty of what he could not say. He could find the mermaid or he could die, or many other things could happen. Everything was and always would be exactly as it should be. He walked on and on.

Then above the grinding of the submarine's engines and the horrible clamour of the minions cursing and ordering each other about, he heard, faintly but definitely, a song.

How he could hear such a song above the noise is one of the mysteries of perception. They say the eye can see a telegraph wire that makes an impression on the retina smaller than the size of any of the retinal cells. In the same way, a lover can hear the song of the beloved through all the chaos of the mind.

The more he listened to that song the stronger it became. He let the mind rest on it with a continuous effort, never letting go. He let it lead him, through more grey corridors, and he felt the heat increase. The agony of the failing engines became deafening. For a moment the song ceased.

Suddenly, turning a corner, Lionel came upon a huge space several storeys high. Dominating the space were the engines themselves, with pipes spitting clouds of dirty steam in many places. The clouds lit up intermittently as unseen sparks crackled inside them. Everywhere there were dials with twitching needles, many of them on red. Towards a bulkhead was the opening of a large cylindrical tube, and sitting in the tube a stubby vessel, like the cockpit of an old-fashioned fighter plane with its perspex window raised. It appeared to be a one-man submarine, an escape pod. All of this Lionel became aware of in a split second, at the periphery of his vision. Resting in the centre of his attention was the mermaid herself, still trapped in her iron cage, magical, unspeakably beautiful. And bending over her, panting for breath, Dr Squidtentacles.

There were ugly scratches in the metal floor where the doctor had heaved the cage towards the miniature submarine, with now only a yard to go to a small ramp leading up to it. At the sight of Lionel he looked up.

"So, you have wrecked my plans this time. By my bad luck rather than by any skill on your part. You are nothing, I tell you, nothing. But I am not finished yet. I have the mermaid, and I have planning permission and all the powers I need to see the job done. I'll be back soon enough!"

Lionel took a step forwards. "She doesn't belong to you," he said simply.

"She's mine. She's my way to everything I want."

"No, it is impossible for you to have her without losing her. She will pine away if you try to trap her. She is a wild thing and she belongs to no-one."

"Then how can you have her? What is your claim on her?"

"I have no claim on her. I love her."

At this the mermaid looked at Lionel with an indescribable expression. There was something of endless peace in that face, and something of agony. Her fishy tail glowed oddly and its boundary with the air became indistinct, as if about to undergo some kind of transformation.

Then she opened her mouth and sang again.

At first Dr Squidtentacles failed to notice. He bent to resume his task of heaving the mermaid's cage into the escape pod, sweating and grunting, ignoring Lionel as if he didn't exist. Lionel ran towards the cage and the doctor's head snapped up. In his right hand was a gun.

Lionel stopped in his tracks. The two men faced each other, for a moment frozen. The mermaid's song continued, moving in some ancient mode, unfamiliar.

"Back off!"

Lionel did not move. The song pushed at the door of his heart and he let it in without resistance.

"I said back off!"

Lionel started to walk towards the cage. The mermaid's song became firmer without ever becoming loud. The notes seemed to penetrate the flesh. The doctor shook a little. He seemed to be hearing it now.

"I could kill you. Self-defence! No witnesses to say otherwise." The sparks from the machinery became more frequent and the lights flickered on his face.

Lionel expressed no emotion. "It would be a long and difficult trial."

The doctor looked extremely uncomfortable. He looked about him as though distracted by the singing. His face looked pale.

Now the mermaid's song rose in intensity. The harmonies belonged everywhere and nowhere. For a moment one might have thought of an Indian rag, then of an Islamic maqam, then of Shetland fiddle music, then of Bach.

Slowly the doctor sank to his knees, tears streaming down his cheeks. "This music is what I've wanted all my life," he said, "but I never knew it."

"It's not the tune that matters, it's the gaps between the notes that count." Where that thought had come from Lionel did not know. Now the doctor seemed in a trance. His right arm reached out as though trying to reach through the gap between the notes in some synaesthetic hallucination. As the doctor's hand approached him Lionel gently relieved it of the gun.

"All will be well," Lionel said.

"I've been looking for the wrong things." The doctor's face was that of a child bewildered.

"The key?" Lionel asked. Meekly Dr Squidtentacles handed him the key to the cage.

Lionel opened it. The mermaid looked up at him with quiet joy. The hinted transformation of her tail now started in earnest. Her scales smoothed out, changing from iridescent blue to *café au lait* tinged with warmth. At the same time her tail bifurcated, starting with the indentation at the top and moving down to the end. One tail became two, then each firmed up into two rounded thighs, well-formed knees, calves, feet. Last of all there were fins shrinking into two rows of toes. There was a large bruise on her thigh where the minion had kicked her, and scratches caked with blood, but these blemishes could not detract from her perfection. She stood up.

"I love you," she said. It was the first time he had ever heard her speak.

He would have embraced her, but awe of her nakedness stopped him. It was a sight that almost blinded him, that shocked him, that removed all doubts, that burned away everything that the old Lionel had been. He saw. He understood.

Lionel took off his jacket and helped her on with it. Then he took off his shirt, and by tying the arms together round her waist made a makeshift skirt, making sure the opening with the buttons was at the unbruised side of her thigh for the sake of the aesthetics of it. She looked quite the fashion. Yet fashion is but the art of revelation of a beauty that is already there.

He had not forgotten the doctor, who might break out of the spell at any time.

"Sing again," Lionel whispered. Tentatively, he reached out and touched the mermaid's hand, and she grasped his firmly in hers, as though never to let go.

She sang: a song of darkness, for they were not yet safe. They walked backwards a few steps, hand in hand, always keeping an eye on the doctor. There was an ominous hiss from somewhere in the machinery, dirty steam began to fill the engine room from above downwards. The grinding of the engines ceased as something somewhere seized up. The doctor looked up in fear and with a great effort hauled himself into the escape pod, as if torn between the song and his fear of imminent destruction. Finally he turned, closed the hatch and punched the controls. With a hiss the escape pod shot along the tube and out of sight.

From Myfanwy

Hello again Corruscating Cockles,
Well I was wrong about the *Saucy Jellyfish* being crushed, wasn't I? But anyway, Lionel isn't out of trouble yet. Ooh! It's a little bit exciting isn't it?

I got my plane ticket and I'm queueing up waiting to go through security at the airport as I type this little note to send to mermaid fans around the world.

Ah! The mermaid!
Love is such a wonderful thing if you can get it.
A big sigh!
Myf
x x x x x x

48. The Quiet Exercise of Free Will

There was now so much steam in the engine room that it was hard to see clearly. Lionel looked to see if there was an obvious 'off' switch. Nothing was obvious. There were banks of levers. Was up 'off' or 'on'? What would happen if the nuclear engine went critical?

Lionel guessed up was 'off' and proceeded to test this assumption by pushing a lever up that was near to one of the dials showing red. This caused the needle to drop back towards the amber zone, which seemed promising, but then some of the other needles started to climb from amber to red. He tried the next lever, but the hiss of steam increased and a staccato alarm started to sound, along with a flashing red light, so he switched it on again. Then the next and the next, and as one dial showed an improvement something got worse somewhere else.

If it all went wrong it would not just be Lionel who would be destroyed—that was something that strangely didn't worry him. But if the submarine exploded Pengoggly and all its inhabitants would be showered in radioactive ash, mummified forever in death like Herculaneum and Pompeii. And his mermaid would die.

He began to panic, switching levers up and down, trying to find the combination that would let everything settle down. Since he didn't understand the machine his efforts were random. Somewhere in his accountant's brain something was counting the number of levers and calculating the odds. If the number of levers is X and each has two states, 'off' and 'on,' then the number of possible combinations is two to the power X. Then if the number of safe states is Y the probability of selecting a safe state at random is... very low, on any reasonable assumption. His eyes glazed over as his hands mechanically moved the levers in a frenzy, sweat beading his brow and streaming down his face.

Alarms added one to another in a dissonant fugue, paining the ears.

To be defeated now....

He felt a hand on his shoulder. It was the mermaid, and he turned. Her eyes were calm. Just as when he had first let himself be changed by her, back at the beginning with the fish tea, they were eyes he wanted to drown in. The panic moved to the side of his mind, like an obsessed actor who is being ignored by the principal characters. Nevertheless he knew that something had to be done, and fast.

For the second time the mermaid spoke.

"To defeat this machine we have to switch everything off. Everything."

Of course. Lionel turned again with a new clarity of purpose. The mermaid stood by his side, and together they set about switching every lever to the off position, working as fast as they could. Now more than two-thirds of the levers were off, but lights flashed and alarms continued to sound in a deafening crescendo.

Then minions appeared in the doorway all talking at once. Several of them ran towards Lionel and started to wrestle with him, trying to turn the levers back on. Others shouted from the sidelines.

"It's a waste of time!"

"Nothing will come of it!"

"You don't know what you're doing!"

"We'll all die!"

"It's too late!"

Lionel fought them, but the more he did so the worse it became. He became locked in struggle with one of the minions while the others switched on as many levers as they could get to. Some of the minions even switched off levers that the others had switched on. They started shouting at each other, contradicting each other.

Once again the mermaid spoke.

The quiet exercise of free will

"Ignore them," she said, "they don't matter."

Lionel obeyed. Free will is like that. When a man is free, he is free to obey. Instead of struggling he simply moved to other levers and turned them off instead. He paid the minions no heed, but moved swiftly, pushing levers up wherever he could, the mermaid doing the same. As the pace increased the minions seemed to lose heart, as though their very existence depended on Lionel's struggling with them, paying them attention. If a minion got in his way he simply patted him on the head and told him to come back later. The screaming of the alarms began to level off.

The minions' efforts slowed almost to a standstill as Lionel and the mermaid turned off the last few levers. Finally the *Kraken* fell silent, the alarms stopped, the lights ceased to flash, and there was just a hiss of steam escaping, like an old-fashioned kettle that has been taken off the hob.

The minions stood there, not knowing what to do. There was a soft muttering as each of them gave his view of the situation and the next one disagreed. Their muttering became quieter as one by one they wandered off, each departing one shaking his head as an expression of sorrow that only he was right and the rest were all wrong.

The floor tilted some more. It was time to leave.

From Prof. Neville Twistytrouser

Ah, well, Philosophical Chums, *free will*.

Now there's a conundrum.

'When a man is free, he is free to obey.' What do you make of that, eh?

In a material universe, does not everything happen by inevitable mechanical laws? And if there is some quantum indeterminacy, that can make no more difference than if some of our actions were to be determined by the toss of a coin! Tossing a coin is not free will.

So how can there be free will at all?

Thinking caps on!

Neville

The little bench under the overhanging willow by the bike sheds, St Doris College, Oxford

49. The power of nothing

THEY RAN THROUGH THE GREY CORRIDORS, confused minions pushing and shoving around them. By following the majority of the minions Lionel and the mermaid found the metal ladder to the exit hatch and climbed up among them. Finally they found the air and the clear sky of Cornwall.

Standing on the slanting deck they saw the steel framework of the planned hotel coming towards them like the vision of some half-built tower of Babel. As the *Kraken* continued to tilt, the side of the submarine locked into the girders, crushing, bending them. Half-finished slabs of reinforced concrete fractured, scoring the side of the *Kraken* as it continued its fall.

The tide of black-suited minions swirled around Lionel and the Mermaid, emerging like ants from a nest that has been stirred, crawling over the hull of the stricken vessel and dropping by handfuls into the sea. Soon the water was full of swimming minions making for the shore.

Hand-in-hand Lionel and the mermaid jumped. The sea was cold and the shock of it took Lionel's breath away. He fell like a stone through the water. He was aware of being squeezed tight. Then he blacked out.

The next thing he knew he was on the deck of the *Saucy Jellyfish* with the mermaid leaning over him, smiling, her salt hair dripping into his face.

"Arr, thanks to your mermaid you still be in the land of the living." Captain Kipper beamed. There was Lola looking radiant, her arm round the Captain's waist as though stuck to him for good. And there was Alf, self-controlled as always, but with his eyes shining.

Nellie was bending over the mermaid, her hand on the mermaid's shoulder. Her expression had not had time to adjust from the fear of loss. She turned to Alf. "Our daughter, Kerensa."[*]

Slowly the *Kraken* continued its descent. The sea wall gave way and the sea flooded into what would have been the underground car park. Falling concrete crashed through the roof of the pink clinic which then caught fire. A gas explosion threw debris high in the air and the crowd ran for cover. The intense heat distorted the steel girders into the semblance of a modern sculpture and a plume of acrid smoke rose up from the tangled remains.

As the minions gathered on the shingle among the boats the noise of an engine could be heard on the far side of the stricken *Kraken*. There emerged a miniature submarine in the shape of a torpedo, racing out to sea. Dr Squidtentacles raised the cockpit roof for a moment to shout: "I'll be back! You haven't seen the last of me!" shaking his fist in the time-honoured manner of defeated villains.

Ramón shouted back from the deck of *El Sueño de la Razón*, "¿Nothing can stop you, eh? ¡Es la verdad! ¡You say Mr Fishface is Nothing and then he stop you!*[†]* ¡Ha!" and with that he shot at the retreating doctor in a gesture more of spirited defiance than bloody intent. In any event he missed.

---

[*] *Kerensa*: a Cornish name meaning *love*.
[†] Thanks to Homer for this joke, adapted from Book IX of the *Odyssey*.

The power of nothing

Myfanwy here! You may skip this boring philosophical rambling from Professor Alphonse Pince-Nez and read my note which follows after. Mwah!

Chères Saltimbanques de la Pensée,
My skeptical friend Professor Twistytrouser is confused about how can there be free will. Eh bien, that is an easy one! If everything is predetermined, then even the efforts of a hero are predetermined. So the hero must make such efforts, including the exercise of will, because that is part of the predetermination.

It is like this. One may think of destiny as a tapestry woven by the Fates, just as Lionel's story is woven by the goddess Aerfen. Within the tapestry are all manner of events. Some of these events could not happen without the exercise of will. Par example, we may see the picture of Odysseus deciding that he must leave the island of Calypso. Eh bien, he decides and then he does! Later in the tapestry we see him sailing away on the raft he has made. He eventually arrives at Ithaka, exactly as decided by the gods. Voilà!

Thus free will exists at the moment of effort, even if, as seen from afar, everything appears to proceed according to destiny. The Greeks, they had no problem with this idea, unlike my English friend! It is a matter of looking at things on the correct scale.

Now, as to this Nothing in this chapter, that is a thing très difficile à comprendre.
   Â bientôt,
   Alphonse

From Myfanwy

Dear Pulchritunous Planktons,
Here I am finally at the bus stop at Milton Keynes railway station, waiting for a number 28 to take me to the Co-op and Milton

Marmalade's shed. I'm all excited. Even the prospect of dealing with his pile of unwashed socks is somehow appealing.

I say socks because he doesn't often change his shirts or other clothing, but socks, well, the sensation of putting on yesterday's socks is seldom pleasant, even for a man.

Not very politically-correct am I? But it's not the socks you see— men can be trained to wash their own socks, given a forceful enough woman. But we have to be resourceful when it comes to affairs of the heart, and sometimes the way to a man's heart is through his socks.

I shall not bore you about the flight, which was in economy. My ankles are puffy and I feel all sticky. I don't know why but international flights make me want to have a long soak in the bath, preferably with a glass of champagne on the side, next to my yellow rubber duck. Brings us back to the beginning of the story, the rubber duck, doesn't it?

I happen to know that the struggle is not quite over for Lionel, as there are still the minions to deal with, and of course Ramón still has his eye on Lola. I have typed up the next chapter and I shall shortly deal with Milton Marmalade, never fear.

love and kisses,
Myfanwy

50. The last temptation

Swimming minions dotted the sea. Others began to fill the shore, moving between the boats like scurrying insects on their way up to the harbour-side. There they gathered, humming and jostling: a swarm of wasps that might attack if disturbed, or might do nothing. They variously lolled against walls, smoked cigarettes, stared into space disconsolately, played with mobile phones or picked their teeth. There was a restlessness about them.

Meanwhile El Sueño de la Razón returned to the harbour, spilling Mexicans back onto the shore.

The flames in the building site died down and in their place billows of acrid smoke rose up. People started to come out from where they had hidden from the falling debris, mostly emerging from the café, and watched in silence as the Saucy Jellyfish coasted gently towards the harbour.

As the side of the fishing boat touched the harbour wall the silence continued for several breaths. This was no ordinary silence, the mere absence of sound. It was a silence of wonder, of depth, of relief from suffering. A silence in which one might feel that anything at all could be accomplished, and yet nothing needed to be done.

Somewhere in the crowd there was a ripple, a little sound of something like joy. Then the Kasteldrog chorus cheered and the rest of the crowd burst into rapturous applause which went on for several minutes.

The crowd of doctors and Mexicans, all mingled together, joined in, not quite sure why they were cheering but enjoying the feeling and the spectacle of it all the same. At least their arch enemy had been vanquished, although the doctors had failed to take him back to London to face the Inquisition and the

Mexicans had failed to retrieve their money. Ramón stood at the front of them next to Lord Fumble. Ramón's eyes were on Lola.

Somewhere at the back of the crowd Edwin Sharck slunk away. There was nothing more for him here. He would undoubtedly be replaced at the next council election and the project was dead. It was time to move on. Smithers likewise faded out of the crowd. If joy had been a detergent Smithers would have been the stain.

Danzel, too, left the milling crowd. There was something more to be done, and he was the man to do it. Dr Squidtentacles's Land Rover was still there, its door open, key in the ignition. At this momentous time he would be forgiven for borrowing it. If not forgiven then he would give himself up to Figgis and face the consequences. One may do what is right and still have to take what comes of it.

What of Figgis? You may well guess that Figgis's little act of courage in the face of Smithers' bullying had softened Mavis's already pliant heart. Mercurial Mexicans come and go, but in the end a woman needs a man who is stable, even if a little less exciting than one might dream of. She placed her arm round Figgis's waist and pulled him to her ample form, and Figgis tried to prevent his smile from becoming wider than would be seemly for an officer of the law.

The *Saucy Jellyfish* was now safely roped to the harbour-side bollards. The cheering became even louder as the seven friends came ashore. First Alf stepped onto the quay and turned to hold Nellie's hand as she disembarked. She needed no help but she accepted this symbolic gesture of manly courtesy. Nellie knew how to reciprocate by being a woman both strong and graceful. She beamed at the crowd, and the beauty of her smile was old and glorious as the sun. Alf cast a wary glance across to the humming swarm of minions, then acknowledged the crowd with a nod. Then there was the minion without a name, still following Alf like a puppy.

Next came Lionel, dripping wet, his hair tousled, not looking like a drowned rat but upright, like a man transformed. Then the mermaid Kerensa, radiant, extraordinary. Everyone, man or woman, fell in love with her at once. A long collective sigh echoed round the harbour.

Then the Captain helped the lovely Lola onto the shore and finally he too stepped onto dry land.

Ramón stepped towards Lola and immediately the Captain was there, standing between them. "Ye shall not pass!" he said.

Ramón stopped. His face was relaxed and his usual grin intact. "I may be a villain in your eyes," he said, "but I know that Lola is no longer mine. I too saw St Doris, and I am a good Catholic, señor. It is no shame to bow before what is holy."

With that he retreated with some dignity back into the crowd of Mexicans and doctors.

Meanwhile Mavis, who loved animals, noticed that Sergeant Spriggan's police dogs were getting restless. Fenrir and Ragnarok tugged on their leads and growled while Spriggan tried to restrain them. As usual Spriggan had neglected to feed them recently and the discipline of police dog training was wearing thin.

Mavis turned to Figgis. "Norman!" she commanded, "those dogs are obviously hungry! Go and get them a burger or something!"

"Yes, dear," Figgis replied, and off he went.

Tracy Truth, the junior reporter from the *Pengoggly Press* was there too. As the *Kraken* had crashed into the girders of the unfinished hotel she had scribbled furiously in between taking picture after picture. She was awed by the story she would have to write, the beauty of the mermaid, the quiet heroism of Lionel and the Captain. She would write the only completely true story of her career, and then, unable to write rubbish any more, retreat to an Ashram somewhere in a remote part of England where she would fall in love. But that is another story.

On the other side of the harbour the crowd of minions still buzzed ominously.

⁂

"Well that's that I suppose," Lord Fumble muttered to Sidney Sinister. Then across the sea of people he saw Lucretia.

"By my green Wellington boot! She's here!"

"Well as I told you, she didn't really die."

"Blast it! You didn't tell me she was here!"

"You'll be wanting to patch things up?"

"Patch things up? Don't whatever you do give her my Chelsea address. I'll see you later. Send your invoice by post old chap. Got to dash!"

⁂

"Time to sort out the minions," Alf said.

Lionel was ready. "Let's go then."

"Not me. My work here is done. You have the power."

"But what do I do?"

"You will know. You found Kerensa, you dealt with the submarine. You will know."

There was no putting off the moment. The minions were the last shadow over victory, buzzing like hornets. Lionel started out towards them alone.

As they saw him coming the buzzing resolved itself into speech. Speech directed at him.

"He'll be back. You can't win every time."

"Well you've won this time. I say you are a hero."

"Yes, you'll be in all the newspapers."

"You'll be interviewed by the BBC. 'It was all down to my friends, I did very little,' you'll say modestly."

"Better start thinking about what records you'll choose for *Desert Island Discs*."

The minions seemed for once friendly. As Lionel approached, their speech became louder. It began to penetrate him. It seemed to come from somewhere inside himself. They surrounded him.

The Last Temptation

He began to dream of fame and fortune, of his little story being written in a book, of that little book becoming a best-seller. Perhaps it would be made into a movie. Buying a bigger house. Perhaps a new car, as the Morris Minor was not very fast. Not a Porsche though—he wanted to stay true to his humble origins—be true to his fans. Although a Porsche would be nice. Perhaps people would come from far and wide to hear wisdom from his lips, how a humble man can be transformed. The friendly buzzing of the minions drowned out everything, the sea, the sky, even the seagulls' crying. A comfortable sleep descended on Lionel, although he still stood there, seeing and hearing nothing outside his head.

Then from somewhere he heard a still small voice, Kerensa's voice. Just as in the submarine, she was saying: ignore them, they don't matter. Don't listen to them. There's something more important than all this. Much more important.

What could be more important than fame and fortune? Lionel knew. He did not risk losing it by giving it a name. "Back!" he said, calmly, "Back. This is not it."

Then he heard the wind and the seagulls crying.

The minions buzzed some more.

"Don't worry," Lionel told them. "There'll be plenty of work for you dismantling the wreckage. Then with your help Pengoggly harbour front can be made beautiful again. There'll be something useful for you to do."

Then in ones and twos the minions began drifting away from the swarm, some heading for the café, others to one or other of the local pubs, some wandering off into the village and the fields and rocks beyond on who-knows-what errands.

As Lionel turned to walk back, there was Kerensa waiting for him, smiling.

※

There was a sense of anticlimax in the crowd. Certainly the events of the afternoon had been dramatic enough, but something more was required, a celebration, a ceremony, something to draw the day to a proper end.

The crowd shuffled about, and a good trade in frothy coffee was made as people waited for something to happen, for someone to take charge and do something. Light clouds scudded across the sea breaking the sunshine with an occasional shadow.

Then all turned to the sound of a Land Rover coming over the hill and down into the village, finally drawing up outside the café in a cloud of dust. Out stepped Danzel, and someone else.

"Old Ben!" the Kasteldrog chorus all cried at once.

The old landlord of the *Piskie and Pasty* stepped onto the pavement, a little shaky but seemingly otherwise in good health. He beamed. "Danzel came a-lookin' for me in the old folks' home. Tells me Smithers be gone and I be needed again. Rescued me from a high-backed plastic chair he did, right in the middle of bingo. A close thing it were, but we made it out the door before Matron could stop us."

He took a breath and continued, "We brought something from the *Piskie and Pasty*."

With that Danzel opened up the back of the Land Rover to reveal several dozen crates of bottled *Hideous Pigsty*. "Drinks on the house!"

A mighty cheer went up.

"Play music!" Ramón shouted. The mariachi band struck up a lively South American tune led by Pedro and José, who were in their different ways very loud and impassioned singers, and the rhythm was such that even the doctors could not help dancing.

Everyone danced.

Alf kissed Nellie tenderly.

Lola looked into the Captain's eyes and her own eyes watered a little. "Everything will work out, won't it?" she said.

The Captain held her tight and nodded. "I could marry another couple at sea, as I am a sea captain," he said, "but for us, we'll have to let the vicar do it, in St Doris's church, if you'll have me."

In the centre of everything were Lionel and Kerensa dancing. Between them there were no words, just unspeakable happiness.

Epilogue

Alf called the minion without a name 'Douglas' and told him that as he now had a name he could safely make his way in the world. Like most people's names, 'Douglas' has no particular symbolic meaning, although apparently in Gaelic it means 'dark water.' Douglas rounded up the few minions who wanted to work and they formed a useful landscaping, odd-job and handyman company.

Gentle reader, you will guess of course that the wreckage of the hotel was transformed into a garden overlooking the sea, with benches settled among tall yuccas, palm trees and salt-tolerant flowers, a place for lovers and anyone with a poetic soul or who needed to develop one.

Research in the local library revealed that the true inheritor of Castle Drog was not Lord Fumble, who was descended from an impostor. The true line descended through a number of Herrings. In the 19th century there was no male heir so the right to the estate would have gone to Fanny Herring who used to smoke a pipe and who married one Cuthbert Kipper. The sole survivor of that line was Captain Kipper. Since Dr Squidtentacles had bought the property from Lord Fumble and the doctor was now missing there was a considerable legal wrangle to remove the doctor's name from the title, upon which Captain Kipper donated the property to the National Trust. This provided several of the inhabitants of Kasteldrog with useful jobs selling local jam and tea towels decorated with mermaids, and the *Piskie and Pasty* developed a regular tourist trade.

All three couples married in St Doris's church to the tumultuous joy of everyone. A collection in the church enabled the statue of St Doris and the sea slugs and fishes fighting the giant squid to be re-painted and gilded to a truly medieval magnificence.

Epilogue

Lola and the Captain lived happily in his little cottage, and she would prepare the fish for sale. The seafood in the local restaurants was among the best in England.

Alf moved in with Nellie and wrote books of adventures about imaginary islands, full of philosophical allegory and whimsical detail. They too lived happily. Nellie occasionally pined for St Doris Island, and when this happened Alf would buy a coconut and they would share it under the banana tree that managed to grow back after every Cornish winter.

Kerensa got a job with Morwenna at the *Frothy Coffee Café*. Inexplicably Kerensa instinctively knew how to make really good coffee and absolutely irresistible cakes (although the fish-flavoured ones were not so popular) and they decided to change the name of the café to *St Doris's Be Here Now*. Kerensa and Lionel continued to live at 7 Marine Parade because why would they want to live anywhere else?

A book was written about Lionel (as you hardly need to be told) but he did not buy a Porsche. He did have the rust in the wings behind the headlights of the Morris Minor fixed and the car resprayed a blue as deep as a cloudless summer sky in Cornwall.

— THE END —

One more note...

A MERMAID IN THE BATH

Just one more note from Myfanwy

Hello again my Sapient Selkies,
Like I said at the beginning, I call you that because if you have understood everything Minty Marvellous has written, divinely-inspired as he is by Aerfen, Celtic goddess of Fate and aided by the gentle guiding hand of St Doris herself, then you will rightly be called wise and you may, like the Selkies, shed your old skins to become something that can move between two worlds.

Ooh! I don't know what came over me when I wrote that sentence. The poetic Muse has touched Milton Marmalade for sure, and to tell the truth I'm feeling a bit touched too. Perhaps I'll write that bodice-ripper after all. I don't actually have a bodice myself, though.

If—and it's a bit of an 'if' isn't it?—Minty Milton were suddenly to acquire all the commanding machismo of Ramón Pimiento el Picante (but not be a bad person of course) then I wouldn't have to work so hard with my Welsh wiles. But then, we have to work with what's available, don't we?

Well here's the Co-op. I expect the shed is round the back. Ooh. Play it cool, now, Myfanwy.

Is there a bodice shop round here somewhere?
Wish me luck,
Your friend,
Myfanwy
xxxxxx
xxxx
x

Printed in September 2021
by Rotomail Italia S.p.A., Vignate (MI) - Italy